SILVER LIGHT

BOOK ONE OF MOTHERTREE

W.K. GREYLING

Paperback ISBN: 978-1-7775489-0-2

Edited by Allister Thompson

First edition: January 2021

www.wkgreyling.com

CONTENTS

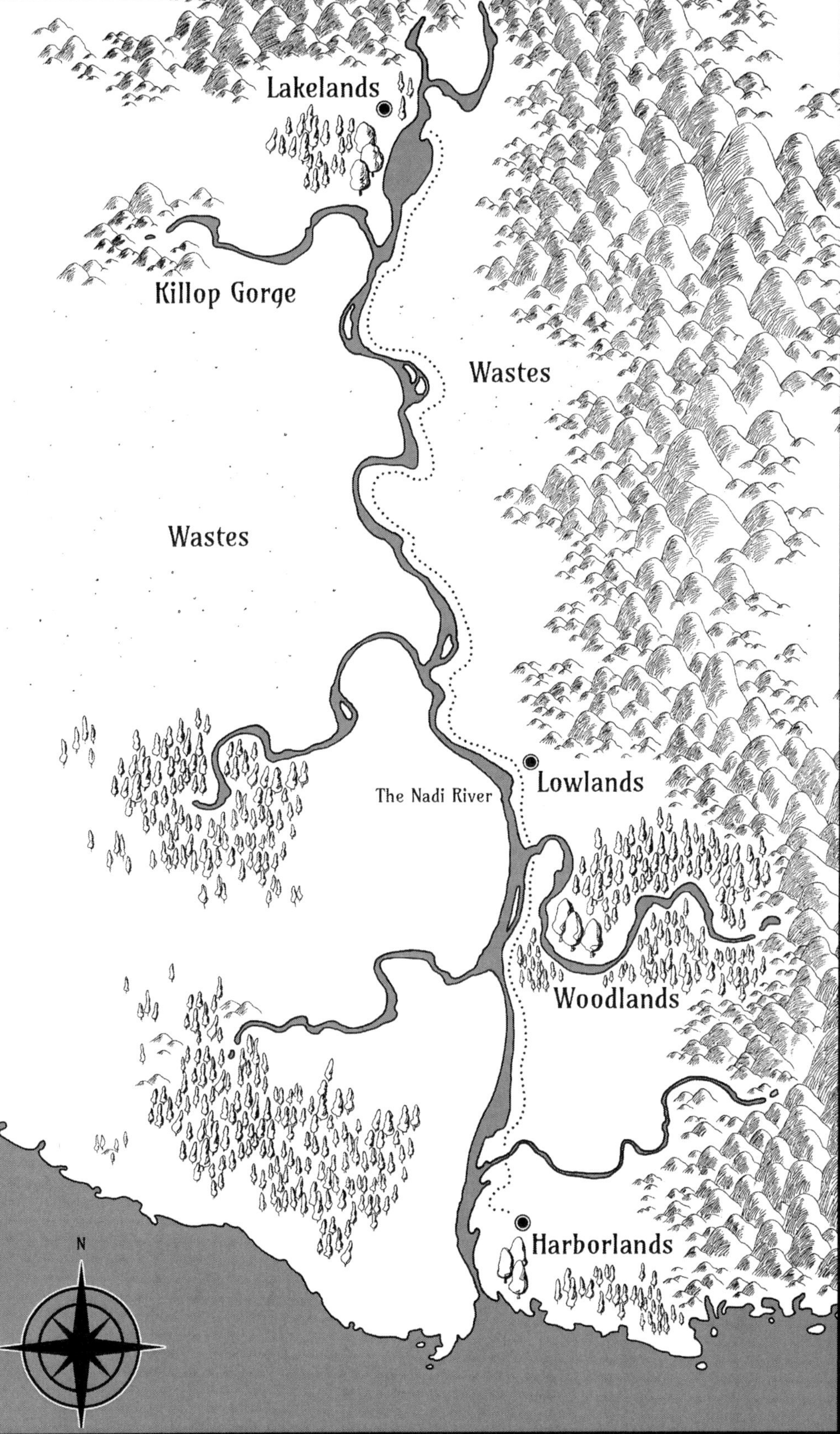
Lakelands
Killop Gorge
Wastes
Wastes
Lowlands
The Nadi River
Woodlands
Harborlands
N

PROLOGUE

"What have you done!" Walde gripped the younger boy's skinny wrists, wincing as purple dye dribbled from Jak's hands onto Walde's clenched fingers. He gripped the boy tighter.

"Nothin. Didn't do nothin'," Jak said.

Walde threw another glance at the overturned pot of dye on the table. He didn't want to think about how much the dye had cost his father to make, the precious blossoms that had been mashed and steeped, now gone to waste. Jak had no clue and probably wouldn't care even if Walde told him.

"You're hurtin' me!"

Walde had glimpsed the boy slinking around the work tent. Jak came from a family of eight, and with the father absent during long hunts, the children often ran wild. Although only a few years Jak's senior, Walde felt infinitely older.

Anger heated Walde's face. He thought about the many ways he could hurt him. Rub dye in his eyes, strip off his clothes, and then write something foul on his back and send him home that way. His lips curled as his mind churned with possibilities.

"Please," Jak whimpered.

Push it down, Walde.

The memory of his father's voice made him flinch. Walde strove to ignore it, but it loomed like a shadow at his back. Watching. Waiting to see what he'd do. The sensation might've made him even angrier if he'd let it. Instead, he drew a harsh breath and pushed his anger down. Little by little, his grip loosened until his hands fell to his sides.

Jak didn't move. They both stared fixedly at the floor, at the dye pooling under the table.

Heavy footsteps made them both jump. The leather walls of the tent swayed gently as Walde's father, tall and stocky with thick brown hair and piercing blue eyes, lifted the leather door flap and entered. He went still as he took in the spilled pot of dye and the boy Walde had cornered.

He fixed Walde with a piercing stare.

"He knocked it over," Walde said tightly. "I came in, and he was playing in it."

His father didn't seem to care about the dye. He looked from Jak's smeared wrists to Walde's purple palms, then back to Jak again. "Are you hurt?" he asked the boy.

Jak stared hard at the floor. "No. He didn't hurt me."

He gave a satisfied nod, then strode over to Jak, threw him over a meaty shoulder, and left the work tent. The leather flap swayed and went still.

Walde righted the pot. He considered scooping the remaining dye off the table, but much of it had already sunk into the bare wood. He shook his head as he gazed at the soft leather hides piled neatly in a box on the floor. There wouldn't be enough dye to stain them now, and without the color, the merchants wouldn't want them. Not a catastrophe, but a terrible blow all the same. Hopefully, Jak's mother would give the boy a sound thrashing.

He was sitting on a chair, staring blankly at his sticky hands and thinking about all the things they would have to do without when the heavy footsteps returned and the door swung open. His father, Carrac, crouched beside the chair so they were at eye level. "I took him back to his mother."

Walde nodded and let his untidy brown hair fall over his eyes. His father's relentless gaze was growing intolerable. "What is it?" Walde muttered at last.

"You pushed your anger down."

"Yes."

"I'm proud of you." Carrac slid a stained cloth out of his belt and wiped the dye off Walde's hands.

"But look what we lost." He gestured sharply to the hides.

"It was a price well paid."

Walde opened his mouth to protest, but something new lay on his father's open palm, glittering in the light that spilled through cracks in the walls.

"This was my father's," Carrac said.

It wasn't made of iron, Walde thought idly. Iron would've rusted after so many years. His father lifted its leather cord and held up the square medallion for Walde to examine. The corners showed no evidence of welding but were as smooth and sharp as the green edge of a new leaf. "Strange," he heard himself whisper.

Carrac grinned. "So I thought when it was given to me." He let it rest flat on his palm.

Walde grazed it with his finger. "It's like a box without a lid or a floor."

Carrac's smile stilled; something deep and wise entered his face. "A box…or a room. I like to think of the sides as walls. Strong, solid walls." He closed his eyes. "In the darkness, I can feel them."

When his eyes didn't reopen, Walde closed his own. A breeze stirred the tent, making the door flap. Then silence descended, and he saw the box in the dark of his mind. Metal walls rose around him, enclosing him as the earth might. But he felt no fear. There was power here. He longed to know if the power was only in his imagination, or if it was real.

His father's voice drifted in. "This is where you keep them, Walde."

"Them?"

"All your strong emotions like anger, fear, pain, and sadness. This is where they go. And the walls hold them in, strong and tight."

"What about the good ones—?"

"If they're strong, they go in, too." His voice caught, and Walde opened his eyes, wondering. "Do you understand me?"

"Yes."

"Good." He pushed the leather cord over Walde's head and tucked the medallion under the neck of his tunic.

"Do other people wear these?"

"No. Nothing like this. Others have their own way to stay calm, but they don't talk about it, because it's theirs."

Secret, whispered the air between them. Only adults shared important secrets.

Walde traced the shape of the medallion over his tunic and in an instant had plunged the sudden stab of joy he'd felt in becoming an adult in his father's eyes into the small box around his neck. "Our secret," he said, smiling.

CHAPTER 1

In the mists of time, the Worldtree seeded us from her womb pods. The summer sun warmed her, the rain wetted her roots, and when she grew heavy with life, she loosed us into the world.
—A fragment of the Seed Pod legend, translated from the old tongue

A lake sparkled in the sunlight. Its southern end opened to become a turbulent river that traveled many miles before pooling in a harbor by the sea. Two smaller rivers flowed into the lake's northern end. Huge deciduous trees lined the west side of the lake. The stone-littered wastes stretched out behind them, home to mountain goats, rabbits, and if one traveled far enough inland, wild horses. The wastes offered neither shade from the sun nor shelter from the rain. The lake's east bank was bare of trees. The same sort of wastes spread out from it until the earth softened to patches of marsh and remained in that state until the mountains began.

Walde glimpsed the hazy line of those mountains through the branches as he swung in his hammock. He was over two hundred feet up, in the largest of the trees lining the lake's west bank. The one called First Mothertree. Hundreds of other people lived and worked in the First alongside him. But as it was nearing the end of seventh day, most reclined as Walde did in hammocks or huts. Walde had strung his hammock in the highest branches, where he could enjoy the best views.

He was a wiry lad of twenty-two summers, dark-haired, dark-eyed, with the sun-browned skin of a wastes hunter. His hands were forever darkened by leather dye. The smell, too, stayed with him—a bitterness edged with something sweet.

His sweetheart, Rona, wriggled out from under the crook of his arm and wagged a finger at the canopy above them. "Leaves are taking their good time coming in. It hasn't been cold. Do you think something's wrong?"

The hammock creaked as wind stirred the branches. Walde scratched the week's growth of hair on his chin, hiding a frown. "They always come in." He couldn't quite manage to sound confident, though. In truth, there were fewer leaves every year. Fewer blossoms. Fewer seed pods. The decline had been happening for decades, and it showed no sign of letting up. The pod harvest the previous spring had been scanty. Some said the changing weather had caused it. Others said the songs were at fault.

Walde anticipated his surge of frustration and doused it. He, like most youths in the villages, took turns playing for the First Mothertree at the song rite. His instrument was a three-stringed lyra, a family heirloom crafted generations ago from scraped seed pod hulls. He played hard during the song rite but the songs were old and tired. If the elders allowed new songs, maybe things would change.

He kissed Rona's sleek black hair and then laid his head back onto the pack that cushioned his head. "What are you thinking?"

She chewed her lip. "Just about something my father said. He thinks that all the Mothertrees are connected somehow, like they all share the same spirit, and that if the Harborlanders really killed their First, then maybe that's why *our* trees are failing this year."

"The Harborlanders *didn't* kill their First. That was just a rumor." He managed to sound confident despite a twinge in his belly.

Half a year ago, a tinker told a barmaid that the Harborlanders had killed their First Mothertree. A guard must have overheard the conversation, for in half a breath, the tinker was escorted to the elder's hut. The tinker wouldn't speak another word about it after that, even for coin.

In the end, no one took the rumor seriously except for the barmaid. Enda threatened to journey to the Harborlands herself to see if it were true. But she never did. The sea was many days south of there. To reach it, one had to travel through lonely stretches of land devoid of shelter and friends.

Of all the villagers, only the hunters knew what wastes travel was like. But Enda couldn't persuade even one of them, either with pods or Ona—the spirit distilled from spring sap—to make the journey. Walde understood their reluctance. Who would dare give credence to such a rumor by acting on it? A First wasn't just another Mothertree. In all three lands, the Firsts were the oldest and strongest. All the Mothertrees alongside them had been sprouted from the First's pods, making them mother to them all.

Rona said, "Don't you think it's possible the tinker was telling the truth?"

"No. I really don't." At least, he told himself he didn't believe it. The very thought of killing a Mothertree made him queasy, never mind a First.

"But what reason would the tinker have to lie? And if he did lie, why didn't he set things straight after coming out of the elder's hut? They hushed him. Plain and simple."

Walde propped himself up on an elbow and stared at her wide brown eyes, the worry lines creasing her forehead. "Do you really believe this, Rona?"

"I don't know. Maybe. The way things are going now, anything seems possible. Think of the Woodlanders."

South of the Lowlands lay a grove of Mothertrees nestled in a forest of much smaller trees. The area was known as the Woodlands, and those who dwelled in the Mothertrees were called Woodlanders.

So it had been from time immemorial. But a few years ago, the Woodlanders had abandoned their Mothertrees and moved into stone huts in the Lowlands—a marshy area peopled by descendants of tinkers. The move was absurd. Unthinkable. And yet, over time, it seemed that more and more people envied the Lowlanders' wealth and space. Rumor had it that some of the Harborlanders had also left their Mothertrees.

The desire was foreign to him. He thought about the wattle-and-daub huts secured to strong branches, the solid, maintained paths. This was all he had ever known, and he loved it. What would it be like to live in a stone house on the bare ground? Cold and lonely, he imagined. Only one stone structure stood in the Lakelands, and it had been built as a prison.

He said, "Moving away from your Mothertree isn't the same as killing it." He snorted and shook his head. "The whole idea is ridiculous. Why kill a Mothertree? And how?"

She threw him a tense, sideways glance then lowered her voice. "Enda told me they used Reachers."

"Of course they did." He loosed another snort, then lay back and sighed.

A cool breeze, common in the early evening hours, stirred his hair and tunic. He took Rona's arm from her side and held it as he would a lyra. Clearing his throat to get her attention, he drew an invisible bow across it. As he did, he made a pitiful creaking sound in his throat.

Rona wrenched her arm back. "You're not listening to me. Or maybe you are listening and don't care."

"Reachers," he said with reluctance.

Every so often, a man or woman born in the Mothertrees developed a strange power. They claimed they could use it to help or hinder the Mothertrees. However, any evidence of help was founded on myths and legends. In every case during the last century, Reachers had done harm—whether intentionally or unintentionally—to a Mothertree. The last known Reacher had caused all the leaves to drop off one of the branches under her hut. Later, the branch dried up and died.

Walde had never met the woman. He had been a child at the time, and the Reacher had been raised in a different tree. He said, "That last Reacher—"

"Marris?"

"Yes, that was her." The price for being a Reacher was death. Banishment, Walde thought, would have been more merciful. But Mothertrees were sacred, and anything that could cause such insidious, ongoing damage was no better than a disease. "Do you know anyone who attended her hanging?"

"My mother did," she said.

"I heard that her palms flared as she died."

Rona's gaze grew distant as she stared up into the canopy. "Mother said that her palms turned as white as lake ice, and it was as if the whiteness itself shone, like something spun from cold starlight."

The hairs on his arms stood up. Walde stowed his emotion with a giddy haste. "That was a long time ago. Fourteen years," he calculated. "And there hasn't been a single incident since. How many Reachers have been hanged here in the past century? Eight?"

Rona seemed to catch the drift of his thoughts. "It doesn't seem like many, but the Lakelands are smaller than the Harborlands. There'd be more Reachers over there."

"Maybe. Or maybe not. Didn't the Harborlands elders round up a group of them a few years back?"

"Those are only the ones they found."

"Still, I wonder how many could be left after that." He shook his head. "I think Reachers are rare, and even if the Harborlanders found more, can you imagine how long it would take to completely destroy a First, trunk and all?"

She stared back at him for some moments before sinking back into the hammock. "When you put it that way, it doesn't make a whole lot of sense."

"No," he said with finality, "it doesn't." Even if there were enough Reachers to do the job, he thought, the very idea was preposterous. As long as a Mothertree produced trade goods, people would fight to keep it. And if the tree didn't produce, then it was dead anyway. Or halfway there. Why hurry that death along in such a complicated, risky way?

"Maybe," she said, "it *was* just tinker-talk. We're so far from everything here. Tinkers can say whatever they want and there'd be no way to disprove it."

A fleck of sunlight had come to settle near her ear. Walde leaned in and kissed it. Knowing the game, she reached up and took light from his jaw. They kissed gently, quietly as the sun lowered and the light faded. As his hand slid under her back, he was tempted as always to let everything go, every emotion.

Sometimes he dreamed of doing that very thing. In his most vivid dreams, the medallion cracked and every emotion went free, like some giant fanged beast let loose from its cage. But he willed it on, even as it raged and destroyed, because it wasn't made only of bad things. The good in it was clean and bright and strong.

All of a sudden, a horn call sounded, and they both jerked upright. "Speak of the devil," she said. "The tinkers are back."

He and Rona climbed off the hammock onto its supporting branches. With the ease of experience, they untied the hammock's ends and Walde rolled it up and stuffed it into his pack. "Should we take the bridges to the stairs?" he asked. "The light is getting low."

Rona snorted and swung effortlessly down onto a lower branch. Walde descended cautiously above her, testing the smaller branches before trusting his weight to them. It was a long climb down to the midpoint of the tree where Walde and his father lived. He enjoyed climbing from time to time, but not at twilight. Despite his caution, though, he was almost at Rona's side when they reached a sturdy footpath.

Other villagers were already ahead of them, some gripping baskets of gifts for visiting officials who might have arrived with the tinkers, others carrying unruly children over their shoulders. The lamplighters were at work now, illuminating the numerous paths that spanned the largest branches.

This was the midpoint of the tree. Poorer folk lived in the upper branches. There, instead of sturdy wooden paths, narrow, lightweight bridges spidered through the branches. The wood for the paths came from a grove of maple trees farmed at the lake's north end; a tidy garden that bore no resemblance to the stately chain of giants the villagers inhabited. The Mothertrees.

"The tinkers arrived just in time for the song rite," Rona said, tossing him a sideways smile.

Walde sighed. Tomorrow would be nothing but trading. The rite would be treated as an afterthought. "Jak and I were supposed to practice in the morning. Now I don't know when we'll find the time."

"You'll both be fine," she promised. "Besides, hasn't he been hoping to get bronze strings for his harp? Here's his chance."

Walde's father would be happy too. He and Walde had just finished staining their last haul. The deep purple skins were coveted by the Lowlanders, and with the scarcity of blossoms, the price for dye rose every year. Walde slowed to glance at the dark windows of the hut he shared with his father. Carrac must have already left.

The tree's trunk was a shadowy wall stretching both above and below them. A wide platform had been built around the trunk. Huts of various shapes and sizes rested atop it, encircling the tree like a bracelet on an arm. Most were centers for the public—an herbalist's tent, a water station (also used for putting out fires, though few ever happened, and if they did, the Mothertree was remarkably resistant to flame), and the elders' meeting hut. There were also two lift stations that worked using a system of levers and pulleys. One transported waste down the tree, the other transported people who had paid the monthly fee or were aged or disabled. Everyone else had to take the uneven wooden stairs that wound around the trunk to the bottom.

Rona groaned as they neared the lift. A long line had formed behind it, and since the lift's basket only supported three people at a time, the wait would be phenomenal. In wordless agreement, they passed the lift without slowing and joined the spill of people on the stairs.

They caught up with Walde's father before reaching the next level down. Carrac grinned at them. He had changed little since Walde was a boy. Some of his hair had migrated from his scalp to his chin, and he had gained a few more laugh lines, but he was the same strong, cheerful, and maddeningly mysterious man that Walde knew as a boy. Walde had no memory of his mother, who had died in a tragic fall only months after giving birth to him.

Carrac shouted to be heard over the crowd. "You're a couple of rumples."

Walde caught the sack his father tossed to him and set it on his shoulder. "We had a lovely evening."

Rona had breezed on ahead of them. She disliked Carrac with a passion that confounded Walde. Carrac was a gruff and private man, but he was also kind-hearted, even-tempered, and industrious, a man who had scraped his way down the tree through his own hard work, leaving his relatives still hanging in the treetops. Walde suspected he would become just like him, but whenever he warned Rona of the possibility, she merely laughed at him.

The stairs ended at the tree's base. They joined the milling crowd on the patio surrounding the trunk and made their way to the floating docks. The boardwalk along the lake's edge was a meeting place for folk from all the villages. During the day, vendors set up tents and street musicians played homemade instruments. Fishermen sold their catch on the docks.

Night had fallen, and the tents were long gone. The lake was hazy with a low mist. The row of lamps lighting the boardwalk flickered as bodies gathered on the planks: Lakeland peacekeeper guards along the edge with common folk behind them.

The First Mothertree was situated at the southernmost tip of the lake, with the fast-moving Nadi River only half a mile away. The tinkers always blew a horn when they arrived from across the lake, and while they waited for a ferry to fetch them, they unloaded their goods. Their horses and wagons would remain on the east bank, tended by their wives and children.

Usually they came in the late afternoon. A night arrival usually meant that officials had traveled with them. This, along with the repeated horn call, told everyone who would be stepping off the boat.

The crowd was unusually quiet as the ferry drifted with excruciating slowness across the water and into dock. Ropes were thrown and tied, and a gangway was lowered so the visitors could disembark. The tribal elders stood in two lines on the dock to greet them. They wore their belted purple surcoats and bore gifts in their arms.

But the familiar men who stepped off the gangway did not resemble visiting officials from the Harborlands. Their traditional surcoats had been replaced by long, flowing robes with broad sleeves that all but covered their hands. The material was not kessa—a fabric spun from the silk of Mothertree pods—or even linen, but something thicker, rougher. Probably kriksa, Walde thought, though he hoped he was wrong. Kriksa was a fabric woven from llonal, a plant that grew in the Lowland bogs. The Lakelanders called llonal "bog thread" and the material spun from it "bog rags." Tinkers didn't even carry it to sell, since no one in the Lakelands would buy it.

Even if the material wasn't kriksa, the officials had made a statement merely by the cut of their cloaks. The treefolk wore short, fitted tunics of kessa or farmed linen, and soft leather hosen or trousers. Such long, loose robes as the ones these men wore were not practical for tree living. It would take nothing for such sleeves to catch on a branch, especially on a windy day.

The reality of the situation landed hard and settled like a lump in Walde's stomach. Could it be that the Harborlanders were following the same course as the Woodlanders? He thrust the thought away before it stirred his anxiety to a higher level than he'd already allowed it to go.

The elders greeted the visitors as if nothing were amiss and then turned and waved folk back a little to make a space for the gifts. Giving gifts to visiting officials was an age-old custom. It was usually done with joy, but there were few smiles as family heads came forward to place gifts at the visitors' feet.

Walde handed his father the sack and watched Carrac join the long line of gift-givers on the boardwalk.

After a while, his gaze drifted to the hazy lights on the lake's east bank. Many of the tinkers would be building fires and settling in for the night. Their children would be laughing and playing.

No one worrying that their way of life might be about to vanish like a fine mist.

CHAPTER 2

Who are the tinkers? That question has haunted us for centuries. Ask a tinker, and he'll give you any number of myths and legends. Among the most famous is that they descended from Stergis, god of wealth and prosperity. Others believe tinkers are descendants of banished treefolk, of men and women expelled from their villages for crimes such as incest and murder.

But this, too, is conjecture. In this treatise, I bring together history and myth with the aim of painting a convincing picture of who these people really are.

–Anon. From a scorched fragment found behind a wood stove in an abandoned Woodlands hut

The officials vanished after gift-giving that night and didn't reappear the next day. They were last seen following the head elders from all sixteen Mothertree villages into the First's meeting hut, and rumor had it they were still there, afraid to soil their bog rags.

With their disappearance, the atmosphere lightened. The Lakelanders set aside the officials like a strong emotion and focused instead on wheedling answers from the tinkers.

Their success, Walde thought later, was spotty at best.

He and Jak sat on stools late that afternoon in a small chamber in Rona's family hut. The room was used primarily for storage. One side held drawers of preserves, the other her father's tools, spare planks, and woodcarving projects. The hut had a lived-in feel despite the fact that the family had occupied it for only two months. Rona's family had moved from a neighboring Mothertree to help renovate the First's extensive network of pathways. Before the move, Walde had known her only as an acquaintance, a little dark-eyed girl with pigtails and a pink, pouty mouth.

She had grown into a strong, wiry young woman who was adept at laying planks and handling heavy tools. One day in early spring, Walde had returned from a hunting trip, sweating and stinking of rock goat. Rona met him on the path to warn him of the construction. In moments, they had both run out of words and stood unable to move, looking dumbly at each other as if there was nowhere else to look. It was enough. For now. Attraction always held things together for a while. Like a birth cord, Walde thought. In time, it wouldn't be enough and the relationship would unravel. At least, that was Walde's personal experience. He wished it were otherwise.

The scents of wood and iron mingled with Rona's enticing herbal smell. She stood behind Walde, fixing his shoulder-length brown hair into a tidy tail. He suspected she was braiding colored cloths into it but said nothing. The back of his head would be against the trunk while he performed anyway.

Walde rewetted his polishing rag in oil and turned his lyra over so he could work on the back. Across from him, Jak set down his harp and rag and stretched his bony arms. He had changed much from the unruly child who had overturned Carrac's dye pot. At eighteen he was quiet, pensive, even stern. His main interest in life was playing the harp. Perhaps he secretly hoped his playing would restore the Mothertree's vitality. He would not be the first to undertake such a challenge. Nor, Walde thought, would he be the last.

Jak's dark eyes flicked Walde a questioning look. "Did you hear anything more? About the Harborlands?"

Jak had only spent a scant hour that day at the market, just long enough to hunt down and purchase his coveted bronze strings. After that, he had rushed home to be with his harp.

Walde's head jerked as Rona tightened something. He said, "Apparently the Harborlands elders moved their meeting hut to the ground. Kriksa has grown popular there, especially with the folk who left the trees. They say it keeps out the sea air better than skins."

Rona snorted but said nothing. Jak's face remained impassive. Only a slight tightening of his lips revealed his irritation. "What about their First? Did the tinkers say anything about that?"

Walde set his lyra down along with the rag. "They all said the same thing. That it's still standing, like the other Mothertrees."

Jak's shoulders visibly relaxed, and he let his harp rest on his lap. "I never believed the rumor about it anyway," he said.

Rona said dryly, "Sure, no one believed it. That's why everyone looks so relieved all of a sudden." She drew something from her waist pouch and tugged once more on Walde's hair. "The biggest piece of news came from that woodlander-turned-tinker. Man's tongue came loose after a few swigs of ona, and he let slip that the Woodlands didn't blossom last year."

Walde hadn't been surprised by that information. Without the song rites, the Mothertrees there wouldn't thrive.

Jak fisted his thigh in an unusual display of emotion. "I can't believe the Woodlanders came back to strip pods from Mothertrees they don't even live in. They have no respect."

Rona grumbled, "Comes from living in the Lowlands."

Walde sighed, wishing the Lakelanders had no connection with the outside world at all. He didn't like the anger and hatred the tinkers stirred with their "news." And how much of it could even be trusted?

The elders must know the truth, he thought. Especially after their meetings with the officials.

Walde lifted his polished lyra to his chest and played a minor chord.

***

A glitter of lamps lit the wooden platform built around the base of the First's massive trunk. Some lamps hung from poles along paths that branched out from the patio around the trunk, others from the low branches spreading above. And if one peered up into the canopy, they would find a sea of lights spreading above them. There was a difference between starlight and treelight. While stars were cool and distant, treelight was warm and welcoming and shifted like a swarm of fireflies in the wind.

Walde was glad that no wind blew tonight. The crowd gathered on the descending platform around him was enough of a distraction. The officials, having slunk out of hiding, were perched on embroidered cushions at the front. The elders and peacekeeper guards fanned out behind them, followed by a line of tinkers. The remaining attendees gathered haphazardly around the tree and in the low branches overhead.

The other villages held their own rites for their Mothertrees, but every musician worth his salt played for the First. The rites were held monthly, with several ensembles taking part. Order of appearance was chosen by pulling sticks.

Jak had the misfortune of pulling the longest stick, so he and Walde lumbered up first. Having arranged themselves on stools placed against the trunk, they waited, quietly checking the pegs on their instruments while an elder uttered the chant that had been given at song rites for generations. The words and phrasing of the chant were so old that no one (save the elders) understood it. Walde had heard it so many times that he thought he could repeat it if he were asked to. Fortunately, such an opportunity would never arise.

The elder returned to his seat and a hush fell over the crowd. Walde exchanged a glance with Jak and then rested his lyra against his chest, lifted the bow to the strings, and drew out a sleepy melody. Jak plunged in at the end of a long, deep note, and together they gradually drove the melody higher and faster, filling it with energy. Growth.

Walde hated the song. It was too blatant. Too simple. Being told to do something was for young children. Not for such a noble being as the First. One could shout *grow* at the tree all day long, and it wouldn't sprout a leaf. How was this song any different?

But Jak liked it, and in truth it was no worse than the other old songs.

Jak liked it, but it was the wrong song for his new strings. The strings themselves were not at fault—they were a fine, shining bronze, and in a few days Jak's fingers would have grown accustomed to them. Days, not hours. Jak had fumbled several times during practice that evening, and the fine beads of sweat gathering on his brow now attested to his intense concentration. When it finally broke, and he fumbled, Walde was ready for it. He might have kept playing and let Jak find his way back on his own. No one would have blamed him. But Jak's pristine reputation would have been tarnished forever. Music was Jak's life. Not Walde's. So Walde made a decision.

At the instant Jak fumbled, Walde buried it with a sharp, strong note. A note that marked the beginning of a new song, one that Walde had heard in his mind one morning while waking from a dream. He and Jak had played that song together a few times just for fun, and Walde was confident that Jak would play it now, and the elders be damned.

Jak's dark eyes flashed on him once, and Walde sensed the gratitude in them. It would be enough.

They plunged on, Walde smiling and swaying as he played. It was a safe bet that the officials didn't know this wasn't one of the sanctioned songs. Not wanting to embarrass themselves, the elders did not interfere. *Would* not interfere.

Walde leaned his head back against the tree as he played. The sea of lights above him blurred, then sharpened, then blurred again into a single, warm glow of light. An odd emotion built in him then, and he resisted the instinctive urge to stow it. He felt…expansive, and at the same time at one with everything. It was a miraculous feeling.

He closed his eyes briefly, not sure if he was still swaying or if he only felt like he was swaying.

And then it was as if he took a step sideways. All feeling in his body vanished, and a vast tunnel stretched out before his startled mind. Something vital was receding away from him down that tunnel. He couldn't see it, but he could feel it, and he would have flung himself after it if he wasn't startled back into his body by someone's urgent shaking.

He opened his eyes to a scene of chaos. Jak, Carrac, and the village doctor were crouched over him, while an elder stood with his arms in the air, trying to hush the concerned crowd. One of the visiting officials stared at Walde as if he were trying to pin him to the tree with his eyes.

Walde registered all of this distantly. The world around him seemed far away. He responded to the three worried men in a way that seemed appropriate. He was ill. Must have eaten something bad at the market that day. He needed to lie down.

Jak and Carrac helped him to his feet. His father took the lyra from him and escorted him to the lift. In truth, Walde was dazed but not dizzy. Neither was he physically ill. Most of all, he wanted to be somewhere quiet and dark, away from all stimulation. He rubbed his hands together idly as he stepped off the lift, wondering if he had burned himself somehow. The skin on his palms felt inexplicably tender.

He groaned with relief when he finally felt his bed under his back.

There was a brief, blessed silence, then the tread of his father's feet returned and lamplight flared. Walde threw a blanket over his eyes.

"Walde." There was a creak as his father sat on a nearby stool. "We need to talk."

Was that suppressed excitement in Carrac's voice? Walde spoke through the blanket. "Not now."

After a lengthy pause, Carrac grunted and rose. "Well, I'm better to you than my father was to me. I don't know if that's a good or a bad thing. Whatever it is, it's too late to change it now anyway. We're going hunting tomorrow, you and I."

Walde had come to himself enough to be surprised by this statement. He pushed the blanket away and rose up on an elbow. "But what about the market? The tinkers are only here for three days."

"We've done what trading we needed to do. The rest can wait until next time."

Walde opened his mouth to protest and then shut it. There was no use arguing with his father when his mind was made up. One stood a better chance of arguing the sun down in the morning.

Carrac closed the bedroom door, and blessed silence returned.

Walde sank back into the blanket. A memory of the tunnel lingered in his mind, as frightening as it was enticing. He wanted to believe that the tree had approved of his song and rewarded him by some sort of communion. But if that were true, then why hadn't Jak experienced the same thing?

The skin on his hands had stopped burning, and he sensed no unpleasantness in his body. The heaviness of sleep weighed down his eyes. He succumbed to it gratefully.

***

Walde rarely had nightmares. He had come to believe that the medallion safeguarded him while he slept, keeping out the negative feelings he strove to bury during the day.

It failed him utterly that night. In one nightmare, his own heart came out of his mouth and tumbled down the Mothertree. He screamed for someone, anyone to catch it, but it vanished into darkness. In another, he rose helplessly into the sky and the world shrank from him until it was no more than a speck of light. He reached for it, like a child reaching for the sun.

The sensation of something vital receding from him played out again and again, each time more intense, until he felt sickened with panic and despair.

He finally woke, bathed in sweat and panting, his heart a livid thing in his chest. A strange light enveloped him, and he looked around for its source. His gaze traveled from the bedroom walls to the blankets, and then to his hands at his sides.

His breath caught. For several moments, he could not breathe at all. His shock was so extreme that his reflex to bury his emotion was completely disabled. He forced himself to gasp in a breath. A stream of whispered curses came out as he exhaled, then a frantic prayer to whichever god would bother to listen.

His palms radiated light, the silvery brightness everyone knew belonged to Reachers. As he glared at his palms, other facts fell into place, the magical experience he'd had while playing, the burning in his hands. His head shook back and forth. How could this be? Why him, of all people? So few Reachers came into the world these days. What were the odds that he would be one of them? It seemed profoundly strange and unjust.

His back stiffened as a new thought occurred to him: Had he damaged the Mothertree?

Push it down, Walde.

The memory of his father's gruff voice calmed him. Walls formed in his mind, and the fear drained away from him. Strangely, the light radiating from his hands faded too, as if it were tied somehow to his emotion. *As if it were tied…*

His eyes widened as he experienced yet another revelation. He allowed the shocked emotion to run free, and sure enough, the light in his palms returned. He thrust the emotion down, and the light faded.

Stunned, he settled back against the mattress. *The power responded to strong emotion.* Carrac had once said that *everyone* learned to bury their emotions. But what if they didn't? What if his father had known somehow what Walde would be and had trained him to combat it?

Questions rained over him. He wanted to wake his father and demand answers. Instead, he lay quiet and still, surrounded by a cloak of his own fear, all the while struggling to beat it down.

Of one thing he was certain: he could not sleep in the tree again. The light in his palms indicated power, and if that power could damage a Mothertree, then he could not allow it to form while he was in the First. Even in his sleep.

"I have to go away," he whispered, and despair battered at him again. Where could he go? This was his home. His life. But what other option did he have? No matter how well Carrac had trained him, he could not prevent Walde from experiencing emotion during the night. He stared malevolently at his open hands. If hacking them off would destroy the power, he'd do it. He'd do it ten times over.

He sighed and dropped his arms. He needed to know more about Reachers and their power. Carrac had never raised the subject or even offered his opinion when it came up in casual conversation. Walde had never thought to wonder why, but now it seemed profoundly curious.

His father knew something. And he'd seemed dead set to speak with Walde alone about it.

Perhaps he had a solution to the problem.

***

Carrac's morning bustle prompted Walde to rise. Walde had not dozed and didn't think he could even if he'd wanted to. He moved with cool efficiency as he strode around the room selecting items to pack. He needed to be ready to leave if his father couldn't help him. He opened his pack and stuffed in a pair of leather trousers and shoes, a flint sack, knives and arrowheads, a length of flax rope...

He paused over his storage chest and ran a finger over a braided length of Rona's hair.

As much as he wanted to, he could not bid her farewell. She would demand to know where he was going, and why. Walde could not burden her with the truth, could not make her weigh her loyalty to him against loyalty to the Mothertree. He shut the chest firmly, wanting no reminder of what he was leaving behind. He swayed, leaning hard on the chest.

After a moment's hesitation, he thrust his lyra and bow into the pack. The narrow end of the instrument stuck out of the top. It would bump his head while he walked, but knowing he carried it with him would make the discomfort worthwhile.

He paused, eyes running over the sparse room that had been his for as long as he could remember. He hoped his father had answers, because if he did not, Walde would have no choice but to leave that very night. He'd already decided which skiff to use and the route he'd take across the lake. Some Lowland lord would employ him as a hunter or farmhand. Or he would join the wretched Woodlanders. He loosed a harsh breath. The despair inched back, but not easily. It felt raw now, a rough blade digging in as it shifted.

He stowed the pack under a bundle of covers beside the bed and snatched up his bow and quiver of arrows.

A soft knock fell on the door.

Walde threw it open and regarded his father with hooded eyes. "I'm ready."

They ghosted down the lamp-lit paths, boots whispering over sturdy wooden boards. Carrac had a hunter's walk despite his broad frame. Walde had spent years learning to imitate the way he placed the balls of his feet, his balance, his ability to find the quietest path.

They passed a dozing guard at the bottom of the winding stairs and made their way around the base of the trunk toward the back of the First.

Dawn lightened the sky, brushing the branches with a soft yellow light. Carrac halted all of a sudden and made an odd sound in his throat. "Look, Walde. The buds are opening."

Sure enough, a delicate purple haze had come to settle on the branches. The sight lifted Walde's mood instantly.

Carrac said dryly, a teasing smile twitching up his lips, "Well, your playing didn't hurt the First any."

Not yet, Walde thought.

They skirted the Lakelands grounds—a hundred-acre strip of rock-sifted earth used for planting a variety of vegetables and flax. The space lengthened every year as villagers removed barrels of stone from the wastes. The families who worked the plot sold a portion of their harvest at the market. The remainder went to the poor.

A bleary-eyed worker set down his hoe and waved as they passed. "Feeling better, lad?"

His deep voice carried over the empty space. Walde replied with a stiff nod. "Yes, thanks."

"'Tis a good day for hunting. Not a bit of wind to spread your smell around."

They left the crops behind and passed the Lakelands' slaughterhouse and tannery, a cluster of work tents, fire pits, drying racks, and soaking tanks encircling a deep stone well. The place was empty now, but by noon, fires would be lit and pungent scents would permeate the air. Even deserted, it stank of blood, smoke, and urine. Lakeland hunters couldn't afford to leave skinning and tanning to someone else, not if they wanted to turn a good profit. Despite the grisly work, Walde had good memories of the place and tried not to stare at it fondly.

After a gentle rise, the land swooped down to reveal a barren landscape of wild grasses, turquoise shrubs, and jutting boulders. Hunters' paths snaked off through the brush, winding around rocks and ridges like water seeking a place to pool. No one owned the wastes, but that didn't stop hunters from laying claim to trails. Some hunters were seventh- or even eighth-generation. After so many years, their trails became heirlooms, well loved and defended.

Though Carrac was only a third-generation hunter, his trail usually yielded well.

Their shadows walked ahead of them as they hiked down a wash and between two massive boulders. Walde scanned the landscape as he walked, alert to every movement. Even if his father's aim that day wasn't to hunt, it wouldn't do to return empty-handed.

Carrac spoke, breaking a lengthy silence. "It's nice knowing we're the only ones out here today." He didn't seem to expect a response, and Walde didn't offer one. "That song you played last night… Was it your idea, or Jak's?"

Walde wondered why he even had to ask. "It was mine."

"Then you'll have to pay Jak's fine on top of your own."

"I know that. I knew it when I changed the song."

"They'll do more than slap a fine on you. You and Jak will be barred from playing at the rites for a while. Jak will get a month, but you'll get six, if you're allowed to play again at all."

No, Walde thought, his father wouldn't have dragged him out here just to discuss the repercussions of disobeying the village elders. He wouldn't have missed a tinker day for that.

Carrac glanced back at him, and Walde forced a shrug. "It is what it is."

"What moved you to do it?"

Sighing, Walde spilled out the story, stopping at the point where he'd passed out of the world for a while. By the end, Carrac agreed with him. Better a month's suspension than a soiled reputation.

They paused at a low, smooth boulder at midday, and Carrac unloaded a feast of cured meats, cheese, and late spring berries purchased only the day before from the tinker's stalls. Carrac said with mock empathy, "If you begin to feel sick again, lad…"

Walde rolled his eyes.

A long silence ensued. Walde consumed what was on his cloth with little pleasure. Much of his attention was focused on keeping calm. Walde had hoped that his father knew something about his problem and had meant to discuss it with him in the privacy of the wastes, but as time went on, that seemed less and less likely.

Finally, he could no longer stand the suspense. He asked in a deliberately casual voice, "Why are we out here?"

Carrac took the empty food cloth from him and folded it into his sack. "We're here to talk about the thing you refused to talk about last night."

"The thing…?"

Carrac chuckled. Then he leaned back, sucking in a heavy breath. As he exhaled, his palms opened to the sky.

They were white. A burning, brilliant white.

Walde's mouth slackened, but years of training compelled him to stifle his shock. His father was a Reacher. Had been, all these years.

"Oh, you're good, Walde. I'm glad. You took to it better than I did."

Walde found his voice with an effort. "Took to what?"

"The training." He patted the neck of Walde's tunic.

Suddenly, it was too much, knowing that Carrac had received the same training as a child, had lived in the First for years without leaving a trace of damage. Knowing that he was content with being a Reacher and apparently wished Walde would feel the same way. Walde sagged forward and dropped his head into his brightened palms. Relief mingled with wonder and confusion.

He flinched when, with a shout of joy, Carrac leapt up and drew him into a fierce hug. "Ah, but this is a good day, lad. A fine day."

A scuffling sound made Walde turn in time to see a startled rock goat bound off down a low rise in the land.

Clearing his throat, Carrac scooped up his bow and pack and continued up the trail as if nothing extraordinary had happened.

Walde hurried after him. "Where are we going?"

"To a place."

The way he said "place" made it seem tantalizingly mysterious.

"You must have a hundred questions," his father said. When Walde didn't respond, he turned and added, "Don't be afraid to ask them."

"Is everyone in our family Reachers?"

"No. My father was, and one of my uncles is. But that's it."

An uncle. Was he talking about Caln? The old man was a bit of a recluse.

Carrac slowed so they were walking side-by-side. "Someone has a better chance of becoming a Reacher if there's one or two in their family, but some have none in their family, and they become one anyway. Of course, if both your parents are Reachers, you'll almost certainly become one. But that situation is rare now. There's just not enough Reachers to go around."

"Another question," Walde went on. "How do you sleep at night knowing your nightmares could damage the branches? Isn't that what happened to Marris?"

Carrac sighed heavily. "Poor Marris. If I'd known she was a Reacher, I would have offered to help her. She had no Reachers in her extended family, you see. No one to talk to her about her power. She came into it blind and paid the price for that ignorance."

"The nightmares," Walde reminded him. He didn't want to think about Marris and how she had died. At least Walde could say that he had never agreed, either verbally or in his heart, with the execution. "How do you keep the branches from weakening?"

"The same way you do with everything. Maintenance. A few days a week I rise early and sit on the floor in the work tent, just above a branch. I feed the first positive emotions until I sense a change, a sort of stretching." He extended his arms. "When I feel that growth, I draw back and return to bed."

Walde shook his head, wondering how his own experience of reaching could be so different from his father's. What about the tunnel and the entity waiting at the end of it?

Carrac was still talking. "Of course, it wasn't easy after your mother died. If it weren't for you, I would've had to leave the Lakelands. But you were such a happy child. You were all the joy I had. But it was enough. Just enough to keep up maintenance. Ah, well." He glanced sideways at Walde's brightened hands. "Still letting your emotions run, eh? It's freeing. But after today, you'll have to keep a tight rein."

Easier said than done, Walde thought. But the knot of tension inside him was easing. "How did you guess what happened last night?"

"Because it happens to a lot of Reachers that way. Music frees some part of us we aren't conscious of, makes us open to wonder. The Reachers used to have songs for that. Passage songs, they were called, because they opened a way into the Mothertrees. Yours was a passage song. Even I felt it and had to be wary. When you leaned your head back and passed out, I knew what had happened. I would've warned you if I'd known what you were going to play." He paused. When he spoke again, his voice was little more than a growl. "The elders will suspect the same thing I did, and they'll test you for it."

Walde stopped in his tracks. "Test me how?"

"The same way they did my father. They'll invite you to the meeting hut and try to shock you so you'll reveal your Reacher light. They might hurt you physically, but in a way that leaves no evidence. Or they might lie to you to make you emotional. My poor father was told his fiancée was sleeping with an elder's son. The elder claimed he'd caught them at it. My father passed that test, but only because my uncle had prepared him for it."

Walde stared at Carrac in near disbelief. "How come I haven't heard about this? These tests should be public knowledge."

"They should be, but they aren't. I doubt the elders do them very often, and the victims are told to keep them secret or be forced to pay a hefty fine."

"Were *you* tested?"

"No. I didn't become a Reacher the way you did, in such a public way. I was sitting alone by the trunk at the time, strumming at my harp. It was a soft, bright summer day and I was happy. The song was good."

A new thought occurred to Walde as his father spoke. He allowed Carrac a few moments of happy reflection before voicing it. "I didn't know emotions were tied to this power until last night, so how do the elders know it?"

The light left his father's face. "They know much more than that, lad. They have the histories, and they're the only ones trained to read them."

"If they know so much about us, why do they keep it hidden?"

"Why does anyone in power hide anything?" Carrac spat. "They've done worse than hide it. Over time, they've spread falsehoods about us and let them fester. And for what?" His palms burned with an angry light.

They had been slowly moving toward the long crack of Killop Ravine. The Killop River started somewhere in the far west and moved southeast for countless miles, its steep walls lowering all the while until they abruptly bent in and formed a low, watery tunnel. The river eventually fed into the Nadi.

This was a low point in the ravine. The riverbank was perhaps forty feet down, a height that a hunter could easily tackle with a knotted rope and hook. *If* he wanted to expend valuable time and energy on a useless task.

No game waited on the riverbanks. The walls were so sheer that even the bravest rock goat wouldn't try them. Walde had only ever spied the ravine from a distance. He stood at its edge now, watching with growing interest as Carrac fixed the claw of his hook into a groove in the rock.

"You've been here before," Walde noted. "That rock is white with scratches."

Carrac did hunt alone on occasion. Walde had assumed he wanted privacy. Knowing he spent the time in the ravine heightened Walde's curiosity to a new level.

Carrac unrolled the attached rope and tossed it over the edge. "I'll go first."

CHAPTER 3

Hunters had to be excellent climbers. The wastes grew no full-size trees, so giant boulders, some as high as twenty feet, were used as perches to stalk prey. Remaining on the rock in all kinds of weather, learning to cling on using ones feet and legs while the arms were occupied with bow and arrow—these were the unique skills of a hunter, and they required solid muscle and a constitution like the rock itself.

Walde had been raised clinging to things high up off the ground, so climbing down the ravine wall posed no challenge whatsoever. "We're trapped here if that rope comes down," he said as he dropped from the rope's last knot to the floor. The riverbank was drier than it had appeared from above, and so firm that Walde's feet did not even leave an impression.

"Nah," Carrac replied. "I have faith you could scale that wall if you needed to."

Walde resisted rolling his eyes.

Carrac set off west, away from the tunnel. Walde was grateful; he had no desire to wade through chill water into a dark cave. He peered around the ravine with interest. The river was narrow but deep, and through its shimmering surface Walde spied fingerlings darting here and there. He would have liked a few quiet moments to study his surroundings, but Carrac forced them both on as if they were a couple of guards on a mission.

A good two hours slogged by. Gradually, the riverbank widened from four feet to eight. The rocky soil softened and became a carpet of meadow weeds and tough grass. Perfect for thatch, Walde thought idly. And for game, if it could get down here. But there was little chance of that now. The ravine walls had risen to over a hundred feet—smooth, arching monsters even a spider would be hard-pressed to scale. The land above would be a sea of broken gray stones.

"No one," Walde said as Carrac paused to drink, "ever comes to this area of the wastes." They had refilled their water skins at the stream. The water was cold and sweet, like lake water after a spring thaw. "What made you do it the first time?"

"I was looking for a place." Carrac capped the skin. "You'll see. It's just around the bend."

The wall did in fact curve, though the river itself didn't shift direction. As Walde followed the wall around, he found himself in a large, open space created by a huge gap in the ravine wall. The ground was a sea of meadow flowers humming with busy bees. And there in the clearing's dead center stood a straight, proud Mothertree. Walde halted at the sight of it and gasped aloud.

It was only sixty or seventy feet high, but its young branches were already dropping from a steeply vertical angle to a horizontal one. In a few years, they would accommodate huts. Walde took an involuntary step toward it, struck with an incompressible urge to touch. More than to touch: to enter, to sink deep, and dredge up life before the heart of all things sank away. Just as it had in his dreams.

Irreverent laughter sliced through his thoughts. "Your face is just a picture," Carrac said.

"Did you plant this?"

"I did. Thirty years ago now."

"You've been coming here for thirty years." He swallowed dryly, ignoring his blazing palms. "The punishment for planting an unsanctioned tree is—"

"Enforced servitude to the community for the rest of your days." The smile hadn't left his face. "I judged it worth the risk." He crossed to the Mothertree and knelt on a thick root at its trunk. His palms whitened as he laid them on the smooth bark, and for several moments he was still. When at last he stood, the sapling's tiny buds had cracked to bare a glimpse of their deep purple innards.

Walde was speechless.

Carrac said, "She responds so well because she's small." He clapped Walde on the shoulder. "You give it try."

"I don't think that's a good idea."

The hand on his shoulder tightened. "This is something you must get used to doing, Walde. You learned to push your emotions down, and now you must learn to push them out."

This is the life of a Reacher. Carrac didn't put it in those words, but the meaning was there all the same.

Walde felt like he stood at the edge of a cliff. What his father wanted for him was dangerous, and more than just to himself.

Carrac viewed reaching as mere maintenance. Feeding it with his hands was like watering. Although Walde knew little about reaching, the very word suggested something deeper than simply feeling. Why hadn't Carrac mentioned the tunnel or the entity Walde had yearned to *reach* for? Walde's own experience, brief as it was, had been powerful. And his dreams were so deep and intense that he doubted their effects could be remedied by "maintenance." His father did not understand.

But perhaps there was a way to explain it to him.

Walde's mouth tightened, and his heart beat hard in his chest. He didn't recall crossing the buzzing space to the tree, but in a moment he was there, and his burning palms gripped the trunk.

At first, nothing happened. There was no treelight, no music to carry him away this time. He lowered himself onto a root and hummed until the dream song blossomed in his mind, harp and lyra mingling. Still, nothing. So he listened to the bees buzzing and the soft tinkling of the river. Even the sun had a sound in his mind, and the curving rock wall sheltering the space. All came together and were one thing. And he was with them like the tree.

And then he was gone.

Was there a way to explain where he went? Walde doubted he could describe it with any satisfaction, neither the place nor the feeling of being there. It would be like trying describe the wind to someone who had never felt it. An invisible pressure might suffice, but it wouldn't convey the icy chill of a winter gale or the gentle touch of a summer breeze.

Walde entered something akin to a tunnel. He sensed its walls as someone might feel a presence in a dark room: instinctively. Other things were harder to explain. The tunnel squeezed, and he moved forward in response to that squeezing, first because he had no choice and then because he wanted to. Yearned with all his being. Something essential was slipping away from him down the tunnel, and if he did not grasp it, he had nothing left to live for.

That was the feeling, and it made no logical sense, but there was no logic in the tunnel, only the reaching and the forceful emotion that drove it on.

And on. He began to feel thin and frayed, but it was so close now… It, or she? Like the tunnel, the being had no physical definition, and yet it radiated life like heat from a burning torch. He lurched toward it, and for an instant he met it and clung on.

In that one, searing moment, the entire fabric of the world opened to him, feeding him a glimpse of impossible knowledge. It was too much. His mind shut down. The tunnel and the being vanished, and he slammed back into his body.

Slowly, painfully, the world took shape around him again.

He was hunched forward on the Mothertree. A bulge in the root jabbed into his calf, and the top of his head felt numb where it was mashed against the trunk.

Aside from these discomforts, he felt oddly calm and at peace. He knew, even before he lay back and stared up into the cloud of purple flowers, that he had done well. The reaching had felt right. Any strangeness could be put down to a simple lack of experience. Idly, he wondered if the being he'd encountered was the tree god, Thara. It seemed likely. But then anything seemed possible just then.

"Walde." Carrac knelt beside him. The evidence of a single tear streaked the side of his nose. "What did you do? The tree hasn't just flowered. It's grown."

"I reached." He closed his eyes, wanting nothing more than to plunge himself back in the tunnel.

"Stand up, lad." When Walde didn't move, Carrac hauled him to his feet and led him over the tree's surface roots to the ravine wall. He unstoppered a skin bottle and held it out.

Walde took a careful swallow.

Carrac said, "Talk to me about what happened."

"I already did. I reached."

"And…?"

He shrugged, looking away. "I don't remember." It wasn't completely a lie. He had forgotten much of the knowledge that had passed to him. As for the rest… He suppressed a sigh. He could never tell his father the truth. It would make a mockery of the decades Carrac had spent doing what he believed was true reaching.

Carrac eyed him for a long moment and then slumped against the rock wall. "You're strong, lad. A century ago, that would have been a good thing. Now it's… Well, it's a danger."

"I know. I know that."

"I'll have to train you to be gentler. As for your nightmares, I'll fetch some daleroot from the herbalist tomorrow. I've used it myself off and on when I felt the need. It'll knock you clean out."

Walde offered a tight nod.

He hated to leave the Lakelands, but he didn't know how long he could stay, even with the daleroot. The slightest lapse in concentration would condemn him to a very public execution, and if that happened, could his father maintain his calm? More than likely he would expose himself as a Reacher and they would both be executed. "How do you live like this?" Walde heard himself say.

Somehow, Carrac understood his meaning. "A tinker asked me that once. He couldn't understand how people could get used to living so high up. A single slip, he said, and you're done." He snorted. "He asked that, not knowing that your mother died that way."

"What did you tell him?"

"I said that we get used to it, and it's just another way to die."

Walde muttered, "There's a bit of a difference between a fall and an execution." He pounded his fist on the rock behind him. "None of this makes a lick of sense. If the elders know so much about us, then they know we could help the Mothertrees. Why destroy the one thing that would help them grow?"

"Power." He caught Walde's wondering gaze and looked aside from it. "What do you know about the time before the purges?"

"Not a lot. I've heard that the Reachers sang for the Mothertrees then, and that their songs died with them."

Carrac was nodding. "They sang, yes. But the Reachers also told stories, moral lessons that taught people how to live. Reacher Lore states that they got this wisdom from Thara." He took a long pull of water as if it were ale.

Thara. Walde's skin prickled. He had given little thought to the tree god before. She was a nebulous figure, meaning different things to different people. Some thought of her as the Mothertrees' spirit, others as just another god among many, one that had little to do with their lives. Most rarely spoke of her and probably didn't think about her much either. Had things been different in the past? He opened his mouth to ask more about her and then snapped it shut as his father plunged on.

"The Reachers and elders had a thorny relationship back then. For the most part, the Reachers tempered the power of the elders, who ran the more mundane tasks of governing. But the Reachers weren't always wise, and depending on the generation, power swayed between the two groups like a badly steered fishing boat.

"Shortly before the purges happened, a dispute arose between three Reachers in the Woodlands, a dispute, they say, over a woman. The young men's families got involved, and sadly, blood was shed. Back then, Reachers were taught to control their strong negative emotions, but there are limits to that control, and the situation was black indeed. So black that their First shed its half-formed pods.

"The Woodlanders were horrified. Such a thing had never happened, certainly not on such a scale. Opinion swayed against the Reachers, and in its wake, the elders took complete control. Straight away, they rounded up the Reachers and slaughtered them. A few escaped to their relatives in the Harborlands and Lakelands, but—"

"Their relatives?"

He nodded. "Reachers were all related back then, Lakelanders to Woodlanders and Woodlanders to Harborlanders, and this proved to be their undoing, for when those in other lands learned that their sons, daughters, and cousins had been slaughtered, they demanded justice from their village elders. Chaos descended as power struggles broke out between elders and Reachers. In the midst of all this, officials from the Woodlands arrived at the Lakelands with their own exaggerated accounts and urged the elders to remove the disease.

"Fights broke out between the Reachers and the visiting officials, and as you can imagine, the elders took the officials' side. By now, Mothertrees in all three lands were suffering, and it had to end. So the purges happened." He dragged in another long gulp of river water.

"The following year, the trees seemed to recover. Pods formed—not as many as before, but that was to be expected, considering what they'd been through. But the year after that, the low numbers were the same. The elders encouraged people to sing, and they established non-Reacher song rites. But nothing worked. Year after year, there were fewer pods and no growth at all. The trees were gradually dying, and no one could do a thing about it.

"People weren't stupid. Many suspected what had happened, and accusations were hurled about. The elders argued that they had merely ended what would have been a long and bloody war. Under such stress, the Mothertrees would have rotted into the ground. But they still lived, and they could still recover.

"Time passed. Those who had witnessed the purges died, and life went on. New lines of Reachers popped up like mushrooms hidden under leaves, and those that weren't extinguished collected knowledge." He looked at Walde and sighed. "So much has been lost, though. Forever lost. Time was when pods were so plentiful that people burned them for fuel in the winter. And now…" His shoulders rose and fell. "Reachers have neither the knowledge nor the freedom to use it."

A lengthy silence fell. The soft meadow and proud, flowering Mothertree filled Walde's view, a surreal counterpoint to his father's dark tale. Walde wrenched his now numb fingers out of gaps in the rock wall. "I don't know what to say. It's a horrible story."

Walde had been taught a truncated version of the tale in which the Reachers, having gone rogue, had held the health of the Mothertrees hostage in a bid to gain more power. Rather than give in to their sordid demands, the elders had executed them. Carrac's account didn't paint the Reachers as heroes, but it didn't paint them as criminals either. No one escaped his father's tale unscathed, and that in itself made it believable. And disturbing.

Even more disturbing, however, was the fact that Reachers had utterly concealed the truth from people. No one knew they did "maintenance" or that they could truly help the Mothertrees if given a chance. As a result, the Mothertrees did not thrive. Ignorant Reachers born outside the lines ended up causing damage and being executed, and these cases perpetuated the belief that Reachers were dangerous. It was a vicious circle, locked into place by fear.

It was disgusting.

Walde asked in a strained but controlled voice, "How many Reachers are alive now in the Lakelands?"

"I know of only fourteen, and that's including ourselves. So many lines have spluttered out over the years..."

Carrac's voice trailed off, and a proud smile lit his face as he regarded his son.

"We should get back home," Walde said briskly and skirted the Mothertree to the bank, where he'd left his bow and pack.

"Yes, I suppose we should. Time flies so quickly."

Once more, Carrac set a fast pace, and the trip back to the Lakelands seemed halved. Walde scarcely remembered it. His mind spun with the idea of starting a quiet rebellion. With a little encouragement, he decided, the other Reachers might agree to a plan. Perhaps a demonstration of power. But first, they would have to reveal the truth to trusted friends and family members. Getting others involved would be essential. With a network of supporters, it would be more difficult for the elders to sweep the whole matter aside—

"Walde."

Carrac halted. They were almost home. Walde could already make out a shimmer of treelight over the top of the rise.

His father met his eyes in the light of their travel lamps. "You look like spring ice about to crack."

"I'm fine." He attempted a wry smile. "Just tired."

"I wanted to talk some more, but that story seemed to have set you off." Carrac shifted, kicking at a loose stone. "I've been troubled lately. About what's been happening down south."

Walde was instantly alert. "Do *you know* what's happening?"

"No. No more than anyone else." His father kicked another stone. "We only get the truth in bits and pieces. See, if we discovered that our pods were the only ones left, we could demand more for them. So we can't trust the tinkers to tell the truth about what's been happening in the Harborlands. But something's brewing, something…" He pressed his lips together and looked out over the shadowy wastes. "They've done away with so many Reachers down there. It'd be a wonder if the trees still lived at all."

CHAPTER 4

It must have been nearly midnight when they took their last weary steps around the trunk to the path that led to Carrac's branch. Many of their neighbors were still up after a long day of buying and selling. Windows were open and voices mingled with the sound of rustling leaves. The walkway to Carrac's hut was shadowy, but cracks around one shuttered window glowed with lamplight.

Carrac said, "I'd wager that's Jak in there, waiting for his money."

Privacy was a rare thing in the Lakelands. Walde had heard it said that Lowlanders locked their doors before venturing out and prosecuted anyone who forced entry. In the Lakelands, people secured their valuables—trade goods, family heirlooms, coins—in chests fastened to the floor. But a hut was a shelter, and hospitality dictated that it be available to passersby.

"Jak…and maybe someone else," Walde said quietly as an angry female growl slid through the closed shutters.

"That woman of yours." Carrac chuckled. "One day she'll flay the skin off your back. It'll happen so fast that you'll look around wondering what happened." He snapped something off the door latch and held it into the light. A strip of bright purple leather hung from his fingertips. "That's your summons to the elders' meeting hut."

"I know what it is," Walde muttered, trying to set his aside his annoyance at his father's jibe at Rona. "No one will be there now. I'll go tomorrow morning."

"Remember what I said about the test."

"How could I forget?"

He clapped Walde on the back and threw open the door.

"Ah, Jak. Poor lad." Carrac's voice trembled with mirth.

The scene that met Walde's eyes was enough to startle a laugh from him. Rona had pinned Jak against a wall so that his face was mashed between two slats, his valuable musician's fingers exposed and vulnerable in her grip. She glanced behind her at Carrac and then dropped Jak's arm with a disgusted sigh. "He insulted me."

Jak turned and looked at her with wide eyes. "No, I just—"

"Shut it." She said something else, but her voice was drowned out by Carrac's booming laughter. Carrac was so amused that he'd buried both his hands inside his jacket. The gesture was so familiar to Walde that he almost disregarded it. How many times had he done that in Walde's life? Walde had considered it a quirk unique to his father. Now he knew otherwise.

The revelation saddened him. How many other aspects of Carrac's personality had formed from having to hide who he was? And how many of those same aspects would Walde adopt? Shaking his head, he strode into his room. He unlocked his chest and scooped out the coin pouch he'd set aside for Jak.

Carrac was holding Rona and Jak apart when Walde returned and placed the pouch in Jak's hand. "Take it, with thanks."

Outrage sparked in Rona's eyes, but to her credit, she held it in. Walde waited until Jak had left before grasping her hand and tugging her outside. He led them around to the back of the hut, where no one could overhear them. He stood close to her, feeling the heat of her breath on his shoulder. A spray of light from a window danced over her defined cheekbones. He said, "Was all that over the coin?"

She jerked away. "It wasn't a small amount. And he had no right to demand it from you."

"Actually, he did. When I chose to play that song, we both knew I'd be paying his fine." He stared hard at her shadowy eyes and told himself that this only seemed petty because of the horrors he had learned about that day.

Rona kicked her boot against the narrow walkway. "I don't like him."

"You don't like my father either. Who *do* you like?" The words were out before he could stop them. He groaned and ran a hand across his face. "I'm sorry. That was out of line."

He waited anxiously for her angry retort, but she gave him nothing but silence. His eyes were closing. "I have to get some sleep, Rona. The elders want me at the meeting hut tomorrow."

"I came here to ask how you were."

"I'm fine. Just tired. I didn't sleep well last night."

"I tried to see you after you fainted, but the crowd—"

"I know." He touched her stiff shoulder. "I understand."

If a fleck of sunlight had touched her face, he would have had reason to kiss her, but there was only darkness and the cold distance she had placed between them. Suddenly they had nothing more to say to one another. He felt the softness of her lips on his cheek, then a breath of wind as she hastened away.

Carrac said as Walde strode back through the door, "I'll fetch the daleroot tomorrow. As soon as I can." The hut's main room held a table and two chairs, a washbasin on a stand, and a few shelves of kitchen supplies. A singed deer hide graced the floor in front of a wood stove. Walde's father sat crossed-legged on it, nudging the remains of a fire Jak must have quickened. "And I'll do maintenance in the morning."

"I think I'll be fine." He took a step toward his room, then halted and looked at his father. "Thanks. For today."

Carrac grinned. "There'll be other days, you know. We'll go back to that tree, you and I."

Walde returned his grin sleepily. "Next time we'll haul back some game."

The bed found him at last, and he passed out the moment his head hit the pillow.

***

Dreams were slippery things. Exhaustion couldn't drive them back or weaken their intensity. Once more, Walde dreamed about losing something essential. It twisted away from him, or dropped like a boulder, or bounded off like a deer hit by an arrow. He thought he had wakened several times, only to find himself still imprisoned.

When he did waken at last, he was drenched in sweat. His heart raced and his palms bathed the room with their cold, silvery light.

He spent some moments calming himself, then rose and lit a lamp. He could not close his eyes again that night. Had he been wise, he would have remained in the wastes until his father could fetch the daleroot. But how could he have known that the nightmares would return? And with such intensity?

He should have talked to Carrac about the dreams. If they were related to being a Reacher, then it was likely his father had experienced the same ones.

So many things he should have talked about instead of brooding over plans that might never come to fruition.

His eyes drooped. If they closed, he might doze off without meaning to and plunge once more into his nightmares. He peeked out the shutters, hoping for a glimmer of dawn, but the only light sprang from the distant path lamps. He needed to take himself somewhere else, away from the relatively small branches just below him. The trunk would do.

He changed as quickly and quietly as he could, grabbed a small goat hair blanket, and tiptoed out the door.

Fog had risen from the lake, burying the lower half of the tree in a white curtain of mist. Walde placed his booted feet carefully as he walked. The boards were slippery with fog; even the handrails were wet to the touch. He came to the trunk at last and lowered himself down in the shadowy space between the herbalist's tent and the meeting hut.

Having spread the blanket securely over his hands, he closed his eyes and, for a miracle, slept.

***

"Walde."

He jumped at the stern voice, got an eyeful of bright sunlight, and shaded his face.

A guard stood over him, waiting. She said, "You are wanted at the meeting hut."

Walde smiled dryly. "I'm here."

She didn't return his smile. Guards never did. Smothering a yawn, Walde got to his feet and, after being frisked for hidden weapons, followed her around a corner and through a pair of tall, polished wooden doors.

The meeting hut was a high-ceilinged hall that followed the curve of the trunk for about thirty feet. It was built of pine beams from the Woodlands. Inside, the wood had been shaped into intricate knot work and polished until it shone. Two enormous chandeliers hung from the ceiling. One was still lit, and it was a good thing since the hut's two windows were still tightly shuttered.

Walde followed the guard past stacked chairs and a locked scroll cabinet to the lit end of the hall, where elders Onyx and Lang sat waiting at a table. Walde wondered idly if they'd drawn the short sticks to be there. Onyx was a tall middle-aged man with thinning red hair and a paunch buried under an oversized ceremonial jacket. Lang mirrored him in height and weight but was several decades his senior. Both had trimmed beards and kept what was left of their hair in short tails at the napes of their necks.

Aside from a gnawing hunger, Walde was calm and well rested. He'd somehow managed to finish the night without having nightmares. The medallion took shape in his mind as he walked, the walls firming, waiting for the test; they would not be breached.

The elders' faces betrayed nothing as he bowed in respect and took the proffered seat before them, draping his blanket across the chair's back. The guard remained at Walde's side, hand resting meaningfully on the hilt of her sheathed shortsword.

Lang leaned over the small table and poured something hot from a teapot into one of three mugs. A sweet scent wafted from the rising steam. "You must be cold from sleeping out in the open all night. Have some tea."

"Thank you, but I'm quite warm." Walde turned the cup, admiring the vivid purple flowers that had been painted around its silver-dipped rim. It was a costly piece.

Onyx cleared his throat. "Have you recovered from your dizzy spell at the song rite?"

"Indeed, I have. Whatever I ate has clawed its way out of me." His mouth stretched in a polite smile.

"Why did you sleep here?" Lang asked.

Walde shrugged. "I got your summons and came, but no one was here, so I waited outside. I guess I must have fallen asleep." He smoothed back his untidy hair with deliberate self-consciousness.

If they wanted to truly challenge his control, they might've forced alcohol on him. He doubted it would have worked, though. The impulse to check strong emotions was so powerful that he usually maintained his control even while drunk.

Lang fingered his white beard. "You went hunting with Carrac yesterday."

"Yes." Offering further explanation would look suspicious, so Walde kept silent.

"You left before dawn and returned at night. In the dark."

"Yes."

The elders exchanged a glance. "When," Lang said slowly, biting off the word, "was the last time you saw the branches under your hut clearly?"

The branches supporting Carrac's hut were visible mainly between the hut and work tent. The messier outer ends extended beyond the work tent and tangled with other branches. "A couple of days ago, I suppose." He frowned, wondering where all this was going.

"That was before the First flowered."

"Yes."

"Your branches haven't flowered. Worse, their unopened buds fall off at a touch. A guard noticed it this morning when he came by to ask for you."

A small, detached part of Walde wondered if that were even possible. Could he have caused that much damage to the branches in two nights? He didn't know enough to dismiss the possibility. But there was this: not all buds on the First blossomed at the same time. Given that fact, Walde doubted that the guard would have taken note of such a thing, especially not from Carrac's front door.

But the elders were leading him somewhere, and he had to go along with it. If he did not react, they would suspect that he knew their game.

How *would* he react to such news if he truly believed it… and wasn't a Reacher? How would he feel, knowing that the branches under his home were failing? Everything his father had worked for, potentially ruined.

Denial.

His brows pulled together, and he gripped the chair arms as if he meant to leap up and look for himself. "I don't believe it. The branches were healthy only two days ago. This must be some sort of mistake."

Onyx shook his head grimly. "There's no mistake, lad. I went there myself and examined them." He held up an unopened bud. It could have been any bud, taken from anywhere.

Walde made a strangled sound in his throat. He snatched the bud from Onyx's hand and ogled it. "How could this have happened? Were they vandalized?"

Lang's blue eyes flicked to Walde's palms, then away. The glance would have meant nothing to Walde if he weren't looking for it. Lang said, "I'm afraid there's a worse explanation than that." His tone became gentle, and sympathy touched his watery blue eyes. It appeared that Lang was as good an actor as Walde. "Your father is a Reacher. We tested him early this morning, and his palms brightened."

Denial. "Impossible! My father is no Reacher. I'd know it if he was." His tight voice echoed through the hall.

"Do you distrust our word?"

"I—" He lifted a hand to his eyes. "Let me see him. Please."

"That's not possible." Lang rose and placed a hand on Walde's shoulder. Walde jerked away as if burned. He stood up, knocking the chair backward.

"Let him be," Lang said as the guard reached for Walde's arm.

Walde demanded in a choked voice, "What are you going to do to him?"

Lang's withered lips compressed. "You know what the price is for being a Reacher, lad. I'm sorry."

Walde focused on a knot in a beam as he shook his head repeatedly. A shuddering breath left him, and he sank down on the polished oak floor.

The elders murmured together softly. Their whispers would have been lost anywhere else, but the hall amplified every sound. If an ant walked across the floor, Walde was convinced he would hear its footsteps.

"Is it enough? He didn't drink the—"

"It's enough. We'll keep him upstairs until tomorrow. Then we'll let him out to see what happens."

One of them must have gestured to the guard, for a firm hand clamped around Walde's arm and dragged him to his feet.

Lang approached him. "Walde, you'll be held here until dawn tomorrow. I am so very, very sorry."

And with that, Walde was led off to the opposite side of the hall. There, a door opened in the paneling and a steep flight of stairs curved up and up to a shadowy crawlspace Walde had never known existed.

"Have you breakfasted?" the guard asked curtly after Walde had climbed in.

"No."

"Then I'll ask if I can bring you something."

Walde made no response, and the trap door banged shut, leaving him in darkness. He shuffled to the wall affixed to the trunk and waited for his eyes to grow accustomed to the lack of light. The space had an airless, musty smell. While the trap door was still open, he had calculated the size to be about six feet by eight, with a ceiling little higher than a yard. The walls let in neither light nor sound. Bright slivers outlined the trap door, and Walde guessed that they would be his only source of air.

He banged the back of his head against the wall in frustration. Everything had made sense until the elders ordered him to be locked up. They had agreed it was enough. He had passed their stupid test. Why allow him to continue believing his father would be executed? Did they do it out of sheer spite?

"Be rational," he muttered. Every action had a motive behind it. The elders would not have confined him for a day unless they considered him a threat somehow. He reviewed the meeting carefully, examining every word and action as he would newly formed arrowheads.

A slow smile bloomed on his face. What a performance Walde had given them! He wished he could have seen himself as they had seen him. Perhaps he had gone too far. Perhaps they feared that if they told Walde the truth about their charade now, he would react with hostility. And with Walde's little act of rebellion at the song rite still fresh in their minds, they might well have worried that he would create a stir on the tinkers' last day.

Yes, his confinement made sense when he viewed matters that way.

Footsteps thudded on the stairs, and the door's bolt shot through. Walde squinted at the brilliant outline of the female guard.

She said, "I've brought you your blanket, a lamp, and a chamber pot. Stand back so I can give them to you."

"Stand?" Walde said dryly as he shuffled away.

A plate of food and a water pitcher joined the other items. Together, they made the crawlspace seem even smaller. Walde thanked her, and the door slammed shut again.

Walde ate quickly then doused the lamp before it sucked up what was left of the air.

The day passed slowly, but the solitude gave him needed time to think. The past two days had brought a whirlwind of change. His entire view of himself and his world had been upended. All his life, he had treaded carefully, as if each new experience was an emotion that had to be analyzed and stowed. He was forever checking himself, and the practice had left him without passion. Jak had spoken of his passion for music. Other men talked in hushed tones about their lovers, their wives. Walde had envied their passion.

Others have their own way to stay calm, his father had said on the day he'd given Walde the medallion, but Walde had long ago dismissed that idea. Others were not as reserved as he and Carrac were. For years, Walde had considered that reserve a strength. What made his father strong made Walde strong, and it was the strength they shared that bound them closer together.

Now that Walde knew the truth, what was he to make of it? Had he lived a century ago, he would've been trained to develop positive passions and channel them to help the Mothertrees. Instead, he was a shadow living alongside other shadows—the Reachers who had tied their own hands back to avoid discovery and in doing so had made themselves into living ghosts.

This couldn't continue. At least not for him. And not while Mothertrees were languishing. If Walde could make no headway here, then he would gather what Reachers would go with him and journey to the empty Woodlands. Given time, the trees would form pods again, and a way of life would continue.

It was a good plan.

He dozed for a while. The guard returned with more food and a gust of fresh air. Walde ate in the darkness, pissed in the pot, then wrapped his hands securely in the blanket and allowed sleep to take him.

A dream came to him after a long space of dreamlessness. He was back in the tunnel, moving forward, but not toward the being. In this tunnel, Thara was absent. Instead, he was surrounded by doors. Each one whispered or whimpered, and Walde feared to open any one of them.

At last, he glimpsed an end to the tunnel.

A shadowy figure stood before him, blocking his way. Walde slowed as he neared it and stared.

It was his father.

Carrac opened his palm. "Walde." Just that. Walde stared back at him. It wasn't a question or a criticism. Rather, it was a simple naming, like a reminder of something lost.

The doors around Walde vanished then, and he slipped into a dreamless sleep.

He jerked awake at the sound of footsteps on the stairs. He shaded his eyes as the trap door creaked open.

The guard said, "Your breakfast, if you want it."

Walde nodded his thanks, and the door closed.

He relit his lamp and dug in, though he'd spent so much time idle that he had little appetite. He was surprised to find a skin of mead lying on its side next to the plate. Did the guard think Walde was a drunkard? He set it aside without taking a sip. When he was done eating, he folded the blanket into a neat, square shape, stacked the plates together, and waited.

At long last, the guard returned. Walde passed her the skin. "I don't drink in the morning, but thanks for the thought."

The guard looked from him to the skin. Then to Walde's complete amazement, she uncapped it and chugged down the entire thing. "Let's get this over with," she muttered. "Leave the blanket. I'll get it back to you later."

Walde's breath stilled. "Let's get *what* over with?"

The guard ignored him and trudged down the stairs. Walde followed on stiff legs, squinting at the light. Unlike the previous morning, the hall's three windows were unshuttered, offering Walde a glimpse of purple flowers in full bloom. The sight would have cheered him if it weren't for the gloom that seemed to hang in the air. The feeling deepened as the guard led him through the door and toward the lift. No one was about. The middle level of the tree would usually be bustling that time in the morning, but now it was utterly abandoned.

The lift operator would not meet Walde's eyes.

The guard said as they stepped into the basket, "I'm to tell you a little about a village meeting the elders held yesterday." When Walde said nothing, she went on, "It was decided that we'd no longer burn our dead, but instead place them on rafts and let the river take them out to sea. The Harborlanders have been doing that for years."

Walde was confused by this and told her so. The river widened and slowed as it approached the ocean. An arm of land jutted into it, creating the harbor that the place was named for. A body couldn't just sail through it all—the boats, the jut of land—and into the open sea.

The guard explained, "Patrol boats will guide the rafts through."

Walde just shook his head.

As the lift sped down, he glimpsed a gathered crowd through gaps in the branches. But there was no cheerful mingling of voices, no movement at all. The guard turned to Walde just as the basket came to rest at the Mothertree's base. "Your father will be the first to go that way."

CHAPTER 5

...are changing. The villagers leave gifts at the First's trunk like tinkers making offerings to Bergis. But you and I and indeed all the elders know that the only way to commune with Thara is through the Reachers. If this bloodbath continues to its finish, we will have to find another way to commune with her. If we don't, I fear that our world will be plunged into a darkness greater than anything we've yet seen.
—A fragment of a letter found lodged under a floor board in an abandoned Woodlands hut

Time slowed. The world seemed to waver and blur, as if through the rippling surface of a river. The crowd parted, and Walde moved through the path they made; he did not know how. His dazed eyes moved from one person to another, and he scarcely knew them. Jak stared at him with burning eyes and a face wet with tears. Rona met Walde's gaze briefly, then her lips tightened and she looked away. And there were others Walde had known all his life. Uncles, aunts, cousins. Faces peering through water.

He glanced at his hands, but they were not burning with a cold, silvery light. They didn't even feel like they belonged to him. He felt nothing. He walked in a dream.

The boats had been cleared from the narrow corner of the lake. In their place floated a single raft with a blanketed body on it. The current tugged gently on the rope that still held it, wanting to propel it toward the river. A horn call pierced the air, and words were spoken in the old tongue. The rope was cut, and the raft began drifting out into the lake.

Walde sucked in a breath. His muscles tightened; emotion roiled in a dizzy swirl beneath the surface. Somewhere in the fog of his stunned mind, an insistent voice whispered that the figure on the raft was his father. That it was Carrac who drifted away from him toward the river, enveloped in a death blanket. His gaze was so fixed on the raft that he didn't notice the archers until their arrows flew. They landed, with hideous accuracy, in the blanketed figure's chest.

The surface broke with a painful snap, and Walde was suddenly running down the boardwalk with blazing hands, shoving through the crowd even as it parted for him. A flurry of raised voices chased him, but they had no more substance than the wind.

The boardwalk ended at a rocky outcrop, which marked the outer edge of the First Mothertree. Walde scaled it, leaping from boulder to boulder as if they didn't exist, and on he went toward the Nadi River. He sensed people trailing behind but didn't fear that they would catch up. Walde could run like a rock deer when the urge was on him. Years of perching on jagged boulders had given him an acute sense of balance, and his long legs could take leaps that others would cringe from. He drew ever closer to the river's edge, eyes darting to the raft, which seemed to be increasing in speed. As soon as Walde was far enough ahead of it, he left the rocks and plunged into the icy water.

The current was startlingly strong. Moving with it, he was able to inch farther out into deeper water. Suddenly, the raft hurtled by. Walde shot an arm out to catch it. His fingers snagged the edge of something, rope or thick bark, and he clung on. In a feat of strength born of desperation, he hauled himself onto it until his upper body was balanced over his father's legs. The narrow raft did not like the extra weight, and it pitched from side to side, the bound logs sinking deeper into the now raging water. Another few inches and most of him was on the raft.

"Father!" He reached up to the blanketed body. With the distracting sway and kick of the current and his own chill fingers, he didn't understand what he felt at first. He prodded the thin blanket, expecting the soft stickiness of blood-soaked flesh. Instead, he touched a firm surface. Heart racing, he drew the blanket off as far as the arrows. His father's face and neck appeared, but the rest of his upper body appeared to be draped in a curved wooden shield. Walde wedged his fingers under the shield's edges and pulled up.

The shield strained under the ropes that bore it down, but with an effort, he managed to lift it a little, which meant that the protruding arrows hadn't gone through the wood into his father's chest. He set his fingers to Carrac's lips and thought he felt a drift of warm air.

Walde's head sank forward, and he sobbed. His father was alive. Must be. Why else would they have gone to the trouble of faking his death? They must have drugged him somehow.

"Father! Wake up!"

The raft bucked violently. Walde barely clung on as it tipped sideways. In another moment it would overturn and his father would drown. Because of him.

With a strangled cry, Walde thrust himself off the end of the raft and let it go.

At once, the raging water took hold of him, and all his energy became fixed on breathing. He could barely keep from sucking in water as the current jerked him this way and that. He broke the surface in time to glimpse the mossy face of a passing rock, then it was behind him, and he was struggling once more to keep his head above water.

The river curved around a bend. Walde knew, with a cold certainty, that he would die if he did not reach the shore soon. The rapids didn't end for many miles; before then, he would lose feeling in his limbs and drown. This may be his only chance.

A woman who got sucked out into the river told Walde she'd survived by floating with her feet ahead of her. Walde tried for the position and failed. The white water tore at his limbs, leaving him sick and disoriented. Another rock hurtled past, and he lunged for it. Missed. As he grasped for another, a submerged stone scraped into his side, making him cry out in pain and shock. Another bashed into his shoulder, slowing his momentum. He grabbed it with shaking hands and clung on. Trembling, he shifted his body so his feet floated ahead of him, then he let go. As the current pitched him forward, he grabbed stone after stone, clawing his way slowly toward shore. At last, he slid out of the water, rolled onto his side, and lost consciousness.

Sometime later, his eyes opened, and he squinted up at the midday sun. He was warm and needled with pain. The shore was bathed in hot sunlight; but for that, he would surely have died from the chill.

Air hissed between his teeth as he rose to a sitting position. His side ached. He fingered the torn cloth and felt the stickiness of blood. He pushed a fist into his eyes.

It was painful to contemplate what had just happened. It was too big, too much.

Of one thing he was sure: he could not go back to the village. And not simply because his palms had flared, exposing him as a Reacher.

The elders had conspired somehow with Harborlands officials to ship Reachers alive down the river. For what purpose, Walde could not guess. He couldn't bring himself to believe that the Harborlanders were using Reachers to destroy their Mothertrees. It made no sense.

His thoughts returned to his father. In time, Carrac would reach the harbour, and a patrol ship would haul him in. Walde wouldn't get there in time to watch that happen. But he *would* get there. As surely as the river flowed, he would find his father and free him.

He tried to stand and collapsed back onto the mossy shore. He felt as though he'd been battered by a mallet. Every part of him ached.

Wincing at the gleam of light on the water, he took in his surroundings. He'd made it through the rapids to the opposite side of the river. A scan of the west bank told him that no one had followed. The elders probably assumed he was dead. Folk died every year by being sucked out into the river. And not all of them were drunk. In Walde's lifetime, only one other person had survived the rapids, and she was an experienced swimmer.

Gritting his teeth, he worked at pulling his clothes off. The sun had dried the cloth in places, and it clung stubbornly to his scratches. He tried to tug off his boots, but the pain in his side made bending nearly impossible. He settled on kicking them off instead. Naked at last, he stared in shock at his mangled body. Scratches scored every limb; some oozed blood, others were a breath away from it. An angry welt had formed on his shoulder, but the skin remained unbroken. As for the wound in his side…

He looked away, swallowing hard.

He dragged his tunic to the water's edge and, careful not to draw too close to the white water, rinsed the blood off it. The wound was perhaps two inches long. A constant stream of dark blood seeped from it. Just looking at it made him queasy. Walde tore two strips off the bottom of his tunic. He bunched the thinner strip into a ball and pressed it snugly onto the wound. The other served as a bandage to hold the ball on. The cloth secured around his waist, he retrieved his leather trousers and rinsed the blood off them while lying down. They were torn in places but still wearable. He had no time to let them dry. He pulled them on with difficulty, trying not to jostle the bandage, then wrung the water from his tunic and shrugged it on too.

After drinking deeply from the river, he climbed gingerly to his feet and considered what he'd need to survive the long journey to the Harborlands.

He peered over the embankment, which ran in a steep line along the shore, and groaned. A bare, rocky landscape stretched away from him, sprinkled only by tufts of stringy grass and field weeds. Without the stunted trees so common in the wastes, he could not hope to fashion a hunting bow or even build a decent fire. The Lowlands might harbor a few trees, but the place was several days away.

Move, he urged himself. He shoved on his boots and walked on the shore beside the embankment, gathering driftwood under his arm. In storms, the Mothertrees shed bits of themselves into the lake. Once dry, they were quite brittle and burned well. Most were set aside to be used in pyres for the dead.

Or they *had been* used for pyres. He grimaced as the guard's words drifted back, followed by everything else that had happened that morning.

What bothered him most was his own stupidity. There he'd lain in the crawlspace, thinking over his life and all he'd been deprived of, while in some dark, hopeless place, his father was being drugged and trussed like some harvest goat. If Walde had not been so cocksure, he might have divined the situation and helped his father. *Or not.* But there was no way to know now. Just as there was no way to know when his father would wake on the raft. With an effort, he set the thoughts aside and forced himself to calmness. The whiteness in his palms diminished until he could make out fine lines again. From now on, he had to keep it that way.

He piled his haul of wood onto the embankment and went looking for an ax. Or rather, he searched for a stone that could become an ax. He had scooped up and examined at least twenty before settling on one the length of his forearm, with a vaguely triangular shape. Snatching up a second stone, he leaned his chest against the embankment and began hacking and chipping out an edge.

The skill came easy to him now, but it had taken years to master. One wrong hit and the entire blade would be ruined.

His face was damp with sweat when he'd finally finished. His trembling hands—caused, no doubt, by blood loss—had made the task more difficult than it should have been. He left the ax with the wood and returned to the river to rinse his bandage. The bleeding was slowly letting up. He could only hope that the wound wouldn't fester.

Satisfied with the bandage, he collected his ax and wood and hauled himself onto the embankment.

After a few paces, he came to the overgrown cart road that followed the river all the way to the Harborlands. Lines of flattened weeds and horse droppings spoke of recent travelers. Walde paused, weighing the chance of being caught against his need for water. If he were not injured, he might have risked leaving the vicinity of the river, but a wound was like an infant; it needed constant tending. As for being caught… If guards *had* been sent over the lake to examine the east side of the river, then Walde was little safer in the wastes than on the road. Both would be examined by the guards.

In the end, he stuck to the road. At first he jogged, cradling the wood and ax under his arm, but pain and weariness overcame him, and he slowed to a walk. After a time, the low hill he walked alongside flattened, and he spied the misty peaks of the distant mountains. A smudge of darkness gathered over them. He scooped up some grass and watched which way the wind took it. North. If he were lucky, the storm would skirt him.

He walked into the late afternoon, stopping twice to drink and inspect his bandages. Thrice he paused to dig up hunter's root—the white, fat root that travelers resorted to eating when they had no other food. He rinsed them in the river and consumed them as he traveled. Until he could fashion a hunting bow, they were all he had.

The nearby hills undulated like storm waves, flattening for a while, only to swell again and conceal the mountains. The cart road was, by contrast, unvarying. He was grateful it sloped down instead of up. Gradually, the sky became overcast and a chill wind smelling of rain bent the field weeds. The few rabbits Walde had spied fled into their holes.

Night was falling, and there was no shelter for miles around. In the wastes, hunters sheltered in the crevices of boulders. But this land was devoid of such large rocks.

In the end, he returned to the river, which had calmed to a deep, steady flow, and walked along the shore until he spotted a gap in the wall of the embankment. There he gathered some dry, dead grass, selected a length of driftwood from his haul, and chopped it in half. After carving a groove down the length of the thicker half, he shaped the end of the thinner into a point. Then, sitting on the fat half to secure it, he rubbed the point of the thin half into the groove over and over until smoke rose from it. He tilted the resulting bit of charcoal into the dry grass and blew while cupping the grass in his hands.

Friction fires were harder to make than flint fires, but without a tinker blade, he had no hope in taking the easy route. He wondered how long this fire would last, given the threatening sky.

With that cheerful thought, he huddled into the warmed hollow and slept.

***

He woke shivering, amazed at two things at once: it had not rained a drop, and he had not dreamed. Or at least, he did not remember dreaming.

A gloomy dawn had broken over the land. Walde forced himself to rise, wincing at every sore muscle and bruised limb. The wound in his side was its own monster. Moving even a little made it throb. He crawled around the blackened remains of his fire and went to the water's edge to drink and clean the bandages.

Carrac might have reached the harbor by now.

The thought halted his hands. Walde was still more than a week's journey from the river's end. What would happen to Carrac in that time?

Don't think about it, he told himself fiercely. Dwelling on what might or might not be happening to his father would only drive him mad. All he could do now was keep moving forward and deal with whatever challenges came his way.

The wound appeared to be healing despite the pain. Walde refolded the cloth rather than washing it—it was not beneficial for the wound to remain wet. After scooping the icy water into his mouth, he scoured the shore for driftwood, peeking around clumps of reeds and river cane. Now that the current had slowed, a variety of plants had sprung up. Tiny frogs clung to the reeds, and minnows the size of fingernails darted in the shadows.

He returned to the embankment empty-handed, thankful that he'd saved the two pieces of wood with which he'd used to start the fire. At least he would travel lighter that day. He kicked rocks over the ashes before clambering onto the embankment.

Four long, lonely days followed. On the fifth day, when the sun was at its apex in the sky, the road suddenly branched into two. The new road led east up a slope.

He had reached the Lowlands.

Wonder moved through him, followed by a twinge of trepidation. Should he venture up that road? He didn't trust the Lowlanders, and without coin he couldn't hope to supply himself with what he needed. But there was always the chance he might find a stunted tree, especially in such a sheltered area. He glanced down at his brightened palms, then tore two more strips off the bottom of his tunic and wrapped them snugly. Anything could happen on the road, and in his current state of mind he couldn't trust himself to hold it together.

He walked between the deep ruts of wagon wheels—a sign that the road was well used. Perhaps it was the only way out of the Lowlands. Walde had seen a map of the place when he was a child, but many of the details had fled his mind.

After perhaps a mile, the slope reached a gentle plateau. Walde paused, mesmerized by the vista that opened before him.

A vast, flat land lay between the mountains and the slope on which Walde stood. Much of it was damp-looking and drab, but stately homes with accompanying outbuildings gathered at the feet of the mountains. Many had what appeared to be gardens and horse pens. Glittering streams trickled here and there on their way down to the low-lying area, which might well be bog.

The Lowlands was a relatively new settlement. A century ago, roaming tinkers who wintered there discovered a use for peat. Who would have thought that the fibrous black earth could be burned? But it did burn, and well. Tinkers sold it in wagonloads in the autumn.

If that wasn't enough of a reason to settle here, another came in the form of precious metals. Tinkers were always looking for iron. This time they found silver, a huge vein of it that would take generations to mine. With so much potential wealth, only a few tinkers had chosen to remain nomadic.

As the full sun shone on their pretty houses and gardens, it also fell on the grubby, ramshackle huts that huddled in the plain's north corner like a skunk's dunghill. Walde's lips pulled back from his teeth. This was the outcome of living away from the Mothertrees—and Thara. This abuse of the poor.

The Woodlanders didn't appear to share Walde's sentiment. Squinting his eyes south, he thought he glimpsed the outer edges of a large settlement. Could this be their new home? Yes, it must be. He wondered how they could be content living alongside such people. Perhaps they were already adopting the Lowlanders' ways. It was an inevitability.

He lingered on the slope a little longer, trying to decide whether to go down into the village. While he could trade his ax for some wood to make a bow, the exchange would stir up gossip. Bad enough that he was a Lakelander, but his torn, blood-stained tunic would make him nothing less than a walking spectacle. No, he couldn't take another step down. He veered off the road and wandered south around some hillocks, pausing to pull up hunter's roots that peeked through the field grass, and all the while he scoured the countryside for stunted trees. He wasn't optimistic. The windswept ground was bare of sheltering boulders. He halted at a stream and drank deeply.

The sun was low but still an hour from setting. He was considering the idea of sheltering there when a muffled scream tore through the silence. Gripping his ax, Walde leapt to his feet and ran in the direction of the sound.

CHAPTER 6

Walde scrambled up the side of a hillock, hoping he was heading in the direction of the scream. He did not have to worry long.

In an area of crushed grass, a young man wearing a purple robe straddled a struggling young woman.

Walde sucked in a sharp breath. For a split second, he considered killing the rapist, but logic stopped his hand. If Walde killed the man, he couldn't in good conscience leave the woman with the aftermath. Nor could he stay. His best course of action would be to knock the man unconscious with a well-aimed blow to the head.

Time slows in such moments. In the time it took Walde to think this through, a slender arm slipped free of its confinement, felt around behind her, snatched a rock the size of Walde's fist and brought it down hard on the man's head. Once. Twice. A third time. The man went still, and panting, she shoved him off her.

The woman didn't waste time weeping but put her cheek up to the rapist's nose to see if he breathed. After a moment's silence, she drew away and climbed unsteadily to her feet.

Walde's bandaged hand dropped from his mouth. He had never witnessed such a display of courage and ferocity in his life. He must have made a sound in his throat, for she jumped as if doused by cold water. Her hazel eyes met Walde's. They held such fierceness in them that he dropped the ax and wood that had been under his arm and raised his hands over his head. He said quickly, "I won't hurt you."

Her gaze flicked from Walde to the bloodied rock and back again. The gesture seemed deliberate, a warning that she could do to Walde what she had just done to the rapist.

She cleared her throat. "You're not from here."

"No. I'm just…just passing through."

"Then keep moving."

Her fierce eyes released him, but Walde sensed a watchfulness about her. It reminded him of an animal who is aware of a hunter while still a safe distance away. Walde fetched his ax and wood and took a few steps back. He knew he should leave but found he could not. He couldn't have said why. Instead, he crouched on the ground to seem less threatening and observed her.

She was a wreck of a woman. Walde judged her to be about his own age, though her face was so filthy with blood and grime that he couldn't be sure. Her knee-length brown frock hung on her slender frame—the neck was torn, but not so that her breasts were exposed. Her bottoms were unsalvageable. She bunched them up and shoved them along with the rock into the neck of the man's robe, then grasped his wrists and dragged him several feet away.

She returned to the disturbed grass and plucked and pulled until much of it stood up again, albeit weakly. Having accomplished this, she snatched up a leather pouch that must have come off her in the scuffle and secured it to a belt around her waist. Walde had no doubt it was hers. All women carried the small leather belt pouch. It held their toiletries, along with other personal items they disliked being without.

She squatted behind the man and pulled his arms up over her shoulders so that much of his upper body draped her back. Gripping his forearms, she struggled to her feet.

Walde looked on in astonishment. The man was not short, and unlike her, he had been well fed. That she found the strength to touch him after what he did to her was incredible, but to carry his weight on her back...

She was fighting for her life, he realized. Her calloused hands and drab clothing indicated that she was probably a lot poorer than the rapist. Even with evidence of her injuries, she might still be punished, and harshly. Lowlanders hung people for all sorts of crimes, and their system of justice favored the rich. His heart turned over as he considered what she was now facing: self-imposed exile or interrogation. Either could lead to death.

The woman took a heavy step forward. She warned in a strained voice, "Go away."

"If I may ask, where do you plan to dispose of the—"

"That's none of your business." She took another step, stumbled, and caught herself.

"The river is a good two miles from here. If you'd allow me..." His voice faltered as she turned her back on him and lumbered around the base of the hillock.

He followed at a distance, stamping his feet as he walked to let her know he was there. A path of light blazed in front of her, and she walked straight into it, into the setting sun, and did not shield her eyes. She could not. All her energy was fixed on hauling the weight on her back another step. And then another. Walde could vividly imagine how it must be. She would not recover from this quickly. Her back would ache. The pain would eventually go away, but it would return in the cold and assail her anew.

Walde thought she was aiming for the river, but as soon as the ground plateaued, she turned and hiked south, shuffling slower and slower with every step.

She had not gone a mile when she paused and swayed. Her trembling legs buckled, and Walde, guessing what was about to happen, dropped his things, lurched forward, and grabbed the body before it collapsed on her.

The woman fell to the ground at his feet, shaking with exhaustion.

Walde peered worriedly around them. They had left the grassy hillocks behind and were nearing a shadowy area of flat land. The sun hovered on the horizon, gracing the low bushes and field weeds with an orangey-red glow. They had no shelter, little to no fuel for a fire, and no food. They could not afford to linger. Walde hefted the corpse onto his back—cringing at the bite of pain in his side—and stepped away from the woman's prone form. "Where do I take him?"

The woman lifted her head, and Walde realized with a start that she'd been crying. "What will you ask for in return?"

He regarded her in surprise. An offer of help to someone in need was given freely. To suggest otherwise was an affront to one's honor. Or at least, it would have been if he were back home. But this was not home. These were not his people. He asked, "What's your name?"

"Brite." She spat the name like a spark.

"I'm Walde." He shifted the corpse, nose wrinkling at the scent of blood wafting from its head. "The only thing I ask is for you to carry my belongings while I walk." He jerked his head at the stone ax and driftwood.

Brite hesitated and then hefted the ax, smiling as she grazed its tip. Her stiff shoulders relaxed a little. She gathered the driftwood and rose on shaky legs to her feet. "Follow me."

Walde had no idea how Brite had managed to haul the corpse as far as she did, the way she did. The position wasted energy and forced one to a constant slouch. Before he had taken five steps, he'd repositioned the body so that it hung over his shoulders like a dead deer. "How long before this man's folks come looking for him?"

Brite didn't answer, and as the silence lengthened, Walde gave up on her speaking at all. He had nearly forgotten his question when her quiet voice bumped up against the shuffling of their footsteps.

"I don't know. Maybe tomorrow morning. But I can't wager my life on that. I have to keep moving, even after we get rid of this body. The man's friends knew he was after me, so when they find both of us gone, they'll be after me too."

"What about your folks—?"

"They won't come at all."

And with those cheerful words, she quickened her pace, forcing Walde to keep up despite the heavy weight on his shoulders. Her gaze darted back at him again and again as they walked. He wondered if that was fear lurking in her eyes, or merely anxiety brought on by her circumstances. Would she feel safer if *he* walked in front and she behind? "I won't hurt you," he found himself reiterating.

"We're almost there."

No sooner had the words left her mouth than a scent akin to rotting eggs filled his nostrils. He looked around for the source, but the earth was drenched in shadow. No, it was not merely shadow; the ground itself was dark. And bare, but for a few tufts of grass. He took a hesitant step, then another. Did he imagine it, or were his feet sinking ever so slightly into the dark mass?

"This is a bog," he said flatly.

"Keep walking."

"Into a bog?" He took another step, for the longer he stood in one spot, the deeper his boots sank.

Brite paused and looked back at him. Her eyes glittered in the eerie twilight. She was like a wraith born from river mist and swamp water. Dark, deadly, and—he guessed—as at home in the bog as Walde was in the treetops. She said, "I know a way through it. Follow me and you'll be fine."

"How far do we go?" He wished his hands were free so he could slap the biting flies.

"Only a little ways. Walk quickly and we'll get there faster."

Walde worked hard to douse his fear as he pressed forward, the body across his shoulders feeling heavier with every step. He trusted this woman about as much as he trusted that the bandages still covered his palms. As soon as this task was done, only her conscience would stop her from slipping off into darkness and leaving him to find his own way out of the bog. She had his ax now. Returning it would benefit her not at all.

A dry smile twisted his lips. Now that Walde was in a vulnerable position, he was experiencing the same mistrust she'd felt about him.

Finally, she halted and waved the ax at a glitter of moonlight in the darkness. Water. "Tumble him into that if you can. But don't leave the path, or you'll follow him in."

"You don't want to search his pockets? He might have—"

"No. I want nothing of his."

Walde, aware that his feet were sinking into the soggy grass, slid the body off his shoulders and hefted it into the bog. As soon as he was free of it, he went to stand by Brite's side. Though she did not step away from him, he would have wagered a bottle of ona that her hand tightened on the ax.

The body sank with hideous slowness. Walde cringed at the soft gurgling of the dark water. He shifted his feet, slapping flies. "Can we go now? It's almost dark."

"I have to see this through."

He nodded stiffly, and they stood together in silence, watching the bog eat the body until nothing of it remained.

"All right," she whispered. "Let's go."

They retraced their steps, and in what seemed a remarkably short time, they were back on firm ground again. They turned in the direction of the river. Words were not needed to understand the thirst they both had.

They crossed the tinker road and scrambled down the embankment to the shore. Moonlight glittered on the water, illuminating clumps of reeds and river cane that huddled at the river's edge. Brite disappeared into one of those clumps, and her vigorous splashing told Walde how much she had wanted to clean herself.

He hoped she had set his wood down somewhere dry.

After drinking deeply, he lifted his tunic and unpeeled the bandage on his side. Part of the wound had broken open, but the bleeding seemed to have let up. He washed the bandage and wrung the water out of it before binding himself up once more.

Brite waited for him by the embankment. Though the night hid her features, he could tell that her face was brighter with the blood washed away. She pushed the wood into his arms and took a swift step back. Walde bit back a sour laugh. Did she worry he would strike her with a piece of driftwood?

She said, "I won't say thank you because that would be an insult. I am in your debt."

He stifled a groan. "You owe me nothing, and adding the weight of an imagined debt to your shoulders won't help you. Better to say thank you and be done with it."

"You're a fool," she said, but there was a smile in her voice.

"Maybe. Or maybe I'm just a Lakelander."

"You're not in the Lakelands anymore. I have to go, and I'm taking your ax with me. I thank you for *that*." She turned and walked along the shore into the night. Walde followed after her.

"Are you heading south?" he asked.

"What's it to you?"

"I'm heading that way myself."

"Oh?"

Her voice was tinged with a friendly sort of skepticism. Walde couldn't blame her. If he was heading south, then why had he been wandering in the lowland hillocks, wearing no jacket or traveling pack, and dressed only in torn, bloodied clothing and bandages? He laughed under his breath. "It's true. I'm heading to the Harborlands to meet my father. As for my appearance…" He dragged a hand through his damp hair. How would she react if he told her the truth? It wasn't a good time to find out. "I was trapped in the rapids for a while."

She slowed and turned a little. "If that's true, then you're lucky to be alive."

They said nothing more for a time. Little by little, the shore between the embankment and the reeds thinned, and they were forced to a slower pace, but Walde didn't suggest moving to the road. The shore was made up of small wet stones, which didn't record footprints easily.

And there was the matter of a food source. Walde had been pulling up reed shoots as he walked and consuming them with a bitter determination. Reeds were a common food in the Lakelands. But they were usually boiled and their seeds ground to make a fine flour. Walde had never eaten them raw, but he would've resorted to worse in order to ease the relentless ache of his empty belly.

It was probably an hour or two before dawn when Brite halted and leaned hard against the embankment. They had just rounded a curve in the river. The bare area of the shore had widened a little, allowing for a space to sit. Walde ran his fingers over his torn sleeve, feeling for biting flies. Fortunately, the river ran too quickly to allow them to proliferate as they did in the bog. Nevertheless, there were still a few.

"Rest for a bit," Brite suggested and sat against the embankment.

Walde joined her. And in the ensuing silence, his head drooped and he promptly went to sleep.

***

The dreams came on him unexpectedly, like pain from a wound he thought had long healed. Once more, the sensation of losing something essential struck him. His mind found new ways to make him feel it, situations that played out again and again until the inevitable and bitter end, each more elaborate than the first.

He woke at last to the sound of his own hoarse moaning. Shoving his bandaged palms under his thighs, he looked around for Brite.

The sun was not merely up but was well on its way to the top of the sky. Walde was alone in the embankment's shadow. Had Brite gone on alone? The thought made him leap to his feet, but he had not taken a step before she appeared on top of the embankment. She jumped down in front of him with a brilliant smile.

Walde's mouth slackened as he looked at her. With the blood cleaned from her face and hair, and the sun shining fully on her, she was the very essence of her name. Her hair was not merely brown, but a deep ruddy red. Her hazel eyes shone with alertness that was perhaps a mingling of intelligence and caution. She was oval-faced, with soft, wide lips and a straight, narrow nose. A scabby cut running from her temple to one sun-browned cheek provoked in him a protective feeling which he at once tried to quell.

Her smile faltered. She had been speaking, he realized, and he hadn't heard a word. He said, "I'm sorry, I think I'm still asleep." He blinked hard, hoping he looked tired.

"You look as if you've been punched in the face. I said I made you a bow." She held up a length of worked wood.

As Walde fixed on it, a smile jumped onto his face. "That's from a stunted tree. Where did you find that?"

"Over the embankment. We walked quite a ways last night, and the land has changed. The Woodlands aren't far away now." She turned the wood, showing off the work she'd done on it. "What do you think?"

Stunted trees looked flimsy, but they were incredibly strong. Old, and toughened by wind and droughts. Cutting one down wasn't easy, and shaping the wood into a bow took skill. He couldn't imagine performing the task with an aching back.

He freed his hands and took the bow from her. It was the right length and thickness. The two ends had been shaped and notched, leaving a thick center. "It's good. You did well." In truth, she had taken a bit too much off the ends, but the weapon would still function. "How did you know I was after one?"

"You're a hunter. I could tell by the way you walked."

Walde's brows shot up. "Are you—?"

"No. But my uncle is—or was." Her mouth twitched down. "He used to take me hunting with him when I was younger. I learned how to make a bow from him. Not well, mind you…"

"Well enough. You chose a straight tree, and that takes a good eye. Thank you."

She motioned to a pile of sticks on the embankment. "I hacked off a few branches but didn't have time to shape them into arrows."

Walde scooped up the sticks and eyed them appraisingly. "Long and straight." He pursed his lips. "Is all this in payment for your imagined debt?"

"No, it's for the ax I—" Suddenly her breath caught, and stark fear entered her eyes.

An odd sound came to Walde's ears, distant still, but growing nearer. "What—"

"Trackers and tracker dogs. They must have traveled right through the night."

CHAPTER 7

Walde had glimpsed dogs across the lake milling about the tinkers' wagons. They were the tinkers' toys, or so the Lakelanders called them. He should have guessed that they'd be employed for tracking.

As he turned to peer in the direction of the barking, Brite grabbed his arm and dragged him toward the river. "We must get into deeper water." She chucked his driftwood into the river, shoved the unfinished bow and arrows deep into some tall reeds, then, to Walde's astonishment, hacked a reed down with the ax and chopped it into two parts, each about half a yard in length. "This is a last resort. Keep one end above water and breathe through the other. It'll be hard but better than holding your breath."

Walde snatched her wrist before she lurched into the deeper water. "The current—"

"You survived rapids, and you're worried about this? Get in!"

The water around the reeds was still and clear. But even a few feet out, it became murky with mud carried along from upriver. The muddy area seemed benign, but Walde knew what hidden flows could lurk beneath its surface. Brite was accustomed to bogs. Did she even grasp how powerful a hidden current could be? The barking had grown uncomfortably close, and now voices joined it. The trackers would be rounding the river's bend.

Brite jerked her arm away and waded in. Walde could do nothing but follow. If he'd had a weapon, he might have crouched behind the reeds and considered his chances.

No, that wasn't true. He would not have waited while Brite fought for her life in the current. He charged in after her.

The river bottom dropped almost instantly. The murky water was ice-cold, shocking him even as he struggled to find the bottom. He was dragged out for several yards before his feet locked around a stone on the river floor. He surfaced and gasped for air.

Brite was nowhere. She could not be underwater breathing through the reed. The current was too strong. Desperately, he searched the shoreline.

No Brite. Instead, a man holding a walking stick in one hand and a rope in the other prodded the clumps of reeds. His animal followed close behind, nose pointed in the air. If the man raised his eyes to the wide river, he would spot Walde at once. Walde dunked his head under and held his breath.

What passed was one of the most uncomfortable moments in his life. The icy water tore at him as he fought to keep his purchase on the rock. The struggle made holding his breath nearly impossible. He finally broke the surface and gasped. A glimpse of the shore told him the man was gone. A woman, three men, and the dog now milled about on the embankment. As the woman turned her head toward the river, Walde dunked back under. Another eternity passed before he broke the surface again.

This time, the embankment was empty. The people were gone.

It was a shabby sort of relief. Brite was still missing, and Walde feared that she had drowned. If she had, then he had no chance of finding her. The current would drag her to the Harborlands, where she would be hauled up like a fish, probably by patrol ships.

These were his thoughts as he let go of the rock and fought his way back to shore. His body felt about as heavy and cold as a rotting branch in winter. The cloths wrapping his palms were missing, but the bandage around his side remained. He tugged his sodden boots off and then forced himself to walk, all the time scanning the clumps of reeds in case Brite had slipped between them, perhaps hiding still. But he saw no sign of her.

He came to the area where they had rested for the night and retrieved the bow and arrows from the reeds. If they hadn't blended so well, the man would have found them. Walde held them a moment, unable to take another step. Had Brite's determination to repay him caused her death? Had the trackers found the tree she had hacked down and traced her path back to this spot?

His fists tightened on the bow, and he very nearly snapped it in half. Only his calming reflex stopped him, allowing him time to think. Why had he already given her up for dead? If he could survive the rapids, then Brite could fight the current.

He jogged down the shore, seizing his boots as he went. He passed the spot where he had emerged from the river and continued on, scouring the river, the reeds, the scruffy wall of the embankment. He had gone perhaps half a mile and was on the verge of exhaustion when he spotted a form huddled against the embankment.

"Brite!"

She shuddered and crouched forward to look at him. Walde slowed, stumbling as he walked. It cost him a great deal to shove back his relief at the sight of her, but he managed it. Just.

"I lost the ax," she muttered.

Walde squatted down beside her, choking out a laugh. "That's all you can think of? You're alive."

Her head hung over her bare legs. "My pride's taken a beating."

"You couldn't have known that the—"

"I did know. Everyone knows about the river's current. I thought I could bear it for a while, but I was wrong."

"Doesn't matter. We're free and alive. If we hadn't been dragged downriver, they might have spotted us. It was the better of two evils."

She threw him a pained glance. "You were dragged out too?"

He groaned. "Look, we need to think about other things—"

"We?"

"The tree you chopped down—how far was it from the river?"

She pursed her lips. "Far. I traveled inland for a mile to find it."

Walde hid his astonishment. Had she slept at all?

She stretched and ground a fist into her back. "They didn't just happen on the tree and come here, if that's what you think. The dogs tracked our scent from the Lowlands to the river. If they track it from the river to the tree, all they'll find is a few twigs and leaves. I concealed the stump."

"Dog."

"What?"

"I only saw one." He stood and peered over the edge of the embankment. The land was flat and shelterless. They would be spotted from afar. "We should lie low here for a while."

She yawned. "I won't argue with that."

Sunlight inched toward them, warming and drying their clothes. Walde suggested that without a body, people might conclude that she and the rapist had run away together, but Brite only laughed at the idea.

"That's the last thing they would think. Rich men rape the women who work for them. They don't take us as wives. That man stalked me for months, always threatening to do...what he tried to do back there. It frightened me to death because I knew he could get away with it."

Walde's brow furrowed. "Don't you have laws against such things?"

"Laws," she mused, "only work if people are afraid to break them. In the Lowlands, people pay fines for breaking laws. The Scats have no money for fines. But the wealthy do."

"Who are the Scats?" The term sounded familiar, but he couldn't place it.

"You'd know if you gave it some thought. At one time, the Lowlands crawled with foxes and martins. The Barans—that's what the wealthy call themselves now—hired poor tinkers to track the animals down."

"Tinkers aren't known for being hunters," he pointed out.

"No, but they're always traveling, so..."

"So they're familiar with animal scat."

She gave a sleepy nod. "The ones who settled in the Lowlands became known as Scats. Some Scats have more money than others, but even the wealthiest of them are poor compared to the Barans."

"But weren't the Barans tinkers once too?"

"They were. Many generations ago."

Walde couldn't help but shake his head. The clearer a glimpse he got of the Lowlands, the worse it looked. Such a culture could not continue indefinitely. In time, it would implode on itself.

Brite was speaking again. "When I heard that he planned to waylay me, I told my family I was leaving home."

"By family, do you mean...?"

"My aunt and uncle," she said softly. "My parents have been...out of my life for some time." She looked down at her work worn hands. "After that... Well, you know what happened. He must have found out and followed me."

Walde tugged on his growing beard. "What if...if you and a witness had gone back and told them what happened?" He had avoided asking this question for fear that she would demand this very thing. In other circumstances, Walde would have been happy to oblige her, but he couldn't risk losing a week or more for the trial. Besides, he suspected that a Lowlands official would have to be sent to the Lakelands to confirm Walde's reputation and identity. Once they discovered he was a Reacher, his testimony would've been thrown out and he would've been hauled back home, leaving his father without aid.

Of course, all of this was irrelevant now that he'd helped her dispose of the body.

A faint smile played on Brite's lips. She took a breath as if to speak, then stopped. Walde was on the verge of changing the subject when she finally answered.

"Even if you *had* testified, they would've still seen it as murder, and I would've been fined. Of course, I couldn't pay the fine, and neither could my relatives. So my life would've been forfeit. Any of the man's family could've killed me then without repercussions. Or confined me somewhere to be used as they liked." Her voice was calm and grave, as if she were reciting a prepared speech. Walde could find nothing to say in answer. It was horrible.

"How do things work where you come from?" she asked.

He sighed and leaned his head back against the embankment. "Crimes like rape and manslaughter are uncommon, but they do happen. In the past, the guilty were either banished or had to spend time in the corpse darkness, but—"

"The what?"

"It's what they call the space between the upper and lower roots of a Mothertree. Mothertrees are so large that this space can hold several individuals. As for the name... Well, they used to throw the charred bones of the dead down there."

Her eyes widened. "You mean, a murderer could be forced to spend his days alongside the bones of the person he murdered?"

"A manslayer. Confirmed murderers were banished. But murder can be a hard thing to prove, and the idea behind the corpse darkness was to deter folk from even contemplating such a crime. No one wanted to be alone with those bones for even a day, never mind a month. Parents still frighten children with stories about that." He shrugged. "Now there's a new prison at the north end of the lake, built all of stone."

Brite had settled back into a curve in the embankment. Her eyes were drooping closed.

"Brite."

They fluttered open reluctantly. "Yes?'

"If that dog traced our path from the hillock to the bog, the trackers would've found two sets of prints—a man's and a woman's. Without a body, they can only assume one thing: that you and the rapist ran away together. What else are they to think?"

"Bog grass doesn't hold prints very well, neither the shape nor the impression. Leave it be, Walde. There's nothing we can do now." Her voice trailed off, and she closed her eyes.

Walde sighed and stared at the softly waving reeds. Talking about the Lakelands had ushered back memories of that terrible morning. He'd been able to hold them back while Brite was awake, but now they returned with a sick clarity.

Odd how the passage of time made the event clearer, as if a mist had been receding from his mind. Gritting his teeth, he forced it all away. The memory. The emotions. He couldn't let any of it trouble him again. Or at least not until *after* he'd rescued his father.

After the length of a few breaths, he climbed to his feet.

He was famished. A bone-deep hunger that came from days of fasting gnawed at him. He dug into the reeds, pulling up young shoots and bundling them under his arm. Some went into his mouth as he worked. After depositing a hill of them by Brite's sleeping form, he went in search of a stone he could form a knife from. The search took him longer than before. The stones were smaller here, and there were fewer of them. But in the end he found what he needed and returned to the embankment to work.

By the time he had finished, the morning had fled. Brite was awake when he crouched down beside her, and Walde noted that half the reed shoots were gone. She regarded the knife with hooded eyes.

He said, "Do you trust me?"

A dry smile pulled on her lips. "The knife, please."

"I'm surprised you didn't bring one when you left home."

"I did. I brought an entire pack with me, but some drunken miners waylaid me on the way out of the village. I was lucky they didn't demand more than my pack." She accepted the weapon from him with a murmur of thanks. "How's your injury?" She gestured to the conspicuous lump at his side.

"I don't know. To be honest, I'm afraid to look at it." He lifted his tunic and unraveled the bandages. The last bit of fabric clung to the wound, but not as badly as it would have had it been dry. Walde took one glance at it and jerked his eyes away.

Brite shook her head. "You're lucky it hasn't putrefied. Don't put that soggy rag on it again. Wait…" She unbuttoned her belt pouch and drew out a small clay bottle, still damp from being submerged in the river. "Lie on your side."

Walde suspected what was in the bottle. He lay down on the stony sand and readied himself for the pain. It came and went, but she was not done with him yet. Needle and thread came out of the pouch, and Walde's protests did not deter her from stabbing him again and again. Another splash of spirits, and the ordeal was over.

"It should heal properly now. Don't!" She snatched the bandage away from him, strode to the river, and tossed it in.

He shook his head, more amused than frustrated. "I was only going to rinse it out and fold it, not use it as a bandage."

"You don't need it."

"Spare cloth is always useful. I could've used it to patch holes in my tunic."

"Or to rewrap your uninjured hands?"

Walde grinned. A serviceable lie came to him, but he couldn't bother giving it. Let her wonder.

She eyed his ragged clothing. "A needle and thread would close those holes as well as they did your wound."

His mouth slackened. "Are you offering to mend my clothes for me?"

"No." She wheeled away, but not before he glimpsed her reddened cheeks. "I'm offering you the use of my needle."

Walde was tempted to say that he'd never learned to sew, but the lie wouldn't reach his lips. "Thank you," he said instead.

There was a moment of awkwardness between them. Walde scooped up his bow and branches and what was left of the reed shoots. "I think we can move on now. But we need to find shelter. If the Woodlands are close, then we should pass through them instead of continuing by the road." He felt a measure of guilt at offering this. If he were alone, he would have continued along the river and reached the Harborlands faster. But the thought of Brite being captured smote him. He told himself that an extra day wouldn't make a difference to his father. If the Harborlands elders wanted Carrac alive, then he would live. Perhaps Walde ought to view his task as it really was: a prison break, one that might take time to plan and execute.

He said, "What do you think?"

She was buttoning her sack. "I think that's an excellent idea. For me."

"I'm coming with you."

"You'll be delayed."

"So be it."

Their eyes met briefly, then she moved past him and clambered onto the embankment. Walde was close behind.

They moved at a brisk walk, gazes scouring the land as they hiked through the trackless wastes. They had traveled for half a mile southeast when the earth began to change. The rocky ground softened and climbed. Stunted trees and wildflowers joined the spiny shrubs and weeds. Walde pulled up some tough lengths of grass and braided them into a serviceable bowstring. Out of curiosity, he offered it to Brite and asked if she'd like to attach it to the bow. He was only mildly surprised when she not only tied the right knots, but also added the right amount of tension to the string.

She tossed him the bow, grinning.

He asked as he unstrung it, "Are you good with a bow?"

"I can use one, but not well. I'm better at knife-throwing."

Walde glanced at her. A wing of auburn hair hung over her face, concealing her expression. With the right question, she would turn and face him full on. He considered what he could say to provoke such a response and then rolled his eyes at his own childishness. He wasn't himself, he decided. Hunger was making him crazy. He scoured the ground for hunters' root, but there was no sign of the long, pointed leaves.

She said, "Are you searching for hunters' root?"

"You've heard of that, eh?"

"My uncle was a hunter."

"Of course. Yes, I am, but without luck." He slipped the last of the reed shoots out from under his arm, gave Brite half, and downed the rest without ceremony. They weren't terrible. Even reeds tasted good when one was hungry enough.

After a time, the discomfort passed and his eyes wandered to Brite again. She had been gathering stray feathers and slipping them into her pouch. Smart. They would come in handy when finishing the arrows. He asked, "What did you do in the Lowlands?"

"I was a bog worker. I gathered peat logs for drying."

"Ah." He should have guessed that.

"The Scats do one of four things: the wealthiest of us are hunters and storytellers—my uncle used to be both—and then there's the builders, the bog workers, and finally the miners. I didn't have to work, but girls who don't earn their keep are married off. Still, there's been so many men nosing about my house lately that I knew it was only a matter of time."

"A matter of time before what? You were forced to wed?"

She flicked him a look that was somewhere between amusement and irritation. "Before my aunt turned me out. After that I would've lost my uncle's protection. For what that was worth."

Walde shook his head as he considered the difficulty of the situation. "Where did you live?" He described what he had seen of the Lowlands from the slope.

"Those hovels you saw house the miners. I lived in the area you thought belonged to the former Woodlanders."

"Then where do the former Woodlanders live?"

"On the edge of the Lowlands, beside a stream. You couldn't have spied them from the slope. They keep to themselves, mostly, and come into town just to do business." She held out her hand. "If you keep watch, I'll shape the arrows for you."

Walde handed them over without a word, and her knife flashed as it came out of her belt pouch.

A companionable silence fell. Or at least a kind of silence. The place was riotous with birdsong. The sound—so unusual in the wastes—made him desperately homesick.

The one thing that had the power to distract him unfolded as they scaled the top of the rise—the shadowy line of the Woodlands. As Walde glimpsed it, his step quickened to a jog. These were not Mothertrees but rather the familiar oak, chestnut, and pine that his people farmed at the far end of the lake. Still, they stood tall and proud, and somewhere beyond them, the Mothertrees beckoned. Walde didn't know if he sensed their nearness or if merely knowing they were near made him think he did. Whatever it was tugged on him. He charged across an old road that skirted the forest's edge and into the trees like a thirsting man into a lake.

Brite's step sounded behind him. "We need to make a fire and finish these arrows before dark or we'll spend another night hungry. Walde—?"

With an effort, he forced himself to slow. As he did, the powerful urge ebbed until it was no more than a gentle prodding. He turned with a foolish grin. "Sorry. I don't know what came over me."

"Home?" She stood in a glimmering patch of sunlight. For an instant, Walde was reminded of Rona. Beautiful, judgemental Rona. His lips tightened as he recalled how she'd turned aside from him at Carrac's "execution." As if Walde were guilty by association. She must have been appalled when she found out Walde was also a Reacher.

He cleared his throat. “Something like that.”

Together, they scanned the undergrowth for old, dry wood. Walde uncovered two paths that were faded from disuse, and nearby, the decayed stumps of felled trees. A sapling had been planted by every stump. Walde reckoned the saplings were a decade old. He hacked some chunks of wood off a stump and added them to the pile under his arm. After settling on a location, he prepared to make a friction fire, but Brite surprised him with a tinderbox.

“I kept the essentials in my pouch,” she said. “Fortunately, the box is watertight.”

They finished the arrows by charring the heads and scraping them to sharp points. Brite bound feathers to them using lengths of thread pulled from the bottom of her frock and some sticky salve from her pouch of wonders. She smiled the first time he called it that, a genuine smile that one might offer to a friend.

After taking a few shots with the bow, he declared he was ready. The sun was low but not yet setting. It was a good time to hunt.

Walde stamped out the fire and walked upwind, knowing that the fire’s smoke would chase away game. He spotted a large patch of clover and suggested that they climb the nearby tree.

Brite chuckled. “Nope. I’ve never climbed a tree, and I’m not starting now.”

Walde just stared at her. “You’ve never been in a tree?”

“Never. My uncle hunted in the mountains. We’d climb rocky ridges and boulders to stalk game.” She hugged herself and looked around. “To be honest, I don’t like being here. The trees make me feel closed in. I can’t see very far, and that makes me nervous.”

"You'd see better from up there." He studied the trunk for foot and handholds, then, stuffing the bow and arrows under the waist of his trousers, he climbed it slowly, showing her where to place her toes, how to grip a branch while pulling herself up.

Brite kept shaking her head, but in the end she gave in. Walde was stunned as he watched her struggle up. It was like watching an adult learn how to walk or feed themselves. On a purely intellectual level, he understood the reason for her difficulty. The Lowlands were devoid of trees. When would she have had the chance to climb one? Still, the sight was bizarre. He ended up grasping her wrist and hauling her onto the branch. She would only go one branch higher before digging her heels in.

Walde suppressed a sigh, and they spoke little for a while.

The sun lowered, casting long, orange rays through the branches. An hour might have passed before a faint rustling prompted Walde to reattach the string to his bow and set an arrow to it. Brite had gone still. She could be very still when she wanted to be.

At last, a fat rabbit appeared behind a distant tree.

Rabbits were infuriating. They moved as if blocked by invisible obstructions, never taking a direct route but zigzagging slowly toward their goal until they seemed to stumble on it by chance.

Once it reached the clover, it was an easy shot. Walde took it and would have hit his mark had the forest not been so still. His arm brushed against some leaves, alerting the rabbit to his presence. It hopped away just as Walde shot, and only his quick redraw allowed him to take another before the animal vanished behind a bush.

Walde helped Brite down, and they traced the blood trail to a thicket. Brite retrieved the dying rabbit and finished it off with one slice of her stone knife.

***

Before the sun was fully down, they had tracked deer prints to a stream, built a new fire, and made a spit on which to cook the rabbit. Brite sighed contentedly as the flames licked the meat. "I feel as if I'm a child again hunting with my uncle. I can almost pretend I didn't kill someone and bury him in the bog."

Walde said nothing. He envied her comfort but couldn't share it. He still held himself away from everything that had happened to him and his father, as one might hold themselves from biting flames. If he let himself dwell on it at all, he wouldn't be able to contain his anger and despair. And fear, for his thoughts would lead inevitably to the Harborlands and what might await him there.

He looked up to find her fire-brightened eyes on him.

"What is it?" she asked. "Why do you look upset all the time?"

"It's nothing." He forced the tightness around his eyes to ease. "I'm glad you're safe."

She dashed a twig into the fire. "You want my trust, but you won't offer it in return."

"I trust you," he said.

"But not with your secrets."

"Secrets?"

"You know what I mean. Lakelanders don't leave the Lakelands. Something big must have happened to you, and I'm guessing it wasn't something good."

Walde turned the spit.

They said nothing more to each other that night.

***

An early-morning downpour put out what remained of their fire, and they rose, shivering, wet, and hungry. Water from the stream quenched some of that hunger, but Walde knew the feeling wouldn't last long. They decided they could not obliterate all signs of their camp, so they left it and walked in a direction they had identified as south the day before.

Even after the rain had stopped, the forest remained dark and misty. Nothing stirred but a few birds and squirrels in the upper branches. Brite was jittery. Even the patter of a fallen leaf made her pause and stare in the direction of the offending tree. Walde had never known anyone so uncomfortable in a forest. It reminded him of his own discomfort in the bog. Comfort, he supposed, was a matter of what one was accustomed to.

They had traveled no more than a mile when the rain resumed, big, hard droplets accompanied by sheeting wind. They huddled against the trunk of an oak and picked wet mushrooms with chilled, trembling hands. Hair and mushroom dirt clung to Brite's face, and her wet, torn frock made her look thin and ragged. She caught Walde looking at her and scowled. "I must look hideous."

He grinned. "You're about as close to a forest nymph as I've ever seen."

"Is that a compliment or an insult?" Her lips twitched in amusement.

He thought about it and decided not to answer. The last thing Brite wanted was another man sniffing after her. Not that Walde would even think of pursuing her. He had far too many complications in his life to drag Brite into it. He wasn't even sure he'd live to see another season. But if these were his last days, he couldn't have stumbled on a better stranger.

He dozed off. When he woke, the rain had slowed and the sky had brightened. They crawled, dripping, from the trunk and continued in the direction Walde hoped was still south.

The land sloped down at a gentle but relentless angle. As the sky brightened further, he halted and stared ahead of them into the hazy light.

"What is it?" Brite whispered.

He shook his head and then started to run. Ferns whipped passed him, spraying him with glittering water. At last, he broke through a tree line and stepped into the stillness of giants.

And they were dead. Completely and utterly dead.

CHAPTER 8

The Mothertrees weren't merely devoid of leaves and flowers; they were gray as aged driftwood. Empty, abandoned huts still clung to them, their planks hanging, dripping in the rain.

Walde fell to his knees and threw up the mushrooms he'd eaten. A horror he had no name for flooded him, and he couldn't push it down. Brite's sharp intake of breath behind him made him lift his head and stare at his blazing palms.

Too late to hide it now. She knew he was a Reacher. She knew.

But what did it matter? The Woodlands Mothertrees were dead.

He didn't glance back to watch her retreat from him, but just sat, staring down at his own vomit. At last, he let out a shuddering breath and rose unsteadily to his feet.

Her voice, so close to his side, made him jump. "I'm sorry. I thought you knew, or I would've warned you."

"You're still here?" he blurted. "You saw what I am."

Her hand settled on his shoulder. "Sometimes the bog gives off light. It's just something it does. You can't help what you do."

Such a simple, innocent answer. It shouldn't have changed how he felt just then, standing in the shadow of death. But it did. He snatched her hand and held it in both of his. "Brite, you're a godsend."

They both looked at her hand then, enclosed in light. One could imagine he held a firefly. He whispered, "You're really not afraid of me?"

He watched her draw a shaky breath. "No. Do Reachers' palms always blaze like this when they're upset?"

"If they fail to stay calm."

She took her hand back and wandered into the clearing toward the nearest Mothertree. Its old paths still sprawled over the roots. Beyond the paths, the ground looked almost as soggy as the trail Brite had forged through the bog. The cleared space had probably been a garden at one time, ruined now. "You know," Brite called back, "if you hadn't been so determined to travel with me, you would've been spared this sight." Her feet sloshed and sucked as she spoke. She paused and looked around. "How many Mothertrees are there anyway? I can only see three from here. The others are too far away."

"There are eighteen in the Woodlands."

"That many? Then how do you know they're all dead?"

"How did *you* know?"

She glanced at him. "Gossip. The Woodlanders still sell the regular trees they harvest from the forest's northeast corner. It's how they make most of their money, or so I've heard. When the Barans found out the Mothertrees were dead, they thought they could convince the Woodlanders to cut one down and sell it to them like regular timber. But the Woodlanders wouldn't do it." She shrugged, probably unaware of how uneasy her tale made him. "That's all I know. Take from it what you will." She mounted the outermost path and walked on with a firmer step.

Walde jumped his way across the mucky space to the path. "All I heard was that they didn't blossom last year." He paused and pressed a board with his boot. "Be careful where you step. These boards haven't been replaced for years. The rotten ones will be slippery."

She inched closer to an old guide rope. "The dark ones are soft and slimy," she agreed.

Walde swallowed back a burning in his throat as he followed along behind. He wondered how Brite would feel if she returned to the Lowlands to find all the bogs drained, the homes and roads empty and crumbling, and the animal pens abandoned. The Mothertrees were home to Walde, no matter where they were located.

And they were more than that. They were passageways to life. He could only hope that Brite's hunch was correct and a few still lived.

The outermost walkway skirted the Mothertree and acted as a bridge to the next. As they crossed over, Walde told Brite about the boardwalk that connected the Lakelands trees. Then he spoke about the treelights, and the song rites, and the sea of purple flowers in the spring. The details brought the vitality of the Lakelands back to his mind, and the grayness around him faded to abstractedness.

Brite stopped all of a sudden and looked around. "I heard something."

Walde listened for a few moments and then shook his head. "The place is falling apart. All the huts are creaking and shifting, and everything is dripping…" He eyed the path, which was strewn with broken branches and withered leaves. This walkway was at the edge of the Mothertree, far enough away from the huts that it was unlikely they would be struck by fallen wreckage. Still, he couldn't rule out the possibility.

She whispered, "It sounded like footsteps." Her eyes darted over the paths that stretched out from the Mothertree's base.

Walde moved to stand beside her. "I'll ready my bow, if it'll make you feel better."

Her lips compressed. Shaking her head, she took a determined step forward.

Walde was at her side when the path dropped out under them and they both plunged into darkness. They didn't fall far, but Walde hit his elbow, and a root jabbed like a fist into his back. Brite curled against his side, making soft coughing sounds. He touched her hair. "Are you all right?"

Breath hissed into her lungs. "Winded."

Walde fingered his elbow. It wasn't bleeding. He forced himself to a sitting position and looked around. They lay in a hole that was perhaps six feet deep and five feet around. A handful of white roots spread out beneath them and along the walls, but these were mere tips, certainly not large enough to have created a cavity in the earth.

Brite said, "Tell me this isn't the corpse darkness."

"This isn't the corpse darkness." He tossed her a weak smile. "It's a dugout." He pointed up at the walkway boards, which hung down crookedly over the hole's opening.

Her eyes widened. "The boards look as if they've been cut clean in half."

"And then reattached somehow." He struggled to his feet, wincing at the pain in his back.

"Are you hurt?"

"I'm just a bit sore," he assured her, and hoped that was true. "Are you okay?"

"My back hurts too, but it's been aching for days. How do we get out of here? I wouldn't trust those boards with my weight."

"We can climb up the sides using the roots as footholds." And do it soon, he thought. Though he hadn't used the word "trap" to describe the hole, Brite wasn't stupid. They both knew that someone had cut those boards and placed them so that an unwary traveler would fall through. And since the hole wasn't deep, the aim had not been to imprison but rather to place one in a position of weakness.

The thought had barely skimmed his mind when there came a patter of footsteps, followed by the sound of an arrow being pulled from a quiver. Arrows, he corrected as two came into view, both aimed at him. Walde had become good at dousing his fear, but even his carefully constructed calm was almost shattered when he glimpsed the archers.

They were children. Young children.

"Don't move!" a girl of no older than nine snapped. "These are tipped with poison. One scratch, and you die."

Few things were as disturbing as a child with a deadly weapon. At least these seemed to have a level of proficiency. The bows had been sized for them, and they wielded them with steadiness and a measure of skill.

The girl had plaited brown hair and blue eyes. She wore a cropped leather tunic and clean leather hosen. The blond boy beside her was the same age, or perhaps even younger. A worn tunic made of kessa hung almost to his knees, and his leather hosen was blotchy with stains.

"Please don't shoot," Brite pleaded. "We won't hurt you. We were just passing through."

"I said don't move. That includes your mouth."

Walde hid a smile. When they were both completely still, a third child appeared and scrambled down into the hole. The boy was perhaps seven, certainly no older than eight. Looking them both in the eyes, he demanded they hand over their weapons.

"If you hurt him, you die," the girl warned from above.

Brite said, "Do you really think we'd hurt a kid?"

"You're a stranger to me, Lowlander. I don't know what you might do."

"Weapons, please," the little boy said.

Walde unshouldered his bow—which turned out to be broken anyway—and tossed it and the arrows onto the floor. Brite's knife joined the pile.

"The pouch, too," the boy said.

Brite's mouth was a mutinous line as she unhooked her pouch and tossed it at him.

The boy upended its contents and riffled through them with his tiny fingers. Satisfied, perhaps, that it held no weapon, he repacked it and tossed it back to her. Then he shoved the arrows and knife into a sack over his shoulder and climbed back up, leaving the broken bow on the floor.

The children stepped back from the hole. "You can come out now," the girl said. "If you need help, we have a rope."

Did Walde detect a note of challenge in her voice? He met Brite's eyes, then took two steps to the wall and climbed out, using the roots as footholds. Brite was right behind him.

The moment they were on their feet, the girl shouted for them to continue along the path. "And watch where you're stepping," she added. "The dark boards are bad."

Walde walked stiffly, hand cupping his sore elbow. Brite glanced at him. "How did she know where I'm from?"

"You have an accent," he reminded her. "And they've been watching us, listening. You were right when you said you heard footsteps."

His breath caught then, and he almost stopped walking. Had the children spied his Reacher light too?

"Turn here," the girl instructed as they reached a fork in the path. The walkway she pointed to led west around the south side of the Mothertree. They had not traveled on it long before they glimpsed a long, shallow valley ahead of them, overhung by dead Mothertrees. Walde knew that a river would lie at its base before he was near enough to see it. Suddenly, he was incredibly thirsty. He swallowed back the residue of vomit he had been unable to rinse from his throat.

The littlest boy appeared at his side, jogging to keep up. "You don't look like my papa," he said.

"That's because I'm not."

His little mouth turned down. "Maybe you're someone else's papa."

"Slow down, Buzz," the girl shouted. "I'm not carrying you back if you slip on a bad board and break your leg."

The boy scowled but fell back without arguing. Walde shook his head at Buzz's words.

"That was bizarre," Brite murmured, echoing his thoughts.

They came to a path that led down to the river and were ordered to take it.

Walde had known about a river in the Woodlands from maps he'd glimpsed as a child, but he hadn't known about the docks. Thick wooden platforms ran along both sides of the river for quite a distance. A mild curve in the river kept him from seeing where they ended, but he guessed they extended as far as the Mothertrees did. The water itself was deep and almost clear, making his throat ache with thirst.

Buzz ran ahead and waved them to a couple of small boats. Walde was ushered into the first and Brite into the second. When Walde asked if they could use the boat's bailing scoops to drink from, the girl tossed him a skin from her pack. Walde eyed the boats as he drank. They were old and worn but still sound. The color and grain of the wood identified it as storm-felled Mothertree, resistant to rot and gnawing insects. Large fishing vessels were commonly made of such wood and were passed down as heirlooms through multiple generations, but these old rowboats wouldn't be worth as much. It was even possible they had been abandoned by the Woodlands' former inhabitants.

He never learned which of the children joined him in the boat. Once he and Brite had finished drinking, they were given blindfolds and told to secure them tightly behind their heads. Walde gripped the sides of the boat as it pushed off, then the vessel steadied and all he heard was the rhythmic sound of the oars.

The strangeness of the situation seeped into him in that space of quiet. Here were children who had been forced to become adults, and not overnight. What had become of their parents? Were they runaways who had fallen under the control of a madman?

If that were true, then Walde and Brite were being escorted to him. He was about to demand answers when a loud horn call sounded at his ear, making him jump and jostle the boat. Moments later, the call was answered by three distant blasts. The horn beside him gave off two short blasts, followed by a long third.

Walde recognized a message exchange when he heard one. Likely, someone knew they'd be receiving guests.

They traveled on for perhaps a quarter of a mile. It was hard to be sure without knowledge of the river's currents. The children seemed as familiar with oars as they were with bows. The paddling was steady and repetitive, indicating that they didn't drift off course. Aside from a few birdcalls, there were no other sounds.

Finally, the paddling slowed and Walde heard the second boat bump against the dock just before he felt the jolt of his own. Someone behind him stepped out of the boat.

The girl said, "Stand up and give me your hand." Walde obeyed, and she placed his hand on the edge of the dock. Walde found the dock with his other hand and clambered onto it.

Someone—the girl, he assumed—grasped his hand again and tugged him forward.

Brite's irritated voice cut into the silence. "I don't like walking blindfolded this close to the water's edge."

The older boy said, "You're not close to the water. I'm between you and the water, see?"

"No."

"You—"

"I don't see anything."

A giggle of childish laughter.

"Shut it, Buzz," the older boy snapped.

"You shut it, Pismire."

"You're going to get it after my report."

"Yeah? What are you gonna say?"

And on it went. The girl didn't interfere but strode calmly along, never easing her viper-like grip on Walde's hand. A din of childish voices drifted toward them down the docks, growing louder with every step.

The girl tugged Walde's hand to the left. "This way."

They veered off the boardwalk and up an uneven path. Walde didn't need sight to know that they walked under a Mothertree. The paths built atop roots were haphazard and bumpy. A root could lift a board in a season, creating a tripping hazard if it was not dealt with. How would these paths have fared after four years of neglect? And from what he had glimpsed earlier, the trunk was fifty or sixty yards from the water. Quite a hike for someone to undertake blindfolded.

A sudden cry from Brite made him jerk the girl to a stop. "Let me take the woman's arm."

"No." The girl tugged on him.

"I'm not moving, so you'd better do as I say."

"I'll shoot you."

"Then do it. After you shoot me, you'll have to burn my bones. Then you'll have to open the corpse darkness and dump me in."

Brite gasped, but the little girl actually laughed, a throaty giggle that took a long time to die.

Someone kicked a board. "I think my papa would've said somethin' like that." Buzz's voice.

"Your papa's dead." This from the other boy.

There was a scrambling sound, and then unfamiliar voices joined in, all, it seemed, from children of various ages. Walde guessed that the two boys had attacked each other, and others were trying to pull them apart.

"Walde."

He felt a warmth at his side and gripped Brite's arm. "Are you hurt?"

"No. I just tripped. You didn't need to say anything."

He loosed a harsh breath and then tore off his blindfold. "I'm done with this."

The scene that met his eyes did not surprise him in the slightest. He and Brite stood under a dead Mothertree surrounded by half a dozen children ranging from four to ten. After Walde removed his blindfold, one after another went still and stared at him searchingly.

"He's too young," a boy muttered.

"Maybe not," another said. "You can't always tell how old adults are."

They pressed closer to him, each striving to catch his gaze. Suddenly, the archer girl shouted for everyone to be quiet and let the adults through. Incredibly, the children obeyed her. An opening formed in the crowd, revealing a sturdy path of new boards.

The girl waited behind the prisoners with a raised bow. "Move. Now."

As Walde helped Brite take a step forward, he whispered, "I took my blindfold off."

She didn't wait another moment but tore hers off and tossed it on the ground.

A chorus of giggles erupted around them.

"Get back to your duties!" the girl snapped, and the children reluctantly dispersed.

Walde found he had lost his worry over the situation. Children as light-hearted as these could not be the tools of a cruel leader or a madman. He still didn't understand what was happening, but his fear had changed to curiosity.

They reached the Mothertree's trunk and wound their way up the stairs. Walde got a good look at the village as he walked. Many of the huts had been repaired, and the walkways showed no sign of decay. Such restoration work would have taken time. Months, perhaps years.

As they neared the tree's middle level, Brite began to slow and glance over the side. "We're so high up," she murmured.

It was true. The leafless branches afforded a view of the winding river and a couple of the stately Mothertrees running along it.

"You won't fall," he promised.

She flashed him an irritated glance. "I didn't say I would." She took another cautious step. Walde wished the lift were operating. But if the tree's only residents were children, then he understood why it wasn't. None of them would have had the strength to operate it. As they came to the middle level, the girl shouted for them to halt. Walde was unsurprised. If this place had a leader, then he would meet his guests in the meeting hut, and that was always at the middle level of the tree.

The doors to the hut were guarded by a life-size wooden statue of a grown man. Its realness was marred only by a lack of paint. He wondered if the children had purloined it from a woodcarver's abandoned hut.

The boy that Buzz had called Pismire scooted past them and ducked into the hut. A long period of waiting ensued.

Walde glanced behind him at the tired-looking girl. Her bow was stowed, and she appeared calm, but her small hand never left the sheathed knife at her side. He attempted a friendly smile. "Is he reporting the number of fish he saw in the river?"

She returned his smile. "Probably."

Finally, the door opened and the boy ushered them through. The windows were shuttered. Light from lamps set in makeshift sconces breathed on the polished wooden walls, and carved panels ran like pillars every few feet. The village's small library bore a few tattered scrolls, some scorched and covered with what appeared to be soot. A shiver ran over him as he regarded it, and a trace of the discomfort he'd experienced when he'd glimpsed the dead, abandoned Mothertrees settled into him again. He didn't know what it was about the emptied cubbyholes that unsettled him. He told himself that the elders wouldn't have burned their collection. Just the scrolls they didn't judge to be important. But he couldn't shake his unease.

"Those are the leavings," came a voice from the end of the hut. "Deemed as worthless as we are. What's your name, Reacher?"

CHAPTER 9

Walde stiffened as the word "Reacher" echoed through the chamber. Soft footsteps pattered on the floor, and a boy stepped out from behind the deep curve in the wall. He halted a few yards away from the visitors.

He was perhaps thirteen, that awkward age where one hovered between boy and man. But he stood with a straight back and a regal bearing. His dark blond hair had been smoothed back into a tail. Steely blue eyes stood out from his sun-browned face. The deep purple of his tunic intensified them so that they seemed to radiate light. A sheathed knife with a worn handle sat comfortably at his belt, and the subtle positioning of his right arm and callused hand told Walde he could pull it in an instant and probably throw it with accuracy.

Footsteps fell again, and a girl came to stand at his side. She was like him in every way, save that she was female. Walde judged her to be eleven, but she might have been as young as ten. Despite this, her eyes ran over Walde as an appraising woman's might. A faint smile tugged on her lips. "Don't worry, we don't punish Reachers here."

Walde found his voice with an effort. "My name is Walde, and this is my traveling companion, Brite."

The boy nodded and spoke in a light but cautious tone. "Well met, Walde, Brite. What brings you through the Woodlands?"

There was a long and painful silence. Walde didn't dare look at Brite's face for a clue as to what he should say. The silence she chose was an answer in itself. He cleared his throat.

"I've been journeying from the Lakelands to the Harborlands to meet someone. When I stopped in the Lowlands, I met Brite. Turns out that she's also on her way to the Harborlands. We wanted to avoid the dangers of the road, so we chose to pass through the Woodlands. We didn't think it'd be booby-trapped." He attempted a dry smile, but the girl's piercing stare made it falter. The boy threw her a questioning glance.

She whispered, "I think we can trust them."

"But their story—"

"Will grow as they learn to trust *us*."

Walde wanted to shake his head. He had never heard children speak so much like adults. Even the way they held themselves defied their ages.

The boy seemed to reach a decision. "Walde, Brite, my sister is an excellent judge of character. An excellent judge of everything, really." He stepped forward and greeted his guests with a handshake. "I'm Albin, and this is Frey. Welcome to our home."

"Where are the adults?" Brite asked as Frey clasped her hand.

A sincere smile lit Frey's face. "We both have stories to tell, but not while you're tired and hungry. And you'll want some clean clothes, and a bath, and a place to be alone to talk about your story."

Brite's mouth opened, but no words came out. Frey still held her hand.

Perhaps, Walde thought, Brite had met her match. He said, "Thank you. That's kind of you."

Albin threw open the shutters, and Walde was startled to find a quiet crowd of children on the other side of a window doing their best to eavesdrop. "Our guests will feast with us tonight. Grella, take them to the chests. Spitfire, prepare the guest huts with bathing water and clean bedding—"

"On the lowest level, please," Walde interjected, thinking of Brite. Knowing her, she'd keep silent to save face, all the while squirming with discomfort.

Albin raised a brow. "If you wish..."

"I do."

Walde caught Brite looking at him, but he couldn't decipher her expression. He gave up and followed the girl named Grella out the door. He felt keenly homesick as he strode up the main walkway beside Brite. "I used to live on a middle level," he murmured. "Back home."

Grella turned up a pathway toward two large huts. The girl was perhaps eight or nine, with tightly braided brown hair and a wide mouth that slid easily into a smile. She gestured grandly to the huts as she approached them. "These are the chest huts. They're full of all the clothes people left behind when they went to the Lowlands. It's all been cleaned and folded, but don't expect the Berg's robes." She waved to the hut on the left. "That one's for women and the other's for men." She knocked at the women's hut and then lifted the latch and ushered Brite in. "Wait here," she called to Walde. "I'll be back in a few moments."

Their voices drifted through the unshuttered windows. Walde withdrew up the path to give them some privacy. The sky seemed to darken as he waited. Not that he could see the sky clearly; even without leaves, a Mothertree's thick upper branches shaded the lower levels well. But a sudden change in the quality of light often hinted at more than a fluffy cloud passing over the sun.

While he listened for the rustling of raindrops, a tinkling of chords from a lyra reached his ears, distant, but unmistakable. He dragged in a deep breath and leaned his arm over a hanging branch. The solitude allowed him to think over his encounter with Albin and Frey, who seemed to be the leaders of this strange village. Albin's first words to him stood out over all others: *Those are the leavings,* he had called what was left of the library. *Deemed as worthless as we are.*

Prickles skittered down Walde's back. The Woodlanders couldn't have abandoned some of their own offspring, could they? Yet the meaning of the words was clear: the children had been deemed worthless.

And perhaps worse.

What had motivated them to maintain those traps and sentinel posts? To memorize a system of horn calls? The place was better defended than the Lakelands.

Why? Who threatened them?

He sighed and stretched. The tug of Brite's stitches reminded him that he still had an urgent journey to make, though the world seemed intent on keeping him from it. The world, and his wretched curiosity. But perhaps he was right to be curious. The children's situation was so bizarre, it might even be connected to what had happened to his father. He loosed a chuckle. There it was. He'd found a reason to stay the night.

The girl slipped out the door and motioned him to the other hut. Good timing, for the rain had finally arrived.

Inside the hut, the walls were lined by chests stacked in twos.

Grella said, "There are four rooms. But that back one's the only room you'll need. The clothing sizes go up from left to right." She flashed a brilliant smile and ducked out the door into the first heavy rain drops. "Have at it."

After sorting through two chests of neatly folded garments, Walde settled on a worn brown tunic that was only slightly tight across the shoulders and leather bottoms an inch too long. But the ragged, stained edges could be trimmed off easily.

He gathered his old clothes into a bundle under his arm. He wouldn't keep them, though they were all he had left of home. No, that wasn't true. He fingered the medallion, then inspected the leather gut cord it hung on. All was well, despite his lack of attentiveness. He was so used to wearing it that he didn't think about the damage the cord might have taken in the rapids, and after.

"Do you need any help?" Grella's voice was loud through the open windows.

"No, thanks. I'm just about done."

"You can leave your old clothes on the floor. I'll get them later." Happy to be free of them, Walde did as she instructed and strode out the door. The rain had ceased, and the warm tones of early evening sunlight filtered through the branches.

He exchanged a small smile with Brite as he fell in behind her and Grella. Brite had stumbled on a purple kessa tunic that fit her well and had only a few holes. The gray hosen had mended holes at the knees but still looked to have plenty of wear left to them. The forest nymph was gone, and she looked like one of the treefolk now. And not a poor one. Purple-stained kessa wasn't cheap.

Grella led them to a couple of hastily provisioned huts on the Mothertree's lowest level. Walde sneezed as he walked inside one. Dust still hung in the air from the vigorous sweeping the floor had likely received. A small tub of tepid water, folded rags, and a bar of soap rested on a washstand. A straw mattress, freshly plumped, sat on the floor, and several worn blankets lay in tidy squares on top of it. These items, along with an empty chest, a wood stove, and a lit oil lamp, were the hut's only occupants. Walde closed the shutters and stripped naked. He was horrified by how dirty he was—he hadn't noticed while changing in the shadowy clothing hut. By the time he'd finished washing, the water was murky and a few small bugs floated on the surface.

He ought to have worn his old clothes here and changed into the new ones *after* washing, but the idea hadn't occurred to him until now. He shook his new clothes out vigorously before putting them back on. Only his boots were still dirty, but there was no helping that. He'd have to ask for boot oil.

Gods, but he was hungry.

"Walde?" A soft knock fell on the door.

"Come in."

Brite swept through the doorway, wet hair draped over one shoulder. She had donned her old frock again and carried the purple tunic under her arm. She held up a sewing needle. "Do you need this?"

"No. But thanks for—"

She closed the door firmly and perched on the clothes chest beside the oil lamp. "Well, I do." She licked a thread and pushed it through the needle. Her wary eyes flicked to his. "We need to talk. About what we're going to do."

Walde turned his head to hide a smile. "I know."

"I can't tell them that I'm a runaway murderer."

"You won't have to. I'm going to tell them *my* story. After that, I doubt they'll think to ask about yours."

Her hunched back stiffened. "You mean you'll tell them the story you wouldn't tell me."

"I couldn't have told you without exposing myself as a Reacher. And I didn't know how you'd react to that."

"You didn't trust me."

"I didn't know how you'd feel about it. That's different from me not trusting you. Brite..."

She looked away from him. "Never mind. It's not important."

A silence fell. At length, Walde lowered himself down onto the chest beside her. He resisted the urge to touch her hand. "I'm sorry. I was still getting to know you then."

Water from her hair splashed her chin as she turned to him. "I said it's not important," she reiterated. But there was a smile in her voice.

They said nothing more. He watched drips gather at the ends of her hair and fall as she repaired her tunic.

"Finished," she announced cheerfully just as there was a knock at the door.

***

The elders' meeting hut had been transformed into a dining hall. Three thick wooden tables, shining with fresh polish, had been pushed together to form one long table. Chairs of various shapes and sizes formed a line down both sides, with an additional two placed at one end. The chairs were filling up with noisy children as Grella led Walde and Brite in. So far, water jugs were all that graced the table. A little girl in a green smock ran around handing out wooden trenchers, cups, and eating knives. She smiled as the new guests entered and bade them be seated.

Walde and Brite looked at each other wryly across the table. The open windows dulled some of the echo from the raised voices and laughter, but not enough that they could've heard each other speak. Walde could think of nothing to say, in any case. The scene was surreal. Low light spilling from the windows brushed everything with shades of orange and gold, intensifying the scene's unearthliness.

Albin and Frey were the last to come through the doors. Each held large wooden platters weighed down with carved rabbit, smoked deer, chestnut bread, and berries. Albin, dressed in a worn leather tunic and brown hosen, contrasted sharply with his sister, who wore a belted purple tunic, dark-stained hosen, and dainty leather shoes. She'd also stained her lips with red paint and darkened the space around her eyes with an oil and charcoal mixture. Walde had never seen a woman under the age of thirty apply such face paint. If Frey wore it to look older, she had succeeded.

They set down the platters, and the other children fell silent as the two took their seats at the table's end. Then Walde was astonished as Albin stood and intoned the ancient chant of thanks to the gods. The moment he sat down, the children snatched up their knives and dug into the food.

There were thirteen children and three large platters. If he and Brite were going to fill themselves, they had to do it fast. *I'm taking food from kids,* he thought guiltily as he piled meat and berries into his bowl. The idea didn't curb his appetite.

The youngest stopped talking. Everything was quiet apart from the sounds of knives scraping against the wooden trenchers and the odd knock to a chair leg. Young children could be remarkably quiet as they ate. It was a phenomenon Walde had observed before. While adults conversed over a meal, hungry children focused all their energy on breaking food into pieces, chewing, and swallowing. Once they were full, their playing resumed.

Despite the many oddities Walde had witnessed, the youngest children fell into this same pattern. The older ones let them play until two started crying, then Grella and the archer girl took them by the hands and guided them out the door.

Walde refilled his water cup and let out a contented sigh. It felt good to be full. "Thanks for the wonderful meal," he said, eyes moving around the table to include all who may have had a part in it. Brite echoed his words and added her thanks for the clothes and hospitality. The girl in the green frock chuckled as she whisked away the platters and wiped the table down with a wet rag.

Albin grinned. "It's our pleasure. We haven't had guests for..." He shot his sister a thoughtful glance. "Actually, we've never had guests."

The room had darkened with the setting sun. Frey removed oil lamps from their sconces, set them in a neat line down the table, and lit them using a flint box from her belt pouch. While she was at it, a girl of about nine rose gracefully from the table, a lyra under her arm, as if she had produced it by magic. She retreated to a corner and, after a bit of tuning, plucked out a gentle, building tune that reminded Walde of his dream song. The other children quietly sipped water while watching Walde and Brite from the tops of their eyes. Albin waited for the two girls to return from putting the young ones to bed before speaking again.

"So. A story for a story. I'll give you our truth in exchange for your truth, and if I say anything inaccurate, my friends will correct me."

The children around the table nodded dutifully. The meaning of Albin's words was clear. Walde and Brite had no friends present to confirm *their* story, so his generosity ought to move their consciences to be truthful.

Such a complex tactic for a boy of thirteen.

"A story for a story," Walde agreed quietly.

Frey slid her hand into her brother's, and Albin gripped it for a few moments, so tightly that his knuckles whitened. He stared at the table as he began to speak. "Almost five years ago now, the Harborlands' elders decided to purge the place again of any hidden Reachers. They did this so quietly that no one knew what was happening until it was too late. It was a horrible time. All the adults were tested somehow, and the ones found to be Reachers were taken away." His mouth twisted. "There was a strong community of Reachers in the Harborlands then. Most of them married other Reachers to keep the blood pure, so when this second purge happened, their children were orphaned. And truly orphaned. No one wanted to put effort into raising children who might become Reachers. So when no one volunteered, the Elders asked the Woodlanders if they would take us.

"The youngest of us had no idea what was going on. Some thought that their parents had moved away, and they were going somewhere to meet them." He shook his head. "The Woodlanders had just finished their own purge, too. So there were orphans here, though not as many. We came just as people were packing up and readying to leave. The children were used as pack mules to carry stuff down the trees to the boats. It took weeks to move everyone. During that time, three of us died from falls and one died months later from a wasting injury.

"The Lowlands came as a shock to us all. It was hard enough being without our parents. Now we had to live without Mothertrees. Our adoptive parents weren't happy either, but they wouldn't talk about it, and some took their anger out on us. It was bad, but it was going to get worse. We didn't age, you see. After three years, people noticed that, and they remembered who our parents were.

"We became known as the cursed children. From that time on, our lives were in danger. Not all our foster parents were cruel, but even the kind ones couldn't protect us from other villagers. Children would just disappear, and no one cared to investigate. My sister and I suspected they'd been killed and thrown in the bogs."

Brite made a soft sound in her throat. "I never heard about any of this," she said.

"No, you wouldn't have. Folk didn't talk about it. They were afraid even to speak about it. It was believed that if a pregnant woman laid eyes on us, she would lose her child. If a child saw us, it would fall ill. And so on. It got so bad that one of the older cursed children killed himself. That was when I decided to take the children and leave. I thought that if we returned to the Mothertrees, we'd start growing again. And if we didn't, at least we'd be away from the people who hated us. We'd heard that the Mothertrees weren't blooming anymore, so there'd be no harvest. The trees would be left alone."

He chuckled. "But it turned out they weren't alone. A lonely old man had stayed behind to take care of his dying wife. He'd spent his life repairing the walkways in his Mothertree, and he kept at that after she was gone. He was a kind old man. He taught us many things before he died. But not everything. Many of us had learned skills from our parents before we ever left the Harborlands." Pride entered his voice. "My father was a hunter, and he taught me how to use a bow and throwing knife."

Another child cut in. "My mother taught me how to make soap."

"And mine taught me how to play the lyra." This from the musician in the corner, who had long ceased playing.

"My mother knew all the herbs in the world and all the poisons too."

The voices went on and on. Walde could not look up. His head had long fallen into his hands. The four walls of the medallion had kept him together during Albin's recounting, but as each new little voice dripped into him, he lost his tight control. His face shook and tears filled his eyes. He blinked against the brightness of his own palms.

The room had gone silent.

Walde wiped his face. "I'm sorry. So very sorry." No one spoke, and when he dared to look up, it was to find every eye on him. Expressions varied from bare longing to entrancement. Even Brite was spellbound, though her gaze was fixed on his face rather than on his palms.

Albin closed his slack mouth and swallowed. "I've always wanted to see that, Walde. Ever since I found out my parents were Reachers."

Brite whispered, "Did you find out during the purge?"

Albin nodded. “We did, though we barely knew what it meant.”

Walde asked, “Then how did you come to think so highly of Reachers?”

“Our parents were good people,” Albin said, and there was a murmur of agreement around the table. “Besides, they brought us up as Reachers, if you know what I mean.”

Walde’s hand rose to the nape of his neck and fell. “I do know.”

Frey had picked a knot out of the wood and was rolling it between her fingers. “I’ll finish the story, Al. Though there isn’t much left to tell.

“Soon after we got here, the old man told us what we should do to protect ourselves. See, the Woodlanders guessed where we went. And many of them still revere the Mothertrees. Even dead ones. Most of them left us alone, but every so often a group came in armed with shiny Lowland metal. The old man warned us not to kill them, and we haven’t. We’ve simply disarmed them and sent them back where they belong.”

Walde asked, “Have you ever met peacekeeper guards?”

“Not that we know of. Thank the gods.”

“Well, I’m grateful that you let us in.”

Albin said, “The only ones we allow in are confirmed Reachers. You see, we never saw our parents die. For all we know, they’re still alive somewhere, missing us. And maybe one day they’ll come find us.” He averted his eyes as if embarrassed. “None of us can tear that hope from our hearts. Not even the youngest, though they don’t recall anymore what their parents looked like.”

A long silence fell. Walde ran a hand through his hair. He suddenly missed his father keenly. Albin’s account was disturbing, more for the questions it raised than anything else.

A sense of urgency gripped him. He would leave this place at dawn, come what may.

Brite broke the silence with a softly voiced question. "How old *are* you two?"

"I'm seventeen," Albin said, "and my sister is fifteen. You can add four years to everyone you see here. Our bodies don't grow, but our minds do."

"Not so for the youngest," Frey cut in. "They get smarter, but they don't mature the way the rest of us do. If the Mothertrees were still alive, then maybe..." She shrugged. "But who knows?"

Walde tried to imagine being frozen for four years on the very brink of becoming a man. It would be its own kind of torture.

"But that's enough of us," Albin said as he refilled his water cup. "Now it's your turn."

CHAPTER 10

Night had fallen. A cool breeze blew through the windows, causing the lamp flames to flicker.

Walde set his mind back to the morning of his father's sham execution. While deciding where to begin, he realized he'd have to explain why he had been imprisoned in the crawlspace, and that led him back to the "hunt" his father had taken him on, and finally to the song rite that had roused his power.

He couldn't have had a more rapt audience. Their wide eyes and appreciative sounds moved him to spin out the tale in greater detail. He found himself relating the history of the Reachers and his own thoughts on why they shouldn't have kept silent. It felt good to express his opinions on the matter, even to such a young audience.

He omitted his trek to the sapling Mothertree. It wasn't his secret to share. The spat between Jak and Rona didn't seem important, but he spoke in detail about his repetitive dreams, his foolish performance in the elder's hut, and his subsequent imprisonment.

His voice grew flat and disbelieving as he related what had occurred the following morning. He couldn't believe he'd just stood passively by and watched what had looked to be his father's execution. What if Carrac hadn't been protected by the shield? Could Walde have lived with himself knowing he'd allowed his father to die? Even if Walde hadn't stood a chance of helping him, he should have done something. Said something.

"You were in shock," Albin said softly when Walde's voice faltered. "It happens."

"It shouldn't have happened." He dragged in a heavy breath and plunged on.

He relived the ferocious, icy water, the struggle on the raft, the shock and relief to find that Carrac lived, and the moment he was forced to let him go.

Albin became so absorbed in this part of the story that he cared not at all about what happened after. He leaned over the table, eyes blazing on Walde. "Tell me again what the guard said to you about burying people at sea."

Walde tried to recall the exact wording. "She said that we'd no longer burn our dead but place them on rafts and let the river carry them out. She said that the Harborlanders have been doing that for years."

"And this came right after the officials left." Albin ran his hand over his hair and spoke in a low, feverish voice. "What are they doing with the Reachers? If they want them alive, then they must be using them for something."

Frey said, "Maybe our parents *are* still alive."

And with those words, the table erupted in a storm of excited chatter. The children pelted Walde with questions, and when it became clear that he knew no more than they did, they ignored him like a useless playing card and went on talking together.

In the midst of all this, Brite remained still and thoughtful, her probing gaze fixed on Walde.

Walde drained his water cup and rubbed his eyes. He told himself that if he'd lied about what had happened to his father, Albin would have dredged the truth from him anyway. And hadn't Walde agreed to Albin's conditions? What good was his word if he went back on it so easily? The legitimacy of these facts did nothing to halt his anxiety, though. What if Albin and Frey asked Walde to search for their parents? Or worse, demanded to go with him to the Harborlands?

He stared into his cup, wishing it were filled with ona.

At last, he stood and offered everyone a tight smile. "Brite and I will need rest if we're going to set out again tomorrow."

Albin stood abruptly. His face held the expression of a boy who'd just been told he couldn't go on an important hunt. He gripped Walde's arm and leaned into his ear. "Meet me back here at dawn."

***

It was a while longer before Walde and Brite extricated themselves from the hall. Albin offered them hand lamps, for the paths and walkways were not lit as well as they ought to be. The children didn't follow their guests out the door, and Walde suspected that they would converse late into the night.

Brite was silent as a ghost as she walked beside Walde down the winding stairs. He refrained from shining the light on her face. A glimpse of her stiff hand on the guide rope told him all he needed to know.

"I'll walk you to your hut," he offered as they reached the lowest level, which was only a few yards up from the ground.

She slowed. "Could I step into yours a moment? I need to talk to you."

Her voice sounded so strange that Walde stopped to look at her, but she'd already gone on ahead of him. She chose the correct walkway off the path, and they were soon inside his hut, their lamps brightening the small space. Walde sat on one side of the clothes chest and waited, but Brite would not join him. She stood with her hands clenched tightly, her eyes everywhere but on Walde.

She said, "I need to know something before I sleep tonight." He nodded, and she went on haltingly. "Are people from your village…hunting you? Is that why you wanted to cut through the Woodlands?"

"No. I don't think so. I'm pretty sure they think I'm dead now."

She met his eyes for half a breath and then seemed to find something interesting on the floor again. "Then you didn't fear the road?"

He shrugged. "I kept to the road all the way to the Lowlands and only left it to see if I could find wood for my bow."

She gave a vigorous, self-conscious nod. "Of course. The road is the fastest way to the Harborlands, and you're in a hurry to find your father, who is in danger."

Walde froze as he realized where their conversation was heading. "Brite—"

"Why did you add a day or more to your travel time by going through the Woodlands?"

He looked away from her searching eyes. "Because people were after *you*, and I didn't want to leave you alone. Where are you going anyway? Can you tell me…?"

She gave him no answer. It was as if she *couldn't* answer. Her sudden stillness reminded him of a rock deer's when it caught human scent. That moment of recognition before flight. He would have given anything to know her thoughts just then.

"Brite…?"

"I'm going with *you*," she answered, and snatching up her lamp, she left the hut.

Walde stared after her, dumbfounded. He had been sure she was going to shake him off like an unwanted tick, tell him she didn't need his protection. Instead, she had merely restated their plan: to travel to the Harborlands together. What was the point then in forcing him to admit the obvious and embarrassing them both in the process?

Heaving a sigh, he shook out the blanket, extinguished the lamp, and lay down on the crunchy mattress. The night was warm and quiet. It was many days since he'd slept in a Mothertree.

A *dead* Mothertree, he reminded himself grimly. A crack in the shutters revealed moonlight on still, bare branches. It sent a chill into his bones. He secured the shutters and tried to relax. The day's exertions ought to have made sleep come easily. But his eyes did not want to close. His muscles were tense, and he felt a dizzying urge to run until he dropped from sheer exhaustion.

Despite his best efforts to steer his thoughts away from what he'd learned tonight, Albin's story slunk back, the words conjuring unwanted images of mistreated and murdered children. His stomach clenched and his palms brightened.

It could easily have been him. Had he been born a few years later, in the Harborlands instead of the Lakelands, he might've been in Albin's place. Would he have had the strength to do what Albin did? Could he have set aside the loss of his parents, the abuse by his foster parents, and all the horrors he'd witnessed around him, to gather together more than a dozen children and steal them away into the night? Even with Frey's help, it seemed a monumental task. But he had accomplished it.

His head shook slowly. He'd never met anyone like Albin. The youth's only weakness seemed to be his fixation on finding his parents. Walde hadn't dared tell him that his parents were almost certainly dead. News of the purge had swept through the Lakelands years ago, and while it was possible that they had been imprisoned for a time, after almost five years the chance of them still living was slim.

Or was it? *They want them alive,* Albin had said. Walde shuddered. No, he would not indulge in useless speculation. Experience taught him that speculation was only as good as the imagination of the one who spun it. And Walde's own imagination was apparently lacking. He couldn't have guessed the real truth about the children, so why think about what might have befallen his father? What he might be suffering at that very moment?

He turned onto his good side and forced his eyes shut.

Time passed, and the tension in his muscles wouldn't ease. He gave up finally and tossed off the covers. He would get a breath of fresh air and stretch his legs. He got to his feet, decided he didn't have the patience to light the lamp, and strode outside without it.

His wandering took him past Brite's small hut. A welcoming glimmer of light danced through a crack in the shutters. He paused, wondering why she wasn't asleep. He doubted she was suffering as Walde was. Brite's life in the Lowlands had been harsher than his, causing her to form a sort of callus around herself. Not that she was heartless. Rather, she didn't let adversity break her. He admired the ability.

He was about to move on when Brite's firm voice slid through the shutters.

"You can't sleep in my bed."

"Why?" a child's voice asked. "I always slept with Mommy when I had nightmares. She'd even tell me stories."

"I'm not your mommy."

"You look like her, though. Couldn't you be her, just for tonight?"

There was a lengthy silence. Walde, curiosity overpowering his conscience, tiptoed down the path and peeked through the front window.

A head of curly red hair came into view. A little girl was stretched out on Brite's bed, hands gripping the mattress as if it were a raft on unsteady waters. Brite knelt beside her and brushed hair from her cheek. "I don't know what being a mommy's like. I never had a mother myself. Not truly."

"Why not?"

Brite shrugged. "She had me when she was only fourteen. After I was born, she left me on my uncle's doorstep and joined a tinker train. Her parents wanted nothing to do with me. As for my father, I have no idea who he is. For all I know he's one of the Barans."

The girl regarded her thoughtfully. "That's dark."

"Dark?"

"A dark story. I don't mind dark stories."

Brite chuckled. It was a deep, throaty sound, free of self-consciousness. "I know some dark stories, but they're not for children's ears."

The girl sat up with a frown. "I'm nine years old. *Not* a child."

"Well then… I can tell you one, but you'll have to promise to go back to bed."

The girl kissed her pinched fingertips and held them up. It was a tree dweller's promise sign, and one that tinkers were usually familiar with. But not, apparently, Brite. Instead of laying her hand over the girl's to accept the promise, she kissed the girl's fingertips.

Walde wasn't surprised when the girl collapsed into the bed in a fit of giggles. Brite watched her with pursed lips. When the girl had calmed, Brite began to speak.

"In the Lowlands, we have quite a few stories about the bone man… He's a hunched old man with a white tuft of hair that stands straight up from his skull. His eyes are black as a raven's, and his wrinkly hands look like claws. All he does all day is gather bones—"

"Bones. You mean human bones?"

She shrugged. "Animal bones, human bones, whatever he finds on the ground. He piles them all into his big leather bag, and when night comes, he hauls them off to his bone house.

"One morning, things didn't go well for the bone man. From the top of a hill, he spied the remains of a dead deer and was so excited about it that he curled up like a beetle and rolled down. But when he straightened, a young man stood over him with a sack in his arms.

"'I have the deer,' the man said. 'What will you give me for its bones?'

"The bone man was shocked. No one had ever taken his bones before. 'Those are mine,' he said. 'Mine by right.' But the stranger didn't care about rights.

"'I have them now, and you're not getting them until you give me something.'

"'But I have nothing to give,' the bone man said.

"'Everyone has something. Think of something fast, or I'll take these bones and burn them to ash.'

"Well, think of the most precious thing you own, and imagine that burned. The bone man racked his brain over what the stranger would want. An idea came to him, but he didn't like it. It was mean, and he wasn't mean. But he had no choice. He said, 'There's a place where I put the things I don't want.'

"'What things?'

"'Things that are over and under the bones. People things.'

"The stranger perked up at the words 'people things.' 'You mean the stuff people had when they died?'

"The bone man nodded. 'Soft things, hard things, *glittery* things…'

"Well, that did it. The stranger wanted the people things very badly and demanded to see them. The bone man guided him back up the hill, then over five more hills, each larger than the last. At the bottom of the sixth, the bone man waved the stranger into a hole in the hillside, which turned out to be a vast cavern. After a few steps, the bone man stopped and pointed to a pit. 'That's the place where I put the people things.'

"The stranger lit his belt lamp and shone it into the hole. Clothing, packs, shiny metal blades, and coin purses were strewn everywhere. And gliding through and around them all were several large black snakes. Now, black snakes are the most dangerous snakes in the world. They like cold, dark holes, and don't like to be troubled by strangers.

"The man snarled and turned to the bone man. 'I have a rope. I'll let you down, and you get me the purses and the blades.'

"The bone man snorted. 'No-wie. Won't do that.'

"'You'll do it, or I'll kill you.'

"'Then what? You'll have a dead bone man and no people things.' He clenched the stranger's arm with a clawed hand. 'Don't lose your bones in that hole.'

"The stranger stared a long time into the pit. 'I'll kill the bastards,' he said.

"So he fetched a rope and hook from his pack and, knife between his teeth, went down into the pit. Now, the bottom was fifteen feet down and the walls were full of crevices. The stranger thought they made excellent footholds, but one held a particularly large snake, and it didn't like being stepped on. It got its teeth into the man's flimsy hosen and bit down hard. The man lashed at it with the knife, but he couldn't do much while he still clung to the rope. And it was too late anyway. Another snake slid out of a crack and landed on the man's neck. The man didn't live long after that. After losing his grip on the rope, he fell into the pit and never came out.

"The bone man was terribly sad and hung about the pit for days trying to think of a way to retrieve the stranger's bones.

But in the end he gave up. Throwing the deer sack over his shoulder, he scuttled out of the cave and into the sunlight."

Walde had ceased watching through the crack several minutes earlier and sat on the ground, leaning against the wall. No other sounds came from the hut. The girl must have drifted off to sleep. Probably for the best, he thought. A story like that might have kept her awake, watching for snakes in the shadows. He found himself smiling softly. Brite was a talented storyteller. She had learned much from her uncle.

While he waited to see if she would wake the girl and force her out of the hut, the window went dark. In the ensuing silence, he closed his eyes.

***

He awoke at dawn, startled and vaguely embarrassed at where he'd spent the night. Hopefully, no one had noticed. The children had taken pains to prepare his sleeping quarters, and he hadn't spent an hour on the mattress. He stood and stretched his limbs, then strode briskly back to his own hut. After splashing water on his face, he pushed a fist into his pillow and thoroughly tangled the blankets. He left the tightly lidded chamber pot outside his door. It felt strange to have no possessions beyond what he carried on his body. Doubtlessly, Albin would stock him with some. In exchange for a favor or two, of course.

He latched the door, turned, and nearly walked into a child carrying a bucket.

"Good morning," the boy said cheerfully. Walde recognized him as Pismire, or rather Spitfire, the boy who'd argued with Buzz. "How did you sleep?"

"Very well, thank you. The mattress was firm and the blankets warm."

"That's nice. Brite told me to tell you she hopes her doorstep was comfortable last night."

Walde's mouth fell open. Spitfire grinned at the look of mortification on his face. Walde cleared his throat. "Is she already up and about then?"

"She was awake when I brought in the water, but I don't think she's left the hut. Do you need water?"

"No. Thank you."

Spitfire turned and headed back to the path. "Albin wants you at the meeting hut," he called back.

Walde's belly rumbled as he trudged up the trunk to the middle level. The life-like statue of the guard greeted him with its colorless gaze.

Albin must have heard Walde's step, for he flung open the door before Walde could knock. He was far from the composed, dignified leader Walde had met the day before. His blond hair was in disarray, shadows lay under his feverish eyes, and a smell of sweat and last night's supper wafted off of him.

"Walde." He clasped Walde's forearm and met his gaze for a long moment. "How did you sleep?"

"Better than you did, apparently."

"A question: Once you reach the Harborlands, will Brite go her own way, or will she help you find your father?"

Walde jerked away at the thought. "She's going her own way, of course. I wouldn't dream of risking her life for this."

"I thought so. But I wanted to be sure. Come." He turned and Walde followed him to the far side of the hall, where a single table now stood. Next to it were a stuffed leather pack, a bow, and a quiver of arrows. Walde tried not to eye them greedily. They would come with a price.

"Look here," Albin said, motioning him to the tabletop. Warm light from an unshuttered window fell on a large square of parchment. "We drew this map of the Harborlands last night."

Walde eyed the sketch in amazement. The tidy lines of the waterways and roads, the opening to the harbor, the eighteen Mothertrees that marched along the river and bent around the harbor's opening—all had been drawn with an expert hand. "We?"

"Well, Frey drew it, and the rest of us told her where things should go. Our mother was a mapmaker, you see, and Frey never forgot what she learned from her." He pointed to the largest of the trees, which stood at the land's southernmost tip. "This is the First. Sadly, it and most of the others are dead. They weren't completely dead when we left the Harborlands, but then neither were these." He waved a hand to encompass the Woodlands.

Walde's mouth had gone dry. So it was true after all. Their First was dead. The tinker had misled them when he said that she "still stood." The Woodlands trees stood too, like a row of icy statues.

He felt the youth's intent gaze on him. "You didn't know this?"

"No." He sagged against the edge of the table. "Gods, will the Lakelands be next?"

"Very likely." Albin toyed with a leather band around his wrist. "The story you told us last night—about the history of the Reachers—it made me wonder if their end will also mean the end of the Mothertrees."

"There won't be an end to the Mothertrees," Walde said firmly. But the words sounded desperate in the wake of what he'd just heard. He rubbed his hand across his forehead. "The elders must see a connection by now between dead Reachers and dead Mothertrees. It's undeniable."

"Of course they see it." Albin's blue eyes flashed angrily. "Haven't they been seeing it for years? But it's too late. They can't admit they did wrong. If they brought back the Reachers, they'd lose all power and credibility. They'd rather give up their whole way of life than do that." He pointed to an area on the leeward side of the Harborlands Mothertrees. "The old guardhouse is here, next to an oak that had been used for hanging Reachers." He ran his fingers out from it. North and east. "There are new streets and houses here. And probably a few pubs. Frey couldn't put all the streets on the map because we've never seen them, but they're there and they probably extend farther than you think.

"Be wary. I'd wait until night, then steal some clothes off a line. If you go in wearing kessa, tongues will wag. People spin flax now or buy kriksa. They still wear leather jackets, but in a baggy Lowlands style. And the women wear frocks, not tunics." He glanced up at Walde's stunned face. "The Lakelands are still pretty isolated, eh? That's probably worked in the tinkers' favor."

"We are, apparently. Very isolated. Have you heard any news that might help me?"

Albin grimaced. "I've been out of touch with the world for seven months, so I'm not the best source of information."

Walde pursed his lips and looked at him sideways. "What about the rumor that Reachers were used to kill the First?"

"Ah." A stillness fell over the restless leader. "You have that a bit wrong. The rumor is that Reachers were used to try to kill Thara, not the Mothertree."

Walde stared at him, aghast. "That's crazy."

"Crazy rumors spread the fastest."

"What did the Woodlanders think of that? You told me that some still revere the Mothertrees."

He smiled darkly. "They don't like it. But they don't understand it either. So they just talk and drink, then talk and drink some more."

"And the elders…?"

He shrugged. "The elders said that if Thara can be killed, she is no god. And if she can't be killed, then no one can harm her."

Walde said, "That's a dangerous bit of philosophy. And people don't know enough to contest it. They don't know what she is or where she is. I've grazed her while reaching, and even I don't know. If she *can* be killed, and it turns out we need her, what then?"

Albin shook his head. "I don't believe the rumor anyway. Reachers wouldn't allow themselves to be used that way." He eyed Walde carefully. "You don't, do you? Believe it?"

Walde's mind whirled. His view of what had seemed possible had changed since he'd left the Lakelands. He knew now that a path of dead Mothertrees had spread from the Woodlands down, and that it had been precipitated by a path of dead or incapacitated Reachers. Something compelling had motivated the elders in those places to act. And it was far from over. Harborlands officials hadn't gone to the trouble of establishing a new burial arrangement with Lakelanders so that a few Reachers per century—whoever happened to slip up—could be sent down to them. No, they'd probably asked for a purge. They wanted the Lakelands Reachers. Could it be they were trying to destroy the being who could be accessed through the Mothertrees? As much as the idea sickened him, he had to admit that it made more sense than anything else. "I don't know," he said hollowly. "You say 'allow,' but someone can be forced to do something against their will. The elders know more about Reacher lore than we do. I don't understand what motive they'd have for wanting to…to do what you said, but I wouldn't put it past them to try."

A grim silence fell. Walde forced his hands to relax from their tight grip on the table. A shine of silver light radiated off them. He'd been far too lax lately about holding it back. He flicked a nervous glance at Albin.

The youth looked as though he'd stopped breathing. Suddenly he straightened, rolled up the map, and secured it with a strip of leather. Having opened a space on the table, he scooped up the pack and set it before them. "I've scrounged together enough dried meat to last you and Brite for some days. And here is an excellent fire kit. And a belt lamp and some oil. A length of rope. A couple of blankets and a water bottle… And here, look at this knife."

He was feverish again, his limbs tight as strung cords. Walde understood his anxiety. His own was a coiled snake in his belly.

Albin offered him a metal knife about a hand's breadth long. Walde turned it carefully in his hands. "My father and I had a few knives like this," he said in a calm, even voice. If he couldn't ease his own worry, he'd strive to ease Albin's. "Do you have a sheath for it?"

Albin held up two armbands connected by a sheath. Each band had a buckle and many small holes so that it could be adjusted to fit any size of forearm. Walde had heard of such a contraption but had never seen one.

Albin motioned to Walde's arm. "May I?"

Walde let him strap the band to his left forearm and then slide the knife into its sheath. "Clench," Albin ordered, and Walde obeyed. The band tightened, but not uncomfortably. Albin said, "You should nab a tunic with baggy sleeves. Or, better yet, a robe. Those are popular now."

Walde drew the knife and held it up to the hazy light. "I've never turned a blade on a man."

"Then you've been fortunate. My adopted father gave me this a year ago. I've had to use it in defense twice. Once, it saved my life."

"Then you ought to keep it." Walde worked at opening the buckles, but Albin stopped his hand.

"Don't." He pinned Walde with a pleading gaze. "I can't let you leave here unarmed. You're a hunter. You understand the value of weapons."

"I had a bow when I came here, and Brite had a stone knife. We weren't unarmed."

"I know. But you won't be able to take such weapons with you into town, at least not visibly. I don't know what's it's like in the Lakelands, but where I'm from, you're not allowed to carry a bow unless you're a guard or a hunter. If the guards see that bow, they'll arrest you and question you. As for the knife, it's too noticeable. People use Lowlands tools now. Metal arrowheads, knives, and ax heads. Stone belongs to the old way of life."

The old way. Walde closed his eyes briefly. He was beginning to feel more and more like a ghost. "All right. So I'll hide the bow before I go into the city."

"Exactly. Will you take the knife then?"

"That depends on what all this will cost me." He looked Albin square in the face.

"Oh." The youth's eyes lowered, and he gave a self-conscious shrug. "Nothing, really. Or just a request. I'd like you to come back here if you can and tell us what you saw. I'd go there myself, but I can't leave the children."

Walde found himself nodding, relieved that it wasn't something more difficult. If he lived through this adventure, where else could he and Carrac go but here? He kissed his pinched fingertips and held them up. "You have my word then. If I can return, I will."

A grin lit Albin's face. He enclosed Walde's hand in both of his. "Thank you."

CHAPTER 11

Three competing schools of thought have developed since the time of the first purges. The first and most popular is that Thara is but the life force of the tree and as such is indifferent to whomever performs the song rite. In this view, the quality of the songs is what makes the difference and not the singers.

The second view holds that Thara doesn't exist at all but was invented by the Reachers in order to justify their own power and importance. This view holds that the only real power exists within the Reachers, who have the ability to either help or harm growing things.

A third, more recent view holds that Thara exists not as a god but as an intelligent parasite that attached itself to the Mothertrees long ago. In this view, the Reachers have the parasite's taint and can therefore commune with it, relaying its will to people on the surface. Given enough time, its influence over others would be complete. From where did this parasite come? Some have pointed to the night sky and to the silvery light of falling stars.

–A fragment from a speech written by one of the Woodlands elders

Walde and Brite ate a quick breakfast at the base of the tree while a dozen children looked on. Afterward, they bid everyone an awkward farewell. The children's eyes followed Walde hungrily. He wanted to promise them he would return, but he doubted he could keep such a promise, and the last thing they needed was another adult breaking their trust.

Walde wore the arm dagger under his sleeve, the bow and quiver of arrows across his shoulder, and the pack on his back. He eyed his bare hands nervously. Albin had offered him gloves with the caveat that he shouldn't wear them in public. In warm weather, wearing gloves would make folk suspicious. Walde had reluctantly refused them. It would be too tempting to wear them all the time, and he needed to learn better control. Wearing gloves would thwart that progress. Still, he almost regretted not taking them.

Brite had discarded her old clothes, retaining only her belt pouch and the stone knife Walde had made her. Before leaving the tree, Albin pressed coin pouches into their hands. Each contained some of the coins the old recluse had left the children before he died. Walde knew better than to refuse the money. He would need every advantage he could get.

Frey, their guide out of the Woodlands, was dressed in a fitted leather tunic and hosen. She carried a sheathed dagger at her hip and another at her ankle. Her tightly braided blond hair had been curled into a knot and fastened to the top of her head. Her charcoal eye paint had been replaced by dark circles. She looked, Walde thought, as if she'd spent the night weeping. But despite her evident anguish, she stood straight and sure.

Walde and Brite followed her down a path to the boat launch. Walde volunteered to take an oar and Frey took the other. Brite said she would have offered, but she had never rowed before. Streams in the Lowlands were too shallow and the marsh too dense to allow for boating.

Flecks of sunlight glistened on the water as they glided south, passing between towering Mothertrees and under an old stone bridge. Walde eased his paddling as the First came into view. His breathing slowed and his back prickled. He sensed something from the towering tree, though he couldn't be sure whether the feeling was real or if his mind played tricks on him. He looked around and then back at the Mothertrees receding behind him.

As his gaze returned to the First, he nearly dropped his paddle. "The First—it's not as gray as the others."

"No," Frey replied without turning, "it's not. But in all other ways, it's as dead as the others."

"Still, I wish I'd known. I might have tried reaching."

She tossed him a wide-eyed glance. "Truly? Do you want to try it now?"

"No. Not now. But I will, if..." His voice trailed. He was about to add, "*If* I come back," but he couldn't form the words.

Brite, sitting cross-legged between them with the pack, must have caught the trailing note in his voice and guessed what it meant, for she reached back suddenly and touched his hand. "You will."

Walde, moved by the gesture, could do nothing but nod.

No other Mothertrees followed the First. The riverbanks brightened for a brief time before plunging into the deeper shade of willow oaks. Frey dug her paddle in, and they drifted to shore. "The river bends east after this. I'll guide you to a path you can use to safely leave the Woodlands."

Brite stepped out of the boat, and Walde helped Frey drag it up onto the bank. They climbed a rocky slope. Near the top, a gap in the trees came into view. Four years of growth had muddied what must have been a clean, well trodden path that ran straight through the forest. Now, only a thin strip in its center was bare of weeds. Still, the cut it made through the forest could not be concealed. The three took it in single file. Frey didn't walk but jogged to compensate for her smaller legs. When Walde offered to slow down, her succinct response was to speed up. The pace must not have been easy for her. Although they had left the steep slope behind, the land continued to gently rise.

The forest was wild and beautiful. In the Lakelands, cultivated trees grew in tidy rows. These seemed to have seeded themselves. Some were so tiny, they could be stepped on, while others were large enough to have accommodated a hut or two. A few of the ancient ones had lain down to rest like reposing statues. Flowering vines twisted around them, and bright green mosses colored their bark.

The undergrowth was dank, rich, and full of life. Too much life for Walde's liking. He slapped at bugs and hopped away to avoid stepping on toads, snails, and even scat. Other pathways crisscrossed through the undergrowth, some almost entirely overgrown.

This was a hunter's wood. The forest on the north side of the Woodlands did not contain the same richness of life. Perhaps it had been harvested for too long, leaving it without the old, rotting trees that made perfect dens for small animals. Frey paused a few times along the way, pointing out concealed traps they might otherwise have succumbed to.

After a journey of perhaps two miles, they came to the ridge of a slope. A faint path led down into a densely wooded area.

Frey halted and pointed down. "That's the path I told you about. Keep to it, and after a short time you'll come to a field full of heath and stunted trees. From there, it'll be a two-day walk to the Harborlands. You'll cross a stream along the way, so there's no need to hoard your water."

"Where does *this* path lead?" Brite asked.

"Probably to the cart road," Walde said idly. He'd been eyeing the branches above him for a hidden sentinel.

Frey touched his arm. "She's up there. How did you guess?"

"It's a good place for a lookout, being at the fork of two paths and at the top of a rise. And if I can figure that out, then an intruder can too."

Frey grinned. "They wouldn't get close enough to think about it. You can't see it yet, but there's a tree over the path down there. The north side of it is booby-trapped."

Brite muttered, "I hope you were going to remember to tell us that."

"Of course."

Walde's brows pulled together in a puzzled frown. "So when the sentinel spies an intruder, what does she do? Climb down and run back to the river to report it?"

"No, she makes a horn call."

"From this far away?" His eyes narrowed skeptically. "Your Mothertree must be a good three miles from here."

"But there are enough sentinels between here and there to relay the messages. And the calls travel well. The horns are loud, and the blasts are made from up in the tallest trees."

"Seems like overkill," Brite said. "Putting a sentinel way out here."

Frey shrugged. "Albin wanted us to have enough time to hide if a big enough force came through. And since this path leads in from the cart road, it's an easy point of entry." Impatience flickered on her face. "It's getting late, and you need a head start."

She bid them goodbye, lingering longer with Walde as she peppered him with blessings from every god she could think of, including some he'd never heard of before.

At last, he extracted himself and followed a chuckling Brite down the slope.

The dugout trap was well hidden under bits of bark and old leaves. Walde would have stopped to examine how it was made, but he would not steal any more time from his father. They made a wide circle around it and continued up the path, swatting at flies as they walked.

It felt good to have been supplied with food and water, a clean change of clothes, and all the tools needed for journeying. And the information he'd harvested from Albin would be invaluable when they reached the Harborlands. "I'm glad we went through the Woodlands," he heard himself say. "I still don't have a plan, but at least I have a clearer idea of where I'm going and how I should look when I get there."

He told her then about the map he carried on his back and about the suggestions Albin had made regarding their appearance in the Harborlands.

"He's right," she admitted, then added, "but I'm keeping this tunic. I'll eat it if I have to."

His lips twitched. "I'd like to see that."

From there, the conversation turned to the possible benefits of eating kessa and whether the body would digest it or expel it whole. Brite's fey mood reached a peak as they exited the forest and stepped out into brilliant sunlight and the rugged landscape of the wastes.

She stretched her arms and sighed as if blown by an enchanted wind. "It's so good to be out in the open again."

"It's nice to be away from the biting flies," he agreed.

They struck out at a fast pace, following an old, overgrown path until it vanished in the heath. Walde found a stick and slashed at the wiry plants, pausing when he uncovered thistles.

He was a long way from the Lakelands now. The distant mountains, which had always looked soft and misty, had gained both height and sharp edges. Some green still lingered here and there, but the overall impression was one of bare thrusting stone cutting against a cheerful blue sky. The wastes had changed, too. The heath had thickened, and despite the look of the mountains, fewer rocks jutted from the ground. They paused to eat and drink and then went on at a steady pace until the sun was low. Not wanting to squander the dried meat Albin had packed them, Walde shot a rabbit and cleaned it while Brite gathered brush for a fire.

"Nothing but kindling," she sighed as she dumped one last load onto a tangled hill of sticks.

"It'll be enough to cook the rabbit. And we have blankets to keep us warm." Summer nights were rarely cold, but when one slept on the bare earth, they had to endure the chill of early morning dew. A goat-hair blanket kept off the chill, if not the moisture.

They made a rough spit from the thickest sticks they could find and then struggled to keep the fire steady while the rabbit cooked. The brush smoked abominably, forcing them to huddle upwind. The cooking and eating distracted them for a while, but once it was over, the intimacy of the darkness and the crackling fire settled on them like a heady scent. Brite sat so close to him that he could feel her body heat. It would have been so easy to let his hand drift to hers. And so wrong.

He had been taking careful breaths, hardly moving, so when she suddenly spoke, his heart bounded in his chest. His palms flashed briefly before he got hold of himself.

She said, ignoring his slip-up, "I've been meaning to tell you something since dinner last night but I never found the right time."

He cleared his throat. "Go on."

"It's just an old piece of gossip that's been floating around." She tossed him a sheepish glance. "Talk is that Harborlands elders have been using Reachers to kill their tree god."

Walde kept his mouth firm for a few breaths longer then broke into a smile. "I know. Albin told me that this morning."

"Hey!" She shoved him playfully with a shoulder.

He wriggled away as if to avoid being swatted, but it served to create a healthy space between them. "Sorry, I couldn't resist." He cleared his throat again. "Have you heard anything else?"

She snatched up a twig and fed it to the fire. "I heard that they've hacked the branches off one of their Mothertrees and set a wall around it. The Barans love that piece of news. They think it brings them closer to establishing trade for Mothertree wood."

Walde rose and fed the last of the brush to the fire. He tried to keep his voice neutral as he spoke. "This only happened to one tree?"

"So I've heard."

He paced through the smoke, pretending to search for stray kindling. "Did they say which?"

"No." Concern entered her voice. "Not that I recall."

Walde sighed and squatted down beside her. "Walls are erected for a reason. I have a feeling that I'll find my father behind this one. My father, and maybe others."

She nodded slowly. "It seems a likely place."

They said nothing more for a time. The air stilled and the smoke straightened. The fire dimmed to a few glowing threads. Walde tried not to contemplate what his father might be enduring at that very moment, but it was like struggling to hold back darkness. Even when he wasn't thinking about it, the fact hung over him relentlessly.

He tugged blankets out of his pack and offered Brite one.

After a long silence, she asked, "Did Spitfire give you my message this morning?"

Walde bit back a groan. He'd managed to thrust the embarrassing encounter from his mind. "Yes. How did you know?"

"Know…?"

"That I slept at your doorstep?"

Her laughter was muffled by the blanket. "How could I not? You snore abysmally."

"Gods, I'm sorry. Did I keep you awake?"

"No..."

"I didn't mean to fall asleep there. It just happened."

"I thought as much. I figured that you came by to talk, but the girl was there so you decided to wait."

There was a question in her voice. "Not exactly," he said. Loosing a sigh, he told her the truth and then waited for her censure.

They lay on their sides around the fire. Walde gazed sleepily at Brite's blanketed form. An ache bloomed in his chest as he thought about when they would have to part. He thrust the emotion down before it grew too strong.

"You owe me for that," she decided.

"Don't I have credits left for helping you disappear that body?"

"That's different. Debts are like food in a market. You wouldn't trade a goat for a handful of berries, would you? Same with this. Stolen words must be paid for by surrendered words."

Walde chuckled. "You can't take the tinker out of the Lowlander. What words must I surrender?"

"I want to know what reaching feels like. In detail."

He ran a hand tiredly over his eyes. It was almost the last thing he felt like talking about. "It's not a thing that can be easily described."

"Then tell it any way you can."

"All right." He rolled onto his back and gazed up at the wash of stars. Something about their otherness reminded him of the tunnel. "I've only reached twice. In both cases I was sitting against the trunk of a Mothertree. It began with a feeling of expansiveness..." He described the moment he'd lost sensation in his body and plunged into the tunnel. What was the tunnel? He had no idea. It was not a physical place with walls and a floor. He tried to describe it and ended up tying his tongue into knots.

"So what happens in the tunnel?" she asked.

"You move forward, first because you have no choice and then because you want to. Something vital is just ahead of you, and you're overcome by a desire to reach it. As you get closer, you sense that the object is not only alive but is also a being of immense power. The urge to grasp her becomes blinding." He paused, reliving the sensation. "I only brushed her, and in that moment I was given a glimpse of impossible knowledge. It was as if the world tore open and bared all its secrets."

"And then?" she asked breathlessly.

"Then I crashed back into my body." His eyes closed against the memory.

"Do you wish you could go back?"

"Of course. It's like discovering a new and powerful sense, then not having the ability to use it."

"It sounds wonderful."

"It is. But more than anything, it feels…right, and once you've felt that rightness, nothing can convince you it's wrong."

They eyed each other across the fire. Brite's face blurred in the flames, but he thought he saw her nod.

***

Walde's nightmare returned that night. Once again, his insides wrenched as something essential fell away from him. He was left feeling sick and helpless, tortured by the knowledge that he could never recover what was lost.

He woke slowly, hands clenched to his chest under the blanket. He didn't have to see them to know they radiated light.

Push it down.

Carrac's voice sounded so clearly in his mind that his eyes burned. He suddenly missed him terribly, his gruff humor and steadiness, his quiet confidence in Walde that never relented. Through whatever he'd suffered these past few days, he must have thought about his son. Perhaps he hoped that Walde had gone on with his life, buried his grief over Carrac's death as Carrac had buried the loss of Walde's mother.

He would never suspect the truth.

"I'm coming," Walde whispered to the hazy dawn light.

The morning was uncomfortably chill and damp. A mist hung over the wastes, and only the distant peaks of the mountains told them which direction to go. They consumed a hasty breakfast of dried meat and berries, then trudged on, Walde carrying the pack again so that Brite could drape herself with the warm blanket.

By midday, the mist had burned off and they were able to correct their course before veering too far east. They refilled their bottles at a tiny stream that wound down from the mountains. The water was sweet and cold, reminding Walde of the river at the bottom of the ravine where his father's sapling grew.

Brite became talkative after they crossed the stream and offered him a thorough account of her childhood. Walde forced himself to listen cheerfully. At any other time, he would have welcomed learning more about her, but with their parting so close at hand, it felt like building a hut that would soon be abandoned.

She still hadn't told him where she was heading or what she meant to do there, and Walde couldn't bring himself to ask her again. Her response, "I'm going with you," had begun to sound a warning in his mind. His greatest fear was that she would refuse to leave his side and he would have to destroy their friendship to get her to leave him.

He was almost grateful when a hunter approached them.

The man was thin and rangy, with a gray beard and a long leather coat mottled with stains. A worn quiver hung from his belt, the bow protruding from its high end. He had been walking north, probably toward the mountains and larger game, when he spotted Walde and Brite.

Walde slowly raised his right hand and reached over to clasp the man's opposite shoulder in a hunter's greeting. Warily, the man did likewise to Walde.

"You don't see many travelers in these parts," the man observed, his eyes running over their clothing.

"We're traveling from the Lowlands. Do you know the easiest way from here into town?"

He regarded Walde thoughtfully, as if weighing whether he should answer. With a shrug, he turned and pointed. "Just head south. When you reach the crops, turn west. After a little while you'll come to a cart road. You can follow that into town."

"Thank you," Walde said.

The man tapped his fingers on his quiver. "I'm not one to pry, but I'm mighty curious about the route you took to get here."

"We cut through the abandoned Woodlands."

His bushy brows drew together. "Did you now?"

Walde glanced at Brite, who had shifted her hand to the blunt end of her concealed stone knife. Walde hoped the hunter didn't notice the movement and guess its meaning.

After a tense silence, the hunter chuckled and slapped Walde's upper arm. "Like I said, I'm not one to pry. A word of advice, though: don't take that bow and quiver with you into town. If you do, the peacekeepers will be on your back before you can speak."

Walde fingered the bow. He'd meant to stow it somewhere as they drew closer to town, but he wasn't sure he'd be able to find it again. Especially if he had to leave at night.

The hunter pursed his weathered lips. "Would you like to trade them for something?"

"What do you have?"

He unshouldered his pack and pulled out some rolled garments. "I'd planned to spend a day or two in the mountains, so I brought a change of clothes. But I'm willing to swap them. You need to dress well for the chill wind that rolls off the ocean. Visitors are never prepared for it." He shook out a brown, hooded robe of woven kriksa. It was hideous—and perfect for Walde's needs. "You're a touch broader in the shoulder, but the height is right. It should fit. I wish I had something to offer your wife..."

"I'll find something in town," Brite assured him tightly.

Walde unslung his bow and quiver and offered them to the hunter. They said little more after the exchange. Walde wished him luck, and they parted ways.

He and Brite traveled in silence. Walde, increasingly annoyed by her frequent glances behind her, was the first to speak. "If he wanted to kill us, he would've done it by now. The wind is right and the field is flat and open. He would've had an excellent shot."

"You can't be too cautious."

Walde opened his mouth and then closed it. Arguing with her on this point would have been useless. Her fear of strangers was deeply rooted, reinforced by her own unhappy experience.

She added, "You ought to be more wary."

He shook out the robe and studied it with feigned concern. "Maybe so. Do you think I should check this for poison powder?"

She elbowed him, but she was smiling.

He pulled the robe over his fitted tunic, shouldered his pack, and carried on. They said nothing more until they reached the farm fields the hunter had spoken of. Walde's step slowed as he approached them. He had never seen such large gardens in his life. Countless lines of green shoots marched across the tilled field. The space was closed in by a low stone wall. Squinting, he could make out the distant shapes of outbuildings.

Brite said, "Lowlanders helped them do this. I'd wager that folk here keep animals too. Some of the former Woodlanders keep them, or so I've heard."

"It would be easier if I could make myself believe these *are* Lowlanders."

"Some of them are. The Scats that came here for work never came back, and talk is that some were given land in exchange for their ongoing building work."

They walked west along the wall. The sinking sun drove a nail of light into them, forcing them to shield their eyes with their hands. When it sank at last, the glow on the horizon revealed a shadowy line of Mothertrees, so distant yet that a stranger to the trees would have been forgiven for thinking they were oaks. Walde regarded them in gloomy silence until darkness swallowed them up.

They reached the cart road just as Walde lit his belt lamp. Like the walls, the dirt road showed no signs of age. It held no deep carriage ruts or even gutters. A few weeds had broken through the soil along the edges, but Walde guessed the local farmers would pull them up before they went to seed.

Brite slowed as they walked past some huts and outbuildings. The night sky was clear, allowing the moon's silvery light to wash over the landscape. They were both keeping an eye out for clotheslines. In the Lakelands, drying lines were hung between branches. In the Lowlands, however, two or three cleft poles were erected. These, Brite explained, were usually the stripped trunks of mountain saplings.

As she spoke, an unpleasant scent wafted by. Walde had caught a drift of it in the Lowlands. Very simply, it was the stench of kept animals.

Without thinking, he brought a hand up to his nose.

Brite chuckled. "Don't like the smell of manure?"

He shrugged. "It's not something I'm used to. Wasteland animals have a clean, wild smell. Fresh droppings stink if you're standing right over them, but the sun dries them out fast and the rain washes them into the ground. Penned animals defecate in the same space again and again, and it's up to their owners to clean it all up." He jerked his head at the distant pens. "I wouldn't want to live like that, confined by a fence, having to eat whatever's thrown to me."

Her lips pursed. "When you put it that way, it doesn't sound nice. But it's all they've ever known." After a pause, she added, "I guess that doesn't make it right."

He shrugged again. "Like I said, it's just not what I'm used to." Not what any tree dweller would be used to, he added to himself. That the Harborlanders tolerated it at all said a lot about how much they had changed.

They climbed a gentle rise in the land and paused at the top. A glitter of lights opened before them like a bright puddle in the darkness. "There's the town," Brite murmured. "I'll have a better chance of finding a frock down there."

Walde suddenly turned and looked at her. The wind had long ago worked her hair lose from its braid. Strands blew across her face, catching in her lips and eyelashes. She seemed to him at once strong and profoundly fragile. How long would she survive in this strange new place? If some of her countrymen lived here, then she'd eventually be recognized, and news of her presence would reach the Lowlands. Her pursuers would come looking for her.

His hand clenched the lamp handle. How could he focus his attention on rescuing his father while worrying about Brite?

"Is something wrong?"

He wanted to say no, but the lie wouldn't reach his lips. Bracing himself, he asked, "Where will you go after this? Do you have friends or relatives here? A safe place to stay?"

She didn't respond at once. Her mouth softened as she searched his face, then she spun away and walked aimlessly down the road. "You already asked me this question. What did I say then?"

"You said you were going with me, but—"

"Then you have your answer."

Walde had opened his mouth to speak again when she snatched the lamp from his hand and crossed to the other side of the road. Her free hand closed over the top of a wattle fence. "I knew I heard the snap of a bed sheet. Look. Do you see the house with the attached outbuilding? There's a two-pole-line not far from the front door."

With an effort, he set aside the problem and all the unsettling emotions it roused in him and focused on the present.

He spotted the line and shook his head. "I'm still amazed that people leave clothes out at night. Where I'm from, they hang them at noon."

"Night's the best time for kriksa," she said, handing him back the lamp. "The sun bleaches it easily, and there's as little shade here as there is in the Lowlands. Hold the fence still for me, please."

Walde dug his fingers into gaps between branches, but the structure needed little steadying. In a moment, she was over it and tiptoeing across the yard.

He reminded her in a whisper, "Don't forget to leave a coin."

Later, he would wonder at how optimistic they had been. That first line contained only children's clothes and a bed sheet.

A second bore men's hosen and some diaper cloths. Brite set her hopes on a third, only to find more children's clothes and a man's large robe.

By then, they'd reached a more populated area of town. Walde no longer needed his lamp, for the roads were well lit by lights suspended on poles. Homes ran haphazardly along the roads. Each had a bit of property enclosed either by stone or wattle fences. Many were only half built, and the workers, or perhaps owners, slept outside on the bare ground. The air stank mainly of penned animals, but every once in a while a scent of fish and brine wafted toward them.

Walde and Brite jogged quietly along the side of the road, keeping their heads down as small groups of people walked—or lurched—by, many of them drunk. It was strange to see so many intoxicated folk so early in the night. A guard appeared, but he was so absorbed in watching the drunks that he paid Walde and Brite no mind.

They turned a corner and strode down a darker road. A large property enclosed by wattle fencing lay on one side, the other was open and under construction. Brite hugged herself as she walked. "That hunter was right about this place. It's cold and windy."

Walde unshouldered his pack and dug out a blanket. While she was busy settling it over her shoulders, his eyes strayed to the approaching buildings, and he caught sight of a line heavy with clothes. He dropped his pack by the fence and grasped hold of the fence's knotted branches.

Brite whispered, "Hey, where are you going?"

He dropped onto the other side and grinned at her over the fence. "To get you something to wear."

"Wait." She scanned the property nervously.

"What is it?"

After a moment, she shook her head. "Maybe nothing. But in the Lowlands, a place this big and this close to the center of town would be guarded."

"I'll be careful then."

He left her at the fence and ghosted across the yard. An herbal smell filled his nostrils as he ran. The origin quickly became apparent. Fully one half of the yard was taken up by a garden of herb and spice plants. Walde recalled that the Harborlands had always grown such plants. He skirted the garden's edge, passed a large stone well, and dropped down under the hanging clothes.

The windows in the nearby stone hut were all dark but one. The light spilling from that single window brightened half the yard. Someone was awake, though no sounds emanated from the window. Walde stilled his anxiety with practiced ease and rummaged through the clothes. He was elated to find women's garments. Not less than three frocks hung on the line. He chose the warmest, left a coin on the ground that was probably worth all three, and started back for the fence. A stiff wind rose, nearly snatching the frock from his hands. Walde paused long enough to stuff the garment under his belt. He took a step, and then froze.

A low growl cut through the stillness, followed by the creak of a chair. A shadow fell across the window, darkening the yard.

Walde ran.

CHAPTER 12

Vicious barking followed him, coming ever closer. Walde was a fast runner, though, and he made it to the fence before the dog caught up with him.

He almost made it over. One more swing and his leg would have cleared the fence. But teeth clamped down on his boot and pulled. Walde kicked, but it only made the dog more determined. Its head shook violently as it gripped him, sharp teeth digging through the leather into his skin. He held himself precariously over the top of the fence, struggling to keep his robe and the frock hanging from his belt from snaring in the wattle. A glimmer of light leaked from his palms. Why hadn't he taken the gloves Albin had offered him?

"Be still!" Brite hissed at him in the shadows. "I'm going to try to get it off you."

A door slammed, and booted footsteps thudded toward him. Walde clung to the fence, trying desperately to stow his rising panic while a growling animal sought to drag him to the ground. Then, inexplicably, it let go.

"Now!" Brite said.

Walde tumbled over the fence, and they bolted across the road. A man's angry shout followed on their heels. They plunged into a dark, empty field and ran on. The exhilaration of the escape made him giddy, and he laughed under his breath.

They came to a mound of worked stone and dived behind it.

"Is he chasing us?" Brite asked breathlessly.

"I don't think so, but I can't be sure." They crouched in the shadow of the rock pile. Brite was no more than a dark shape at his side. Distant, drunken voices rose and fell. Walde dug the frock out from under his belt, found her hands, and pushed it into them. "I hope this isn't torn. How did you get that dog off of me?"

"I tossed it some dried meat."

A grin broke on his face. "That's brilliant."

"You wouldn't say that if you knew more about guard dogs. That one shouldn't have let you go to take the meat. It's been badly trained."

"Good thing." He was still a little shaken by the encounter. He had never been attacked by a large animal, let alone one trained to hunt people.

He patted his bitten leg and winced. The dog's teeth had punctured the leather and broken the skin. He tore a strip of material off the hem of his robe, hiked up his trouser leg, and went about binding the cuts by feel.

"How bad is it?" Brite asked.

"The bites aren't deep." He secured the bandage and let the trouser leg fall. Thankfully, the leather was stained so dark that the blood probably wouldn't show.

"Thank the gods. Could you turn around while I change?"

He didn't bother reminding her that it was too dark to see anyway. He turned and waited, listening to the rustle of fabric against skin.

"The frock fits well," she said at last. "Thank you."

Walde turned too sharply and crashed into her. He drew back, mouthing a hasty apology.

Brite either didn't hear him or chose to ignore it. "So. Where do we go now?"

We. He drew a heavy breath. He considered raising the issue of her remaining with him, but set it aside for later. They needed to find a safe place to spend the night. He could tackle the thornier problem tomorrow. "A guest hut or whatever version of that they have here."

She chuckled. "The Lowlanders call it an inn."

Walde frowned as he shouldered the pack. Tinkers used that word when referring to the village pub. Was there difference in vocabulary between the two peoples?

They made their way cautiously back to the main road and into the brighter, noisier part of town. Brite had finger-combed her hair, and it swung behind her now like a dark cape, mimicking the sweep of her skirt. Walde wished he felt as comfortable in his long kriksa robe.

A couple of drunks passed, shoving each other as they walked. Brite pulled Walde to a sudden stop and whispered, "We should follow them. They may be heading to an inn."

He shrugged, and they fell in behind the pair. After a couple of turns, the drunks ducked into a large, two-story stone building. Light, music, and laughter flowed through its open windows into the street. Brite did a little dance and grinned. "I was right! There it is."

"That's a pub."

"No, it's an inn. Folk sleep in the upper chambers."

Walde looked from the noisy first floor to the dark second. "That's absurd. No one in their right mind would put a guest hut above a drinking establishment. The guests would be better off sleeping in the field."

Her mouth gave an irritable twitch. "You don't know what you're talking about. Come on." She threw open the heavy door and dragged him in. *Inn.* Walde heaved a sigh. But his reluctance to enter the place was instantly overcome by the heady scents wafting from the kitchen. He was sure he had never smelled anything that good.

They strode into a large, well-lit room with a blazing hearth on one end and a polished counter lined with stools on the other. A handful of small, round tables were scattered about the room, some with chairs around them and some not, but every one occupied by folk eating and drinking. Two men sat on stools in a corner sawing on five-string rebecs while a woman sang her lungs out. The sight of the musicians set his mind back to Jak, and he briefly wondered how the youth fared. A haze like that of smoke gathered around the ceiling beams.

No one looked up as Walde and Brite swept through the door. Indeed, the place was so noisy that a thunderclap would have been lost in the ruckus. Walde smiled wryly as he considered the pub's furniture and décor. While the building was new, the establishment's owner had clearly taken pains to dismantle parts from an older pub, probably one from an abandoned Mothertree, and install them here. The liquor cabinets, counter, stools, tables, and chairs were all ancient. Even the mantle over the fireplace was blackened and cracked. Only the floorboards and ceiling beams appeared new, and they had been darkened with some sort of stain.

A wiry old man stood behind the counter, washing mugs and chatting with some men seated on stools. A woman about the same age loitered by the hearth with a tray under her arm, listening, apparently, to a conversation at a nearby table. Brite made a beeline for her.

The woman's face brightened as she spotted her new guests. She was a slender woman with work-roughened hands and eager brown eyes. Her limbs contained a restless energy so that even standing still she seemed in motion. Her gray hair lay in a tidy bun at the nape of her neck.

She spoke before Brite could call out a greeting. "A Lowlands girl if I've ever seen one. Am I right?" Brite admitted she was, and that set the woman to trying to guess her family name. “You do look familiar,” she said with a sly twinkle in her eyes. “If I hadn’t been away from the place so long, I’m sure I would’ve recognized you straight away.”

Walde shoved down his anxiety at the thought and glanced around as if interested in the décor.

“We need a couple of rooms,” Brite said after a pause.

The woman looked from Walde to Brite. “We have only one room available, and you’re lucky for that. The previous lodger left early.”

“We’ll take it,” Brite said just as Walde opened his mouth to ask if there was another inn in the area.

The woman glanced at Walde, then turned with a shrug and led them through a swinging door and up some stairs to a shadowy hallway broken by many doors. She halted at the second door on the right, knocked once, then lifted the latch and went inside. Walde had expected a small room, but even he was surprised by the cramped space. The chamber couldn’t have been larger than six feet by eight. A narrow bed had been shoved into a corner, and beside it stood a small, stained clothes chest. A bowl of wash water, a single candlestick, and an empty chamber pot completed the room’s contents.

Their hostess said, “There’s a few extra blankets and some cleaning cloths in the chest. Chamber pots are emptied every morning, so don’t bother to do it yourself. Same goes with the wash water. Folk like to keep the streets clean here.” She gestured to Walde’s pack. “Don’t leave your possessions behind when you go downstairs. They will be stolen, and I won’t be held responsible. Any questions?” She looked pointedly at Walde.

“No. Thank you.”

“Very well. My name is Ava, and the old man you saw behind the bar is Cawl. We only serve the stew for another hour, so—”

“We’ll be down,” Walde assured her. “Thank you.”

The door closed, rattling a dead bolt nailed to the inside. The room was quieter than he'd expected. "Our guest huts have no locks," he heard himself say, then felt a fool for the remark. It was a pointless comparison. "I'll take the floor," he offered.

Brite tugged her rolled-up tunic and hosen out of her overstuffed pouch and tossed them on the bed. She stepped toward him. Lamplight from the open window shone on her hair and lit one side of her face. Without thinking, he brushed a few dark strands from her moon-brightened cheek.

Her eyes closed briefly, and at that moment, Walde knew she would not draw away if he kissed her. He wanted to, so very much, but doing so would bind them even closer than they had been growing, and Walde couldn't allow that. It would make separating from her next to impossible.

She asked, "Are you all right with this arrangement?"

He dropped his hand. "You ask me this now."

"I'm sorry."

He chuckled. *Was she?* "I'm kidding. All I care about right now is eating whatever they're serving downstairs."

She closed the shutters. "You understood what she meant about being lucky, didn't you? She meant that this town is full."

"I understand." He went to the door and opened it. "I'm not angry, and I'm all right with sleeping on the floor if you're all right with my snoring." He tossed her a rascally grin and then strode down the hallway toward the stairs.

They found two empty stools at the counter and ordered stew and watered mead. Walde caught a man farther down the counter eyeing Brite and scowled at him. The man took his eyes away.

The stew tasted as good as it smelled. The meat was tender, the gravy thick and fragrant with fresh herbs and spices. Green beans and baby carrots gave it flashes of color. Fearing there wouldn't be enough left over for a second bowl, Walde shoveled it into his mouth.

Ava leaned on the counter across from them. "So, what's new in the Lowlands?"

Brite shrugged. "You must get a lot of visitors from there."

"Not as many as you'd think." She scooped a wet mug off a hook and wiped it with a stained cloth. "The Scats here have been around for months, some of them for years. The ones who can afford it rent a room from us while the others sleep outside. Come winter, the braver souls will go up the Mothertrees and find abandoned huts to sleep in. There are fines for that, but they always do it anyway."

A bearded middle-aged man seated next to Walde nodded at the hostess's words. "If the fines don't get them, the falls do. Five were killed that way last winter."

Brite shuddered. "I see. Well, I'll tell you what news I've heard." And with that, she went on to lay out a spread of village gossip that would have made a wizened Lakelander blush. Births, deaths, and marriages were rhymed off, followed by murders, robberies, arsons, suicides, unfortunate accidents, failed attempts to kill the "Berg," conspiracies, and executions. The hostess nodded along, an eager hunger in her bird-bright eyes.

Walde could not have imagined such a den of misery and vice. Brite, he decided, had made the right choice in leaving it.

The musicians had paused, and several lodgers had abandoned their tables to crowd around Brite. Walde shifted his stool closer to hers and kept a hawk's eye on the men. His newfound knowledge of Lowlands culture made him doubly cautious. Brite hadn't mentioned rapes, but Walde put that down to her not wanting to relive her own experience.

Brite took a long pull and wiped her mouth on her sleeve. "That's all I remember. Now it's your turn."

"What would you like to know?" the man sitting next to Walde asked, eager, it seemed, to offer information. Trade, Walde reminded himself, was everything to these people. Brite had tipped the scales with her generous outpouring of gossip, and now they had to be balanced.

The man's eyes narrowed as he waited for her answer, and a faint smile touched his moustached lip. "The name's Brite, isn't it?"

Ava slapped her drying cloth on the counter. "That's it! Barnett's niece. I knew you looked familiar."

Walde swallowed his mouthful of stew a little too sharply. This was exactly what he had feared. But there seemed little she could have done to prevent it. With so many Scats in this city, her discovery would've been inevitable. Knowing that, why had she chosen to come here?

Perhaps, he thought grimly, because there *was no* safe place. The Woodlands had been the nearest thing to a haven they'd come across. She ought to have remained there.

If Brite was troubled by the disclosure, she didn't show it. Ava refilled her mug, and the three Scats chatted pleasantly about people they knew. In a short time, though, Brite steered the conversation back to the Harborlands. "I heard that one of the Mothertrees here was chopped up."

The hostess snorted. "If you've come here hoping to make a deal for that wood, you won't get it. The elders don't have dealings with middlemen."

Brite laughed into her mug. "I'm just curious, is all."

"No harm in telling her 'bout it," the man said, and Ava nodded in agreement.

"The Reacher tree was the one," she said, "and all they did was strip the branches off it so no one could climb to it from the neighboring tree."

The man shook his head at her. "You make it seem easy, but it took them years to do. Those branches look small from a distance, but each one is fatter than a willow oak's trunk."

"So what's left of it?" Brite asked idly.

"Just the middle part of the tree," Ava replied. "The trunk. You'll see the top of it in the morning. Looks like a sharp black nail sticking up into the sky."

"Black?" Brite said.

The man nodded. "They smeared the cut areas with pitch, maybe to try to keep it from growing. It's still alive, you see."

Walde forced himself to swallow one last bite, then he pushed the bowl away. His appetite had fled. "Why is it called the Reacher tree?" he asked carefully.

For a moment, they just looked at him, and he wished he'd spoken earlier.

Ava was first to answer. "Because that's where they tie up the Reachers. It used to be called 'First,' but that was before my time here."

"I heard they're using Reachers to kill their tree god," Brite cut in. "Is that true?"

The lodgers behind them had wandered back to their tables. Walde hid his expression in his cup. His ears, though, were wide open.

The man leaned back and stroked his beard thoughtfully. "Not a god. Or at least they don't think of her as such. To them, she's a parasite that fell from the sky and burrowed into the earth. She attached herself to the Mothertrees' roots and can either help or harm them. The trees grow well if Reachers commune with her, but if not..." He shrugged. "They die. It's like a noose, of sorts, with the Reachers at one end, and the parasite on the other. So the elders fire back at both by torturing the Reachers."

Walde closed his eyes briefly and forced himself to breathe, to avoid thinking about his father.

Brite's hand fell on his under the counter and tightened. "What do you mean," she said, "by 'it fell from the sky'?"

"You must have felt the quake that happened six years back," the hostess said.

"Yes. We all felt the quake. It happened after that star fell out of the sky."

"Stars give off a bright, silvery light. Same light, they say, as Reachers make." The man pointed a finger upward. "They call her the starseed—a being that once lay at the core of a falling star. After she fell long ago, she burrowed deep into the earth and attached herself to the Mothertrees. Given enough time, they say, she would have wielded absolute power through the Reachers. That's what they say."

The room seemed to have darkened. Walde had long ago dived into the medallion. Now he wanted nothing more than to retreat to the room upstairs.

Brite's voice sounded, as if from a distance. "The tree god has been around longer than six years."

"I didn't mean that she arrived then," Ava said. "Only that the starseed idea came from that event."

"And you believe it?" She looked from their hostess to the man. Ava shrugged and resumed drying mugs.

The man snorted. "I believe I need to piss out this drink."

He emptied his mug, stood unsteadily, and smiled at Brite. "It's been a pleasure, darling." Nodding to Walde, he lurched off toward the door.

Brite got to her feet the moment he was gone, and Walde followed her stiffly up the stairs.

"Do you want to talk?" she asked as she latched the door and drew the deadbolt.

Walde edged around the bed to the window, opened the shutters a crack, and looked up at the night sky. If the stars had been hidden by cloud cover, he would have turned away. But it was clear as spring ice. He opened his hand. A star lay in his palm, silver-bright as the ones in the sky. The light was the same. Not similar, but exactly the same.

"Walde..."

He closed his hand tightly. "Not now."

"You don't believe that man's story, do you?"

He couldn't turn and meet her eyes. He kicked at the wall. "The words were said, and I can't unhear them. Do you understand?"

The floor creaked as she made her way around the bed. "You told me that the being gave you knowledge," she said tentatively.

"I communed with her. Just like the man said."

"But is that a bad thing? You told the children that Reachers used to sing songs, story songs that taught people how to live. If the wisdom in those songs helped shape your culture, it can't have been bad."

"How would you know?" he retorted stiffly.

"Because I've lived in a place that never had it." Her voice shook. Walde turned and was startled to find her face flushed and her mouth soft as if she were on the edge of tears. "Didn't you listen at all to the horrible gossip I spilled down there? It hurt me to spill it, because you were there and I didn't want you know just how awful the Lowlands are. Look around you, Walde. You know that this place will become just like it." He allowed her to grasp his hands. "The elders want power, the same sort of power that the Berg has. Think about what that means."

It meant that they would subdue any power that competed with theirs, even if that meant twisting the truth into a very convincing lie. He squeezed his eyes shut. "I'm so tired. I feel like I can't think straight anymore. I'm worried about what's being done to my father. I'm worried about you. And on top of all that, I've been fed a story that upends everything I believe in. Even if it's false, the Harborlanders believe it. Enough to allow torture. How long will it be before the Woodlanders and Lakelanders believe it?"

He sat down heavily on the bed.

Brite's hand rested on his forearm. "Not everyone is stupid. If I can see through it, others will. And there's still the Woodlands…" Her voice trailed as a knock fell on the door. Walde lurched to his feet. "Who is it?" Brite shouted.

"It's Ava, your hostess."

Walde pulled the deadbolt and lifted the latch.

He scarcely knew what happened then. One moment he stood looking at Ava in the shadowy hallway and the next, he was pinned against the doorway with his hands twisted behind his back.

CHAPTER 13

Two strong men bore Walde against the door frame, one shouting curses in his ear. Brite's screams and the crashing of overturned furniture added to the chaos. Walde managed to turn his head enough to glimpse two guards struggling to pin Brite to the floor. "Don't fight them!" Walde shouted.

The weight increased on his back, but Brite's scuffling ceased. Desperately, he shoved down his rising panic. He found the medallion in his mind and retreated behind its walls. *Good, now breathe.*

And think. If the guards were here to arrest Brite, then they wouldn't hold Walde indefinitely. He could make plans to free her.

The guards shackled his hands behind him and frisked him thoroughly. His arm knife was confiscated, along with his other possessions. All the while, they said nothing of substance, not a word to explain why Walde and Brite had been arrested. Brite, flanked by two guards, one female and one male, was led off ahead of Walde down the hallway. The drift of music from downstairs had ceased, and an eerie stillness fell over the building. The only sounds were the thudding of boots and the jangling of manacle chains.

Every eye in the pub was fixed on Brite and Walde as the guards marched them past the counter to the front door. A sturdy closed-topped carriage waited outside.

As Brite climbed in, she paused and glanced back at the inn's door, where Ava stood looking impassively on. "Bitch," Brite spat. Then the guard shoved her in.

Walde had never set foot inside a carriage. The contraptions perched across the lake every six months like exotic birds, drawing the gazes of curious children. He had imagined sitting in one, even driving it. But his imagination could not have conjured the stink of hot urine as one of the horses pissed or the sudden jolt as the carriage lurched forward. One of the guards seated on either side of him grabbed his bound arms to keep him from tumbling to the carriage floor. Brite sat on the bench across from him, flanked by her guards. Walde tried to meet her eyes, but her head hung down and the dark curtain of her hair concealed her face. Walde forced his attention away from her before misery took hold of him.

His jaw tightened as he focused on the guards. "Where are we going?" he demanded.

Silence. It was as if he hadn't spoken at all. He raised his voice so that anyone on the street would hear him. "I said, where are we going?"

He was rewarded with an elbow to the ribs. He bent over, hissing out an imprecation. A moment or two later, he asked in a quieter voice, "Is this how you treat visitors? We weren't even accused of anything."

The guard to his right snorted. Walde expected some cutting remark, but whatever he was thinking, he kept it to himself. Walde leaned his head back against the carriage seat.

After a time, the air gusting through the windows cooled and the darkness deepened. A stench of fish and tar filled his nostrils. Walde couldn't see up to the sky, but he guessed that they had entered the Mothertrees' shadows and were not far from the harbor. He closed his eyes briefly and let their stillness settle over him. When one was anxious, there was a saying among his people to "feel the tree." It involved more than becoming aware of its presence. Mothertrees were not merely huge, but also ancient. Their roots ran deep. They had weathered every storm, witnessed every birth and death, over countless generations. There was a quiet wisdom in such steadiness. Even dead, they gave Walde a measure of peace.

The horses slowed and turned. The soft thudding of hooves on dirt changed to loud clopping on wood, and the carriage juddered as it rode over unevenly laid boards. Brite, who had not moved during the whole trip, suddenly gripped her stomach and moaned. During storms, some Lakelanders experienced wind sickness. The motion of the swaying branches made them nauseous, and some even emptied their bellies. Walde was about to lean forward and ask Brite if she was ill when the carriage turned again and came to a sudden halt.

The guards opened the doors and prodded their prisoners out, ignoring Walde's pleas for them to be gentle with "the woman." He was careful not to name her. If they weren't sure of her identity, he wouldn't hand it to them like a fat goat.

He had no time to take in his surroundings. A large stone building loomed in front of him, lit by two outdoor lamps. A guard standing by the entrance opened a heavy wooden door, and Walde and Brite were led through it into some sort of vestibule. They passed an unoccupied desk littered with scrolls, through another set of doors and down a shadowy hallway. Walde's guards halted at the first door they came to, opened it, and nudged him through. He managed one last, desperate glance at Brite before the door closed behind him.

The room was shadowy and damp. A barred window placed high on the far wall cast a square of moonlight on the floor. One side of the room held three small cells, the other a couple of chairs and a card table. A single lamp burned above the table, spraying the cold stone wall with light. The room appeared to be empty, but as the guards entered the chamber, a tiny, frightened whine emanated from one of the far cells. Walde drew in a steadying breath and lowered his chin to the space between his collarbones.

The medallion was gone.

He went still, frozen as if in sudden pain. He didn't recall them taking it, but then they had frisked him so soundly, he probably hadn't noticed. An easy slice to the leather band would have freed it from his neck.

With a great deal of effort, he held its loss at a distance. Doing so made him feel as if he stood on a bare crag in a windstorm. He was so unsteady that he nearly toppled over when a guard seized his arm and hauled him to the nearest empty cell.

The iron door slammed shut behind him, and the guard secured it with a padlock.

"I want to speak to your superior," Walde demanded. But he was soundly ignored. The chamber door closed, and booted footsteps tapped away to silence. The remaining guard approached Walde's cell. Walde forced himself to remain still and calm, even as his manacled hands balled into fists.

The man regarded him coolly and then said, "You think you can hide what you are from us, but you can't. You *will* fail." Leaning closer, he almost whispered, "It'd be better for the girl if you failed now. Understand?" An icy warning brightened his eyes.

Walde said nothing as the guard claimed one of the two chairs by the table. It hadn't taken much for his mind to work out the guard's meaning. If Walde didn't admit to being a Reacher, the guards would hurt Brite to make him betray himself.

He stumbled backward and slumped against the stone wall. The reality of the situation was seeping into him, battering his carefully constructed calm. "Ava" must have eavesdropped on their conversation, either through the door or through a wall. Once she learned that Walde was a Reacher, she must have called in peacekeeper guards. There was probably a reward for reporting Reachers.

And Brite? Walde doubted now that the guards knew anything about her. If she had gone her own way, she wouldn't have been captured. But Walde had foolishly allowed her to remain with him. He couldn't allow her to be punished for it.

That left him with two options, either escape the cell or reveal he was a Reacher. The first would be nearly impossible, and the second…

He steered his mind away from the thought of being tortured. He'd rather die than be used as a tool to hurt Thara. The very idea recalled his dreams to him, the feeling of something essential slipping away, again and again.

He gripped his palms together behind him. This was its own sort of torture. He couldn't see his palms to know if they seeped light, and without the medallion to aid him, he couldn't form walls to protect himself.

Or could he?

His eyes closed and his father's voice slipped into his mind. *Close your eyes and imagine walls. Strong, solid walls. In the darkness, you can feel them.*

He did feel them. Once he had chased back his awareness of the medallion's absence, they formed at once.

He had never needed the medallion.

He dropped his forehead against the cell wall and swallowed tightly. His father must have known all that time. Gratitude for him swelled in Walde's heart. The emotion wasn't strong enough to require dousing, but he was careful all the same.

He straightened and looked around. The cell was newly constructed from stone and mortar. The cell door was bolted into solid stone. An iron padlock held it fast. As he expected, there was no hope of escaping this cell. If they dragged Brite into the chamber, he would have to confess. After that, they would likely escort him to the Reacher tree. As for Brite…

His hands clenched again as he stowed his swelling fear. How could he trust that they'd let her go? If they wished to torture him, they would have no better tool on their hands than Brite. No, he had to assume that they'd continue to use her.

The thought had barely registered when the chamber door swung open and an aged man dressed in a long, hooded robe entered the room. A serving man walked behind him carrying a food tray. "Uncuff him," the aged man said coolly to the guard, who had stood the instant the door opened.

Walde's muscles tensed at the prospect of the cell door opening, but it was too good to be true. The guard merely waited for Walde to turn so he could unlock him through the bars. Still, it was good to be free of the manacles. He stretched his stiff arms and rubbed his sore wrists. The guard slid open a food slot in the cell door and passed him the tray. Briefly, Walde considered shoving it back at him, but the act wouldn't have accomplished anything. He set the tray on the cell floor. "I have no appetite," he said flatly, then he turned and looked the old man full in the face. His skin was a pale pink. A bridge of heavy white brows shadowed his penetrating eyes. Probably a village elder. The guard wouldn't have responded with such deference to anyone else. Walde sniffed as if he'd detected a foul odor. "I had no idea how low the Harborlands had sank until I came here and smelled its stench. Kept animals. Guard dogs. A rumor of outright torture. And now I find myself arrested without being charged for any crime. I traveled here from the Lakelands to confirm some rumors. Now I'm afraid no one would believe me. It's too outrageous to be believed."

Anger contorted the guard's face at these words, and his hand moved to his dagger, but at a wave from the elder, he stepped back and straightened his arms.

The old man clicked his tongue disapprovingly and closed the food slot. "You won't get any more food or drink, so I suggest you take advantage of this." Walde made no reply, and the elder didn't wait for one. He and his serving man swept back through the chamber door, and the room fell silent once more. Or nearly silent. Voiceless sobbing emanated from a far cell.

Walde took advantage of a stained chamber pot in the cell's corner, then lowered himself to the floor and eyed the sausage and bread balefully. He picked up the steaming mug and sniffed it. A sweet floral smell tickled his nostrils. Where had he detected that odor before?

When the answer came to him at last, the hairs on the back of his neck stood on end. He barely managed to stow his horror before it betrayed him. This was the same tea the Lakelands elders had offered him on the morning of his "test." At the time, he'd thought nothing of it. He had been so absorbed in his "performance" that he hadn't even tasted it.

Hadn't tasted it.

Walde went deadly still again. A memory tugged at him. Words that he should have hearkened to danced back into his mind. *Is it enough?* one elder had asked the other while deciding whether to press Walde any further, then he had added, *He didn't drink the–* The other elder had cut him off before he could finish, but the answer was obvious, just as obvious as the implication. How had Walde missed it? The tea must have contained an herb that stifled one's ability to control emotion. The Harborlands officials likely brought it, and the Lakelands elders had been eager to test it.

He let out a ragged breath. This was the key to so many unanswered questions. It explained why so many Harborlands Reachers had been caught when tested five years ago. With such an antidote, elders could wring emotion from Reachers with ease. And they *had* used it. Ruthlessly.

Walde drove himself further and further behind his walls. It was monstrous. Unable to control their emotions, Reachers were being forced to spill their fear, anger, and pain into the First, and then to feel the response from Thara—the sickening drawing away, and the slow death of the tree that followed. His father—

No, he couldn't contemplate it, not if he wanted to maintain control.

The cup rattled as he set it back down. He wanted to smash it and crush the pieces under his feet, but he doubted he could maintain control if he did so. Hot anger lapped at his walls. If he didn't calm his thoughts, it would begin to spill over.

He snorted. Did it matter? He was trapped. If he didn't drink the tea, they would force it down his throat anyway.

He pushed the tray away from him, then almost jumped as the chamber door opened once again.

Brite stepped into the room. Alone.

CHAPTER 14

Brite's wild eyes met the guard's for the briefest moment before a knife flashed in her hands. Walde's control slipped. His fists clenched over light as she flung the knife at the guard.

Brite's throw was masterful. The weapon shot sleekly from her thumb and index finger and would have caught the guard squarely in the chest if he hadn't jerked away at just the right moment. The blade either went into his side, or into his jacket. Brite didn't wait to find out but ran straight to Walde, a ring of keys in her bloodied left hand.

"He's behind you," Walde warned just as the guard slammed into her. Brite struck the bars then somehow managed to twist away so she was no longer pinned against them. The guard unbalanced her with a leg lock, then slid his arm around her neck and gripped her in a chokehold. He had her now, but he wasn't loosening his grip on her throat. He would choke her until she died.

Rage flooded Walde. Unchecked, it crashed against his senses so he hardly knew what he was doing. His blazing hand shot through the bars and claimed the knife that had lodged itself into the guard's jacket. Before the guard could turn, Walde grasped the man's belt with one hand and plunged the knife into his back with the other. The guard grunted—a strange, animal sound that would have disturbed Walde if his vision wasn't still misted by rage—then he dropped, leaving Brite hunched over, gasping for air. Walde snatched up the keys that had fallen to the floor and after several tries opened the padlock and heaved open the cell door.

Brite had recovered by then, and despite trembling, had the presence of mind to wipe her bloodied hand on the guard's tunic. Walde wrenched the blade out of the man's back, cleaned it, and offered it to Brite. She accepted the knife and kept it ready in her hand rather than return it to the sheath she'd fastened to her belt buckle. How she'd managed to escape her cell, kill her prison guard, and steal his knife was a mystery to Walde. He unbuckled the man's sheathed dagger and secured it to his own belt. Walde's palms still blazed, and it cost him some moments of concentration to find his calm. He touched Brite's hand. "Are you hurt?"

"No."

He nodded, swallowing. "We'll have to fight our way out of here."

"I understand."

He nodded again and then slowly opened the chamber door, which thankfully had closed after Brite entered the room.

The hallway was dark and quiet, but as they stole toward the vestibule, Walde could just make out a smattering of voices from some room at the far end of the hallway. Brite was at his side as he set his hand on the vestibule door latch. "Ready?" he breathed.

"Yes."

Walde's hand stiffened around the hilt of his own blade. He drew in a long breath and loosed it slowly, then quietly lifted the latch.

The space between the front door and the vestibule door was no more than fifteen feet. A guard who appeared to have been pacing in the soft light of a wall lamp turned at the sound of the intruders. His hand jerked to his dagger, but Brite's knife caught him in the chest before he could draw it. The man took one step back before crumpling to the floor.

Walde stared at the man's prone form. How many guards had they slaughtered now? His own killing hung over him like an angry storm.

Brite retrieved the knife and cleaned it. As one, they dove for the heavy oak doors and braced themselves to meet another guard. But the porch outside was still and empty. They closed the door, sheathed their blades, and ran down the building's path to the wooden cart road. A Mothertree loomed over them, its massive, empty boughs webbing the sky. Reaching the road, Walde tugged Brite south, away from the town. A stone warehouse reeking of fish emerged from the darkness on the left side of the road, its roof shadowed by the Mothertree across from it.

"Where are we going?" Brite hissed.

"Away from where they expect us to go." Albin's map unfurled in his mind. The cart road stretched north to south alongside the line of Mothertrees. If the guardhouse was where the map indicated, then the First was only three Mothertrees away. Paved paths cutting across the space between Mothertrees allowed access to the harbor. It would be a good area to lie low for a while. The guards would assume that the fugitives had run out of town, not huddled close by the station. But where could he and Brite hide? By morning, every guard in town would be out searching for them.

An unexpected gust punched into him, slowing his pace.

"That's a storm wind," Brite muttered and then added, "It's a good thing. If the rain falls hard enough, the dogs might lose our trail."

"Dogs." He groaned.

"If the guards don't have them, they can get them." She tripped on the edge of a board and managed to right herself just as Walde grasped her arm.

The thought of falling set an idea into Walde's mind. He slowed and peered into the shadows under two Mothertrees. The path that cut between the trees wasn't lit. Perhaps it was only used to bring fish hauls—and the occasional boat—to the warehouses. "We should have nabbed the guard's belt lamp," he heard himself say and then cursed himself for a fool. He could make his own light.

"I'm not climbing a bare Mothertree."

He shook his head. "No. I have a better idea." His chest tightened as he slid a single blade of darkness from the whirling mass of emotions that lapped at him: the feel of the knife entering the man's back. It was more than enough. Grasping her hand with a faintly glowing palm, he tugged her off the cart road into the jumble of roots and old boards toward a Mothertree's trunk. Light from his palm whispered over the ground, revealing the weedy gaps between roots.

As Walde had suspected, much of the wood around the base of the Mothertrees had been torn up and repurposed. The only boards left were those too decayed to be useful. The lower portion of the stairs was also missing, though Walde guessed it had been ripped off to prevent folk from wintering in the branches. Many of the huts had been removed as well, probably over the course of years. He half carried Brite as they stumbled toward the elevated trunk. It was not a short distance to travel, yet she allowed herself to be dragged along without knowing what he had planned. It both warmed and troubled him to think that she trusted him so. He ignored the reflex to stow the feelings. Better to concentrate on Brite than on a memory of killing.

The trunk was a dark, undulating wall. As they neared it, Walde glimpsed a line of lights from the boardwalk that ran parallel to the road but on the other side of the Mothertrees. No sound emanated from the distant harbor; folk were probably bracing for the storm.

"Well?" Brite sighed as she dropped against the trunk.

"Would you mind staying here for a little while? I have to look for something."

She snorted. "The temptation to wander is great, but I'll manage. Be careful."

He nodded and then rested his hand briefly on her warm shoulder. Light flared under his palm, as if in response to that heat. Her mouth opened, and Walde smiled dryly. He added embarrassment and guilt to his mire of emotions before wheeling away from her into the darkness.

He began a methodical search of the ground, shining his light on the shadowy spaces between roots. It was a long, grueling task, and he was acutely aware of the passage of time. The elder would've allowed Walde perhaps an hour to consume the tea and food on the tray, and after that, he would return. Finding the guard dead, he would sound an alarm. Guards would be called from their posts in town, and there would be a manhunt.

He shone light down into a wide crack between roots. Vine and brush tangled together in the shadows. He almost turned away, but a colorful smudge of rust made him pause. He lowered one foot into the gap and gradually paid out his weight until a soft creak broke the silence.

His light flared out his excitement. He had found it at last. Squatting down, he swept away bits of rotting iron and brush until he found the outline of a door and the indentation of a handle. The loop and padlock had disintegrated, but Mothertree wood lasted an age, and these doors had always been made from such material. He thrust both hands into the groove in the wood and heaved. The door didn't budge, and he was forced to unsheathe his dagger and slice through several fat vines along the entire door's length. At last, with a sigh of creaking wood, the door burst open.

A scent of earth wafted up from the darkness. Walde paused, shuddering. The charred remains of countless bodies lay at the bottom of that excavated hole. It was one thing to imagine spending the night with them, another actually to do it. But what other choice did he and Brite have? The boughs of every Mothertree would be searched, but no one would consider looking underground. Generations of treefolk had been taught to associate the corpse darkness with imprisonment and death, making it the last place a fugitive would wish to be. If he and Brite could bear it, they could hide down there in relative safety.

Balancing the door on a shoulder, he dropped an arm in and peered around.

Root hair hung down around the entrance. The floor was perhaps seven feet down. The depth indicated it had only been used for a few decades before being abandoned. The older ones were shallower. When they grew too full, they were covered over with dirt. Walde caught a glimpse of dark moss and mushrooms over a lumpy floor. The air inside was damp but calm. Without the driving wind, it would feel positively warm. He let the door close gently and climbed to his feet. The corpse darkness was on the west side of the tree. He couldn't tell how far away the boardwalk was, but he judged it to be at least thirty yards, perhaps even forty. The wind dragged him backward as he made his way back to the trunk. Brite knelt inside a cleft, arms wrapped around her knees. She rose as Walde approached and met him on the remains of an old path that led away from the trunk.

"I've found what I was looking for," he said, voice raised to cut through the wind. A raindrop splashed her cheek. The fact that it had traveled through the branches above indicated it had already been raining for some time.

He was drawing breath to say more when a horn sounded, distant but clear. "We have to hurry!"

Brite gave a tight nod and let him guide her toward the gap between roots where the trap door was hidden. He crouched down to show her the opening.

"That's the corpse darkness, isn't it?" Her voice quavered as if she spoke through chattering teeth. "You want us to hide in the corpse darkness."

"It's the only place they wouldn't think to look."

"When was the last time they threw bones down there?"

"I don't know. Probably years." The rain fell like drops of ice. The wind drove it, a damp, briny blow the likes of which Walde had never experienced. If they didn't find shelter soon, they would freeze. He opened the door and lowered his arm into the space. "Look, it's just like regular earth."

She squatted down and peered in. "What if it floods?"

"It never does. The water filters through the bone fragments. If it didn't, they wouldn't have kept prisoners down there." He pulled his arm up and regarded her hopefully.

Just then, another horn call threaded through the wailing wind.

Brite loosed a curse and gripped the door with pale fingers. "How do we get down there?"

Walde scrambled down first. The roots dangling around the door were still dry, allowing him an easy grip. He had barely touched the floor before Brite clambered down, the door leaning heavily on her head before slamming shut.

An eerie silence followed.

The pit was perhaps five feet wide by eight feet long. Pale mushrooms peppered the floor. Walde ran his light over the space. The door rested on ledges that had been carved into two massive roots. The two short walls had been shored up with cut stone, while the two longer walls—brushing aside dangling root hair, Walde found more cut stone. Large Mothertree roots didn't shift much over the years, but even so, the walls showed evidence of repeated repair work. Words had been scratched into every smooth surface that remained. Names, signs, curses.

"They must've used bones to scratch all that in," Brite whispered, then jumped back with a gasp.

Walde, following her gaze, spotted the moss-covered eye sockets of a skull. His palms flared, showering light on the ghastly image. He uncovered a few more as he circled around. All in the corners. The center of the pit was almost level. He wondered if consigning the skulls to the corners had been a custom in the Harborlands, or if it had been the work of prisoners.

Brite's expression was ghastly as she lowered herself to the floor. "I couldn't have stayed here for weeks."

Walde crouched beside her. He tried not to dwell on how many insects probably squirmed under him. "You wouldn't have had a choice. For prisoners, it was either this or banishment. An escapee couldn't just disappear, not in a village." He paused as his eyes landed on the familiar shape of her belt pouch. "They didn't take your pouch."

Her lips twitched. "They did. But I got it back."

"How? How did you escape your cell at all?"

She brought her knees up to her chin and spoke quietly. "Before they cuffed me, I nabbed a hair pin from my pouch and stored it in my mouth. After they uncuffed me, I used it to pick the padlock."

"Pouch of wonders," Walde murmured. The turn of phrase won him a small smile. "How did you pick the lock under the guard's eyes?"

Brite chuckled. "I didn't have her eyes. She and another guard were...occupied for a while. He gave her my pouch in return for her favors. She had emptied my change purse and was counting coins when I finally managed to pick the lock."

Walde shook his head grimly at the account. It was disturbing to think that Harborlands guards would perform such vile deeds in front of prisoners. "How did you escape the chamber?"

She drew breath to speak, then her mouth hardened and she shook her head. "She's dead, Walde. And that's all you need to know."

He nodded reluctantly. He wished she would confide in him. Not knowing what had happened made his imagination run wild.

After a time, they both became aware of an incessant dripping.

"It's probably coming in from the door handle," Brite said, and sure enough, there was a small, dark area directly below the door handle. If rain entered through that gap, then light could.

With an effort, he herded his emotions behind the imagined walls, allowing only a tiny glimmer to leak through.

Brite gasped at the sudden gloom. "Not yet! Let me fall asleep first."

"The guards might be out there. If they look this way and see light..."

She dragged her hands over her face. "Gods, but this is horrible."

Walde hesitated and then curled his arm around her taut back. He spoke without thought. "I'm here. You're safe."

She sniffed out a dry chuckle, but he thought he felt some of the stiffness in her shoulders ease. Awkwardly, they stretched out in the center of the corpse darkness, Brite's back against his chest. It was difficult to find a comfortable spot. Bones poked into him, but he refused to dig his hand under the mashed mushrooms to wrench them out. Brite's breath hitched several times as she struggled with the same problem. The muffled snap of a bone breaking made her flinch and whimper, but after a while they both stilled and Walde heard her breathing steady. He didn't trust himself to touch her, even to give comfort. Despite his depressed state of mind and the bodies beneath him, he was still keenly aware of her. It was challenging enough to stow his uneasiness, let alone desire and all the incidentals that accompanied it.

"I owe you my life," she whispered, just as he contemplated shifting to his opposite side. "How am I supposed to repay you for that?"

Walde shook his head. "It's more the other way around." He told her then about the real reason they had been arrested. About the tea, and how they would have used her as a weapon against him. Brite stiffened but said nothing until his whispered words drained out.

"So it wasn't me they wanted," she said.

"No. But they'll want you *now*." He almost added that she should've stayed in the Woodlands, but it seemed pointless.

After a long pause, he spoke again. "Tomorrow evening, I'm going to climb the Mothertree next to the First and look down over that fence they've erected around the trunk."

"Won't that be dangerous? They'll still be looking for us."

"I know. But we can't stay down here anyway. Even if we ate all these mushrooms, we'd still need water." His mouth went dry before he found the courage to ask, "Is there a safe place in town for you to stay? Perhaps with a relative?"

"No." Her answer was curt, and Walde sensed she would say no more about it. For now. In time, he'd have to bring up the subject again. But first, he would need to work out her chances of slipping away from the area unnoticed. Tomorrow, he would venture out of the corpse darkness alone and find out just how difficult it would be for either of them to leave the area.

He thrust his concerns away and tried to clear his mind. To find the sleep his body craved. Brite was still, but her breathing didn't deepen. Walde sympathized with her. Even without the knowledge that they lay on a bed of bones, the space was confining and damp; a faint scent of ash hung in the air like a memory of fire. Despite these discomforts, he felt himself drift. A muddle of thoughts and images swept through his mind. Suddenly, he felt as if a heavy shadow bore down on him. It was the body of the man he had killed. His hand spasmed. He gripped a knife, his fingers sliding on blood. With a choking cry, he flung the knife away and clutched at the weight on him, but it wouldn't move.

"Walde…"

He gasped awake, air thundering into his chest. Light flared from his sweat-dampened palms. He buried them under his side. But would they stay there? He had forgotten how little control he had while sleeping.

"Walde." Brite's sleepy voice repeated. A glimmer of light escaping his side illuminated the profile of her face. "Are you all right?"

"Yes. It was just a nightmare."

She propped herself up on an elbow. "I know what it's like to try to sleep after killing someone. You can run from it while you're still awake, but when you close your eyes..." Her head shook. "Remember the night after I killed that man?"

"Yes. We walked all night. I thought you'd collapse."

"I almost did. But I couldn't stop moving. And even when I did lie down, I couldn't sleep."

"That's right. You got up before I did." He recalled wondering how she'd found the energy to hack down a stunted tree and fashion a bow from it.

"Even if you don't regret killing someone, it hurts you. It's as though you've also killed something inside yourself."

Walde, refusing to explore his own feelings on the matter, asked, "Do you feel like that now, after…what happened tonight?"

She took a long time to answer. "No, I don't. And that's what worries me. I shouldn't be able to sleep after killing two people. It shouldn't get easier."

Walde didn't know what to say to that. Unlike Brite's fear of heights, this wasn't irrational. On the contrary, it was a real and deeply disturbing specter.

He could only find one thing to say, and he spoke to himself as much to her as he said it: "The fact that you're disturbed by it says something about your conscience. It's still there, and it's not going away."

Her eyes glittered in the light. "I hope so."

He reached out and brushed her hair back from her forehead. "You're a good person, Brite."

She stilled at his touch. Throat tightening, he dropped his hand and turned onto his other side. "Good night."

The night marched along. Brite's breathing gradually deepened, and she slept peacefully. Walde did not. As Brite had warned, the memory of the killing haunted him. He wondered if the guard had a family. Children to feed. And what about the other two guards? How would Carrac feel, knowing that three had died so he could be rescued?

Suddenly, the shallowness of the thought sickened him. This wasn't merely about rescuing his father. It was about innocent men and women being tortured, about the more than a dozen children who had stopped growing, and above all, it was about the destruction of an entire way of life. Others might have to die before this was over. But that was the price, whether he wished to pay it or not.

He lifted himself up to allow blood back into his hands. A glimmer of light from his palms shone on the wall. Water trickled down the old stones, following a white path of mineral deposits. The leak probably came from a gap around the fat wooden dowel joints that acted as hinges. Holes drilled into the massive roots served as sockets for the joints. But the holes were old now and may have widened around the edges, letting in more water. He rose up on an elbow and surveyed the other leak at the front end of the pit. The dripping from the door handle had slowed, and a faint brush of light illuminated the moss directly below it.

Was it dawn already?

As he stared at it, hardly breathing, a loud thud shook the pit.

CHAPTER 15

Brite jolted awake and looked wildly about her. Walde grasped her arm. "Ready your knife."

His own blade was already in his hand. He allowed Brite only enough time to unsheath her knife and grasp it before plunging them both into near blackness.

He didn't know how long they waited, backs taut as boards, watching the puddle of daylight on the floor gradually grow brighter. Little by little, the dripping ceased and Walde thought he detected the faint chirping of birds. Brite relaxed and lay back down. Though he couldn't make out her features, her shadowy outline was clear.

"If someone was out there, they've left," he breathed.

"I thought you said no one would think to look here." Her tone wasn't accusatory, but anxious.

"They wouldn't. Or at least, they shouldn't."

"That's comforting."

"They shouldn't have discovered I was a Reacher either, but strange things happen."

"Eavesdropping happened." A bone cracked as she shifted, but this time she only sighed. "It's amazing how a little sunlight and birdsong can make breaking bones sound cheerful."

Something loosened inside Walde at that, and he laughed into his arm until his palms flared and his whole body trembled with the effort of keeping silent. When he was still at last, he didn't know what he felt. Amusement and anxiety had blurred into one thing. He lay down with his back against Brite, the dagger ready at his side.

"Walde, are you all—"

"I'm fine. I just need to sleep."

And incredibly, he did.

***

He woke to the muffled sounds of the bustling harbor. He sat up and found Brite gathering mushrooms. She was so close to the light radiating from the door handle that he could easily make out the shadowy pile of mushrooms in her skirt.

"How long have you been gathering those?"

She jumped at the sound of his voice. "Long enough. I've eaten quite a few too."

He stretched his legs, ignoring the hint of guilt in her voice. "That's good."

"Would you like some?"

"Maybe later." He felt for his dagger. It was a comforting weight at his side. "It's time I took a peek outside."

Brite rose and moved to the opposite end of the pit. "Be careful," she warned.

Walde grasped root hair with both hands, then swung his legs up and walked up the wall until he was high enough to be able to push the door open with a foot while bracing himself against one of the massive roots.

The door didn't budge.

He seized some higher root hair and pushed up using both feet. Little by little, the door inched open, showering him with light. Gritting his teeth, he gave it a firm shove. There came a scraping sound, and the door burst open.

"What's happening?" Brite's concerned whisper issued up from the darkness.

"Nothing. Something must have fallen on the door during the storm, and now it's shifted."

"Can you see anything?"

He struggled to find a more comfortable position while propping open the much lighter door. "No. Only the hollow between the roots. I'm going to climb out and take a better look."

"I'll wait here," she said dryly then added another, "Be careful."

Walde scrambled out of the door and lowered it until it closed.

The object that had caused them such anxiety turned out to be part of a branch. It lay across one of the roots like a pair of scales, tipping slightly in the breeze. Walde must have shifted it when he opened the door. It was a good thing a larger branch hadn't landed on the pit, or they would have joined the ranks of the deceased.

He gave the branch a push so that it settled on the other side of the root, then squatted in the hollow between roots and peered around. A vague brightness in the branches above him indicated it was noon or a little later. The docklands bustled. A cluster of fishing boats obscured his view of the estuary, but the boardwalk, while perhaps forty yards from where Walde hid, was still clearly visible. Two men hauling wheelbarrows wove between groups of chattering women and vendor's stalls to a man waiting at a horse-drawn cart. The man shoveled what might have been fish onto the cart, closed a hatch, and drove the cart up the steep, rickety path that cut between the Mothertrees. Walde flattened as it passed, thankful for the shadow under the Mothertree. He guessed it was heading to the outbuildings near the cart road. When it was out of sight, he sat up again and fixed his eyes on the boardwalk. At once, he found what he was looking for. A guard stood by one of the floating docks, eyeing the passersby. He was well armed with a bow and shortsword, but he was alone. Without a dog.

Walde lowered himself back into the hollow and stared thoughtfully at the lacework of branches overhead. Very few guards would recognize Walde and Brite by their faces. That left the Scats who'd been at the bar, a village elder, and a servant. Given the size of the Harborlands, one could slip out of town under the cover of darkness without being recognized.

Brite could return to the Woodlands.

Pain nudged at him at the thought of parting from her, but it was distant. Contained. As it should be.

Quietly, he lifted the door and slipped back into the pit.

"Well, what did you see?"

Walde told her as his eyes adjusted to dimness. Afterward, Brite walked to the space under the door handle, still holding mushrooms in her bunched skirt, and peered up at the spray of light. Flakes of dirt and dried mushrooms tracked down one side of her cheek, reminding Walde of her appearance after the rainstorm in the forest.

"Did you recognize the guard?" she whispered.

"No, he was too far away."

"But you didn't see any dogs…"

"No."

She let out a relieved sigh. "That's good. I feel better about us leaving this place."

Walde squatted on the floor, and after a moment, she joined him. He didn't insult her with meaningless phrases like "we have to talk" but cut right to the chase, laying out how she could escape and why he thought she would be safe in doing so. "Once you're out in the fields, you'll have your knife to hunt with and your tinderbox to make fire. You should travel at night to avoid hunters. But if you do meet someone..." He drew a breath and halted, staring at the stiff line of her back, her hanging head. When she spoke at last, her voice could've cut stone.

"I'm not leaving you here."

"Brite—"

"No." She seized his arms. "We've already talked about this, and the answer is no. It will always be no. Do you understand?"

Walde's eyes closed briefly. He was both surprised and ashamed by the relief he had to force down. "All right," he relented. "I won't speak of it again."

Her hands loosened and then fell. "Thank you."

And that was that.

They consumed the pile of mushrooms and then gathered more in Walde's silvery light. While they foraged, Walde felt out his power, learning to isolate one emotion from another, then to call up each one. To do so, he had to learn which thoughts prompted which emotions. It was much like plucking and stilling strings on a lyre. Once one grew accustomed to the feel of the strings, it was easier to still them.

The practice session was a welcome diversion from his concern for Brite.

They were both thirsty and weary of sitting when they finally ventured out. The sun—gleaming from behind a cloud—was low, and the boardwalks were empty but for a few fishermen repairing their nets. A roar of distant laughter echoed off the water. Did it come from a boardwalk pub, Walde wondered, or from some men drinking on one of the many boats that cluttered the harbor?

"It'll get busier as night closes in," Brite promised.

They were hunched low in the hollow. Though the roots were wreathed in shadow, being out in the open again was as unnerving as being thrown into cold water.

"Very likely." Studying the sky, he judged they had only two hours until twilight set in. "We should get going." He tugged on his scruffy chin as he eyed her skirt. "We'll be traveling over roots for a while..."

She caught the direction of his eyes and nodded. "I'll tuck the hem under my belt."

"Your blue tunic," he reminded her with a sigh.

She stuck out her lower lip. "I should've eaten it."

"Now you'll never get the chance."

Grinning, he rose warily, and together they made their way up to the base of the Mothertree's trunk. Brite paused there long enough to draw her hem up through her belt, then to tighten the belt so the hem wouldn't shift. The dress now hung a couple of inches above her knees. "Scandalous," she said with a faint smile.

Walde sidled around the huge trunk and looked around. Even if the walkways had been maintained, traveling from a Mothertree to its neighbor would take time. At least one hundred and fifty yards yawned between trunks—in this case, a space of overgrown weeds, rotting boards and massive roots jutting and coiling like serpents. To make matters worse, the ground sloped down from the base of the trunks so that the earth was never level.

Brite's voice at his ear almost made him jump. "If someone sees us, do you think they'd care enough to abandon their nets and report us?"

He shook his head. "It's the guards I'm worried about. If you spot one, get down low and wait until he passes."

It went without saying, but he felt better having voiced it. She gave a curt nod, and Walde urged her to go ahead of him. That way he would travel at her pace.

Brite took her time. She kept her head down and treated every safe stretch of root as its own bridge. Walde was bemused by the dance of her bare legs, the swaying of her arms. She forded the space as if it were a bog, the roots as grassy islands.

They reached the stone path that connected the boardwalk to the cart road and darted across it. Horse manure bit into Walde's nostrils, and he kept a close eye on where he stepped. Then they were on roots again and racing toward another trunk.

There was only one mishap. A raised voice from the harbor startled Brite, and she tripped, falling hard on a knotty length of root.

"I'm fine," she hissed as Walde dropped down beside her. "Did someone see us?"

He glanced around. "No. There's some men talking on a boat..."

"That far away? It sounded closer."

"The water makes things sound louder than they really are. Are you sure you're all right?"

In answer, she pulled herself up and limped ahead of him toward the trunk. But before she reached it, a clopping of hooves from the cart road made them both dive down into a weedy space between roots. It seemed an eternity before the mounted guard passed and the sound faded to silence.

The sky was darkening. Walde sensed a growing stillness within him, an anticipation akin to dread as he arrived at the trunk and dug his fingers into its bark. He glanced at Brite. "The First is just ahead. We'll see it when we round the trunk."

She nodded as she fiddled with her hem. Some of it had come down and now hung at her calf. "Should I wait here, or do you want company?"

Walde made no reply at first. He was both warmed and chagrined at her perceptiveness. "Do as you wish," he suggested.

In the end, they rounded the tree together, Brite limping only slightly as she moved behind him.

The first thing he glimpsed was the edge of a tall wattle fence. Then the First's trunk peeled out behind it.

He halted in shock. Though he'd heard it described, seeing it was like a physical blow.

A massive black column rose out of the encircling fence, bending a little here and there as it narrowed to a jagged point in the sky. Walde didn't want to believe this had been a Mothertree, once home to hundreds of treefolk. The place where the best song rites had taken place, where people had huddled, overhung by its heavy boughs full of treelights and life. And now, a stripped, blackened pole standing over the Harborlands like an accusation.

His head was shaking. But inside, his anger had hardened to steel.

He felt Brite's hand on his shoulder and turned to face her. "I'm going up this tree to get a better look at what's going on at the First," he said.

Her hand fell, and she offered a solemn nod. "Be careful."

He forced a small smile. "You say that a lot. I'm beginning to think you mean it."

"Don't get your hopes up." She shoved him playfully and then crept back around to the north side of the tree. Walde peered up into the tangle of branches. Unlike the other trees, this one appeared to have been stripped not only of its stairs, but also of its huts and paths. Of course, he was only viewing one side of the tree, but it made sense to assume that if the huts and paths had been removed on one side, they had been removed on the other.

It was an easy climb. The removal of the stairs had left a rising spiral of holes in the trunk's surface, many of them larger than the toe of Walde's boot. He was tempted to follow them up as they spiraled around, but caution won out. If he climbed on the side facing the compound, a guard might spot him and shoot him down. In the end, he had no trouble finding footholds in the lumpy bark. Attaining the second level, he inched around to the opposite side of the tree and then swung up onto a branch that would give him a view of what went on inside the fence.

He was not able to follow it to its natural end. The branches facing the compound had been shortened, some by a third of their length. The reason for such trimming escaped him. It might have been to keep people from seeing exactly what went on inside the compound. It certainly made it impossible to shoot arrows at guards with any accuracy. With the branches trimmed, the First's blackened trunk stood at a good eighty yards away. He edged as close to the end of the branch as he could while remaining hidden in a tangle of twigs and let out a tight breath.

The sky seemed lighter up here. Before he forced his eyes downward, he found the ragged outline of land's end, and beyond it, the vast gray ocean. For an instant, all thoughts vanished, and he hovered there at the edge of the world, shivering as if touched by a parting curtain of mist. Then, steeling himself, he forced his gaze downward.

CHAPTER 16

Walde was too far away from the prisoners to see detail, but what he could see made him grasp at the empty place at his neck where his medallion once hung.

There were five of them, likely more around the other side of the tree. They sprawled in a variety of lax positions over the natural folds in the trunk's base, their wrists cuffed to a chain that encircled the tree like a silver choker. Their hands were bound with some sort of bright cloth. He couldn't tell whether they were awake or in slumber, if they were at peace or in pain.

He tore his eyes away. For some moments, he could do nothing but hold his face in his hands and struggle to calm the harried strings of his emotions. *Father.*

But no. He would've recognized his father had he seen him. Even from such a distance. Carrac must be on the other side of the tree. But even if he wasn't, Walde told himself, he wouldn't abandon those poor suffering creatures. He hoped they'd be well enough to walk. If Walde had been bound and tortured, he would've done anything he could to get free.

Of one thing he was sure: if he found his father, he would get him to safety one way or another, even if he had to carry him on his back.

His mouth firmed, and he found the strength to lift his eyes again.

A distance of perhaps twenty yards stood between the First's trunk and the wattle fence. Its open gate was manned by a single guard armed with a bow and short sword. If another gate existed, then it was concealed behind the First's thick trunk. But Walde doubted there was another. In fact, the guard was little more than a doorman, for the compound's real defense was the sentinel who manned a platform affixed to the trunk. The narrow walk was perhaps twenty feet above ground, high enough to give the sentinel a view of the entire compound while still providing him a good shot with his bow.

Walde would have welcomed three gates over that platform.

The sentinel had one weakness. While he marched around the First, he always left one side of it unguarded. This period of absence might've given Walde enough time to scale the fence and duck into a shadowy space between roots. But again, he was stymied, this time by several feet of what appeared to be spikes driven in the ground along the inside edge of the fence. Anyone who climbed over it would be in for a painful surprise. He couldn't make out if there were gaps under the fence, but he doubted they would've overlooked such an obvious way in.

He could take out the gate guard while the sentinel was on the other side of the trunk, however, once the sentinel glimpsed the empty gate, he would sound an alarm blast.

Walde shook his head. The longer he studied the compound, the worse his chances looked. But he'd throw himself over the sea cliffs before giving up.

As the sky darkened, the guard left his post and lit torches on poles that ran along the inside of the fence. Walde counted under his breath while he walked the circumference of the compound. If the man paused after disappearing behind the trunk, he might be conversing with another guard.

But he didn't pause. There probably wasn't a second guard. If there had been, the two would've split the job of lighting the torches. Walde sighed and straightened his stiffening back. It was growing late, and there wasn't much more to see from here.

He crawled out from the tangle of twigs, rose to his feet—and then went deadly still. A glimmer of light hung in the branches below him. He grasped a nearby branch and bent to look down. The corner of a hut peeked at him through the branches. Walde swore under his breath. How could he have missed it?

This was looking worse and worse. The hut must belong to someone employed by the elders. No one else would've been permitted to live within direct view of the compound.

Brite. He had to warn her about the hut.

The thought energized him, and he had to force himself not to race down the branch to the trunk. If he dislodged a chunk of bark, it might alert the hut's occupant.

He was only steps away from the trunk when he heard a soft grunt. A slender hand appeared, fingers gripping the edge of an empty knot in the wood.

"Brite!" Walde hissed, stunned and horrified that she had climbed the tree. A traitorous wisp of light escaped his palms, and he stowed it instantly.

"Help me," she whispered.

Walde grasped her wrist and pulled her up onto the branch beside him. She clung to him and panted, her warm, sweat-dampened body shivering with either fear or exertion. "Can you stand on your own?"

She drew away from him and grasped the trunk. "I came to warn you that someone's living up here. I saw lamplight and the outline of a hut."

"I know. I was about to warn you of the same thing."

After an awkward pause, he leaned on the trunk beside her. Despite the horrors he had just witnessed, a faint smile touched his face. "I can't believe you climbed that trunk. Two levels."

"Let's not talk about it. What did you see down there?"

Quietly, he reported all to her, not sparing a detail. Whether for good or ill, she had become his partner in this endeavor. Her wide eyes held his, taking in every word until words ran out. He gestured back at the glimmer of light in the branches. "Since the hut faces the gate, we can't take the guard down without being seen, even if we crawled around the outside of the fence."

She nodded calmly. "Then we make sure the person in the hut can't see us."

It was the obvious solution. Probably the only solution. And yet he wished it hadn't been voiced.

"Walde…"

He had been looking down at his feet. "Yes."

"Are we doing this tonight?"

He looked back through the branches toward the Reachers. "We shouldn't," he admitted softly. "It'd be wise to wait another day and think this through. But I don't think I can. I can't allow my father to spend another day being tortured." He found her eyes again. "It's getting dark, and there aren't any paths up here. Even if we pulled this off, how would you climb back down in the darkness?"

Her lips tightened. "I'll do it if I have to."

Yes, he thought. She would. Even if she died trying.

"We could follow those holes down around the trunk," she suggested. "By then it'll be too dark for anyone to see us."

He gave a reluctant nod. More than anything, he wanted her to climb back down and disappear for a while. The prospect of her negotiating a bare Mothertree while being chased by an unknown assailant set his teeth on edge. But he knew her well enough now to know she wouldn't be dissuaded.

The dregs of sunlight filtered through the branches as they edged around the trunk and then down to what used to be the tree's first level. Brite trembled as she stretched from one handhold to another, all the while making small, voiceless sounds under her breath. The sight reminded him of her slog to the marsh, carrying a dead man on her back. He had never met anyone with such determination.

They rounded the trunk again and alighted on the branch that bore the stranger's hut. No, not hut, he thought, but a watcher's perch. Why else would someone occupy a hut on a first-level branch facing the compound?

Brite clung to a fist of twigs and panted. Walde didn't ask if she was all right but waited until she caught her breath. The branch was almost flat on top. Centuries of employing it as a walkway had smoothed its surface, making its bark thin and dark in comparison with the rest of the trees'. Since the branch bowed a little, the watcher's perch was almost invisible. Only a glimmer of light betrayed its position.

"Why are we waiting?" she whispered as she edged away from the trunk.

He met her eyes squarely. "Do you know how dangerous this is?"

She stared off at the hazy light. "We have the advantage of surprise. And that's about all. We don't know how many people live in the hut or what weapons they have. If they come out with bows and arrows, we'd have no cover. Even if they aren't armed, they might call out to the gate guard. And if we do manage to kill them, they might fall out of the tree." She chewed the inside of her lip. "Have I left anything out?"

He flashed her a grim smile. "No. You've summed it up nicely."

"So what do you suggest?"

"I'll spy it out first, then—"

"No. We stay together."

"But—"

"Together."

The firm set of her jaw warned him that she would not be dissuaded. Walde's head bent, as to a judgment. "All right. Together." At least they would get a good look at the perch before approaching it.

They ghosted forward, Walde leading with Brite closely behind. He was impressed by the softness of her step. If he didn't know better, he would have assumed she was a hunter. Her uncle had trained her well.

The branch rose at a slight incline before curving over and sloping down. The hut was closer to the tipping point than Walde had anticipated. He pulled up short, hand on his dagger, afraid even to whisper.

The tiny hut rested on top of the main branch and one of its thick offshoots. Oddly, it had no front door but only a small shuttered window, too small to allow a body through. Narrow side paths probably led around to a back door.

A gap in the branches showed an indigo sky. It was a calm, quiet evening, and the distant sounds from the harbor only added to that note of peace. Of normality. It was utterly surreal.

Walde was about to take a step forward when the silence was shattered by a scraping of metal against metal: someone sharpening a blade. He glanced back at Brite. Her knife was already out and poised in her hand. He quietly drew his own blade, and they started toward the left side path.

Walde had grown so accustomed to looking out for rotting boards that he automatically glanced down as he stepped onto the path. And that was what saved him. Light from a back porch shone on a gut line that ran across the path. It was an alarmed trip wire. Walde halted, inches from the wire, and carefully stepped over it. A glance at Brite told him she'd seen it and understood.

As they passed another shuttered window, the sharpening ceased. Someone set a tool down and picked up another. By now, Walde was sure that the guard was sitting on a back porch. Gripping the dagger, he took another careful step.

Crunch.

A leaf of some sort—likely placed by the guard—disintegrated under his heel.

There was a shocked silence, then a sound like a chair overturning. Walde veered sharply around the corner, only to find the back porch empty. A quick glance through the door told him the guard wasn't inside the hut either. Was he hiding around the hut's right side? He turned to motion to Brite, but she wasn't behind him. She was nowhere.

Anxiety battered against his carefully constructed calm. He licked his dry lips and stepped toward the hut's west corner.

The creak of a drawn bow stopped his heart, and almost at the same instant, there came a soft but decisive thud. Walde swung around the corner, fists clenched over a glimmer of escaping light.

He was just in time to grasp the attacker's robe before she tumbled over the edge of the path and out of the tree. Her bow slipped from her limp hands and landed at Walde's feet.

"Is she dead?" Brite whispered behind her.

Walde sheathed his dagger so he could use both hands, then lay the woman on her side against the hut's wall. He judged her to be in her early sixties but strong and hale, her slender fingers untouched by arthritis. She was dressed in a hooded brown robe and black boots. Her long gray hair had been coiled tightly to the top of her head. Her bow was no toy, but a weapon that any guard would have been proud to carry.

Brite's knife stuck out of her back, right up to the hilt. His lips tightened. Although Brite had succeeded in killing their attacker, she had abandoned Walde in order to do so, giving him no sign of her intention. The fact bothered him more than it should have. "I think so."

"She was going to shoot whoever came around the corner. I sneaked up behind her."

They had been speaking in whispers, wary of the guard and sentinel. If it weren't for the distance and the fact that the door guard knew someone lived here, Walde and Brite would surely have been noticed. He met her eyes in the fading light and managed a tight smile. "Does that mean we're even now?"

"Not quite." She knelt down and retrieved the knife. Her hands shook as she wiped it clean on the woman's robe. "The only reason you came barreling around the corner was because you thought she'd shot me, so you can hardly say I saved your life. Who was she, anyway?"

"Possibly an elder or someone they hired." He sheathed his dagger and rose to his feet. "Let's take a look inside the hut."

They paused at the back porch before going inside. A chair and low table stood near the door. A sentinel horn hung from a chair arm. Three sinister-looking tools lay on the table, their metal gleaming in the light of the oil lamp beside them. Walde hastily looked aside. He didn't want to believe they were a torturer's tools, but he couldn't deny his suspicion. He crouched down. Sure enough, a gap in the branches afforded him a clear view of the Reachers. The woman could have watched her prisoners while seated in her chair, sharpening her tools.

"What are they?" Brite whispered.

Walde couldn't form the words to reply. Instead, he turned and strode into the hut.

The only occupants of the cramped space were a narrow bed, a chest, a wood stove, a few shelves, a chamber pot, and a wash basin. A familiar scent assailed his nostrils the moment he entered. It didn't take him long to find the source. Bundles of drying herbs hung from the tops of every shuttered window. Walde calmly tore them off their hooks and crushed them under his feet, grinding the bits into cracks in the floorboards.

When nothing remained, he turned to Brite's shadowy outline in the doorway. "It's what they've been using to poison the Reachers."

"I'd guessed that."

An uneasy silence fell. The air was filled with the herb's sickly sweet scent. And with it came the knowledge of who the woman had been. "I don't feel so bad now about killing her," Brite whispered, echoing Walde's own thoughts. "I wonder if she grew the plants too. And where she grew them."

Walde just shook his head.

He found a water pitcher on the floor by the wood stove, and he and Brite took turns drinking from it. A store of dried meat and berries was tackled next, and when they could find nothing else, they took turns washing from the basin. Walde hadn't realized how much his gnawing thirst and hunger had affected him until those needs were met. A haze of sorts lifted from his mind, and the situation lay starkly before him. While they had removed the threat in the tree—and gained a bow and arrows in the process—there was still a gate guard and sentinel to tackle. The only way to approach the guard without being seen was via the fence's deep shadow. But that same fence would block Walde's view of the sentinel platform all the way to the gate. If the sentinel faced the gate when Walde took out the guard, he would sound an alarm and it would all be over. Walde could try shooting the sentinel first from several yards beyond the fence. But even if he managed by an extraordinary stroke of good luck not only to hit a moving target from twenty-five yards away, but also to kill with his first arrow, the sound of the body clattering to the platform floor would probably alert the guard.

Brite was silent throughout these musings, her gaze fixed pensively on the pool of lamplight through the door. After a time, she turned and met Walde's gaze. Her eyes were oddly clear. "I have a plan," she said.

CHAPTER 17

Walde waited for her to elucidate, but all she offered was a sly smile. "Turn around—or sit in the chair outside. I have to alter my clothing." She retrieved the lamp, set it on the floor inside, and closed the door.

Walde folded his arms across his chest. "I'm not moving until you tell me your plan."

She shrugged. "Fine. I'll undress in front of you." She unhooked her belt and deposited it on the floor. Holding his eyes, she gathered up the skirt of her frock and slowly lifted it up her legs to her hips.

Walde wheeled away before it came off entirely. It cost him effort to hold his frustration and worry in check. "Why are you doing this? I've been open and honest with *you*. I thought we were a team."

He heard her unsheathe her knife. Fabric rustled, and the blade cut into something. "A team." She snorted under her breath. "You've been trying to get rid of me since we left that hunter in the wastes." A harshness underlay her words, and Walde recognized that he'd hurt her. Not deeply, but enough to damage their friendship. He opened his mouth to apologize and then snapped it shut.

Why had she raised the issue now? Could this be a ploy to guilt him into going along with her plan? The more he thought about it, the likelier it seemed.

The silence stretched. Fabric rustled, and the blade cut against the floor. At last, she spoke again.

"Prostitutes are common in the Lowlands. Most of them are Scat girls who've been sent out by their parents to help pay off family debts. Their customers are other Scats. Barans don't touch them. I imagine that this place has its fair share of prostitutes. Take a stroll down the boardwalk at night, and I think you'll find more than one trying to get your attention."

Another cut. Walde's eyes closed briefly, and he loosed a shuddering breath. "Brite, don't tell me that you mean to—"

"Your people must have prostitutes too. They can't be that precious."

"In the Lakelands, there are huts marked by a purple loop on the door…" His voice trailed. He heard the creak of a chest opening and a soft exclamation. The lid fell, and a bottle was unstoppered.

"Can I turn around now?" A heady scent of spirits wafted through the air, mingling oddly with the herbs.

"If you like."

With a great deal of presentiment, Walde turned and regarded the figure leaning against the wall.

Brite had transformed herself. The frock now hung three inches above the knee. The neckline plunged, and her belt had been fastened above her waist, causing her breasts to lift so that twin moons peeked out from the neckline. The sleeves were gone, leaving little more than straps to hold the frock up. It was appalling. And undeniably arousing. Her unbound hair fell softly around her bare shoulders, inviting to be touched.

She took a swig from the bottle and then tipped it until spirits dribbled down the front of her frock. Satisfied, she set the bottle casually on the lid of the chest. "Is it effective?"

His nails bit into his palms. "Why?"

"To distract the guard while you go in."

"Do you really think he'll allow that while the sentinel looks on?" Even as he said it, he remembered what she told him the two guards had done in full view of their prisoner.

"Of course he will. I'd wager that all the guards here have dirt on each other. If the sentinel squealed about such a petty thing, he'd risk getting mud on his face."

She had an answer to everything. Or almost everything. "What if the gate guard was one of the ones who arrested us? What if he recognizes you?"

Her lips compressed. "There's only two who would, and it's unlikely that either of them would be the gate guard."

Night had fallen, and the warm lamplight huddled around them like a blanket. Walde gazed sullenly at her down-turned face. In some ways, Brite was still a mystery to him. Part of him enjoyed that inscrutability, that dark wildness. But this went beyond what he was comfortable with. How far did she mean to go with the guard? And what would she do if he tried to rape her before Walde could take out the sentinel?

He lurched forward suddenly and grasped her arms. "You don't have to do this. We can find another way."

"Really? *Is* there another way?"

There wasn't. Not then, at least. And without others to help him, maybe never. He snatched up the bottle and took a long pull.

Brite unhooked her sheathed knife and shoved it down the front of her frock so that it rested under her breasts. She attached her pouch to the front; somehow it obscured the knife's slight bulge. "Once you take down the sentinel," she said, "I'll kill the gate guard and take his keys. If he doesn't have the keys..." Her voice caught, and her gaze fanned over the room.

Walde caught her train of thought. "The keys could be here."

They quietly scoured the place. The trunk was emptied, its contents strewn over the floor. They upended the narrow mattress and knocked softly on the bottom of the trunk and on the floorboards. While they searched, Brite's plan danced around in Walde's mind until at last he reluctantly accepted it. Freeing the Reachers would be dangerous, no matter what he and Brite did. And he consoled himself with the fact that she would never be far away from him. The compound wasn't so big that he wouldn't hear her cry out—if she allowed herself to cry out.

After a thorough search of the body, they returned resignedly to the hut—Walde now bearing the dead woman's bow and quiver of arrows—and lingered restlessly, reviewing their simple plan in hushed tones. His immediate concern was finding a way for Brite to get down the dark Mothertree without falling. But even talking about it made Brite stiffen and peer out the door as if a monster waited.

At last, they left the lamp on and exited the hut without closing the door. Walde had unstrung the bow and shoved it into the quiver, removing some arrows to allow room for it. The extra string in the quiver's side pocket gave him a measure of relief.

Brite all but clung to him as they made their way slowly in the darkness down the branch. It was a novelty to walk in a bare Mothertree without lights. Without a human's touch. Certainly, the branch had flattened from use, but in the near darkness he saw only a nakedness that evoked an earlier time. They reached the trunk without mishap, but the worst part was yet to come. It had been hard enough for Brite to climb the trunk in daylight. Now the trunk was a black wall, the handholds invisible. Walde felt around until his fingers sank into one of the holes left by the removed stairs. The next one was only a couple of feet away. He found Brite's hands and placed her fingers into the holes. "Just follow these as they wind down." He tried to make his voice soothing, confident. Brite's hands were chill and damp, and she trembled like a frightened rabbit. "If I had your respect for heights," he said, "I might have gotten fewer bruises in my life."

"How far down is it? I don't remember."

"Not far. We're on the first level, so…"

"Twenty-five, thirty feet?"

"Perhaps twenty-five. You'll reach the ground in no time."

"That's what I'm afraid of." She drew her hands back and rubbed them on her frock, probably to remove the sweat. "I'll go first. If I don't, I might not go down at all."

Walde didn't argue. His teeth clenched as he listened to the scuffle of her hands and feet on the trunk, her tight breath. It went on for a long time. Thankfully, no one would see her in the shadows. When he was sure she was far enough away that he wouldn't interfere with her descent, he started down. Footholds were easy to find. The bark was riddled with small cracks and protrusions, and if it weren't for the bit of moss that tickled the surface, the climb would have been effortless.

He found Brite in a trembling heap on the north side of the trunk, curled into a gap between roots. He touched her damp shoulder and then flinched at the touch of her soft, heated flesh. Easy to forget in the darkness what she'd done to her frock. Once more, he chased down a stab of fear over what the guard might do to her.

He rose and looked around him in the faint brush of light from the harbor. The paved path that cut between Mothertrees was a dark finger in the distance ahead of them. Since their plan was to approach the compound from the boardwalk, they had to make their way to the path first. From there, it would be a smooth jog to the boardwalk. But getting to the path would be difficult. The Mothertrees cast a net of shadows over the entire area. Jutting roots and boards were like dark shapes in a heaving sea.

Brite straightened and leaned on the trunk. "Shall we go?"

"May as well. Try not to step on the rotten boards…"

"I know."

"Do you think you'll be all right on your own?" He remembered how she'd clung to him the last time they'd struggled over roots in the darkness.

She hissed out a laugh. "I've just climbed a Mothertree. This is paradise."

The words "this is paradise" rang oddly in his head as they threaded their way toward the path. He found himself mouthing them while a bubble of laughter rose from the pit of his belly. Was this what happened when a Reacher smothered his emotions too long? Or was it a natural reaction when the world sank into darkness around you? Why weep at evil when you could laugh at it?

Carrac would have laughed. He'd already been laughing at the world for some time. "This is paradise," Walde whispered as he walked along the thin edge of a root.

He reached the path ahead of Brite and waited guiltily while she slogged her way over. The stench of spirits wafting from her frock reached him before she did. "Sorry. I should've stayed by you."

"There was no need. I have the knack for it now."

He chuckled. "A bog sprite knows where to step."

"Is that how you think of me?" There was a smile in her voice.

"Always."

He glanced down the path at the lit cart road. It was empty. The harbor, on the other hand, was more alive than it had been hours before. Music drifted from more than one location, and as he and Brite neared the boardwalk, it became apparent that some of the large, docked fishing boats swarmed with people.

A woman's angry shout drew their attention to a dock, where a scantily clad woman stood, fist raised at someone in a boat. Brite cocked a brow at him meaningfully. *Prostitutes.*

Walde's answering smile was closer to a grimace. It was comforting to know that Brite's role in their plan wouldn't be questioned, but that didn't ease his anxiety.

It was time. He loosened the quiver's strap so that it hung as low as possible, then shifted the quiver itself so that it faced his front right side. All the while, Brite kept an eye on the boardwalk. Enough light spilled from the harbor now to betray them if someone bothered to look. Or care. "Ready?" he whispered. She offered a brisk nod.

Walde dropped his arm over her shoulder, and they stumbled forward onto the boardwalk, aiming for tipsy. Brite curled against him, concealing the quiver as they walked. For a time, they simply focused on finding a balance between careful and casual. It was like a dance, knowing how to step without treading on each other's feet, all the while feigning drunkenness. The Mothertree they had just climbed loomed on their left, the tips of its branches casting a shadowy web over the boards. The scent of the harbor drenched the air: fish, weeds, oakum. The boats floated calmly on the water, most of them dark and still. The party boats were moored, and many were encrusted with a thick layer of barnacles.

He was distracting himself, trying to force what he was about to do from his mind. He clutched Brite to him, and in what seemed like moments they arrived at the path that cut between the intact Mothertree and the black pillar of the First. The compound's fence was perhaps a hundred yards off. Still, the silhouetted figure of the sentinel was clearly visible in his platform. The gate guard was hidden by the bend in the fence.

As Brite pulled away, Walde's arm tightened around her. "Don't let the guard hurt you," he whispered fiercely into her ear. "I don't care how close we are to success. It's not worth getting hurt over."

In answer, her hand fell on the concealed knife at her belly.

Walde's hand slid over hers, and it felt as if they both stopped breathing. "Promise me."

"I promise."

He nodded once, stiffly, then took his hand away.

"I expect the same from you," she said.

They both waited for the sentinel to vanish behind the trunk, then, throwing a glance behind him to make sure no one was watching, Walde left Brite at the path and made his way over the First's roots to the fence. All the while, he counted under his breath. When he knew the sentinel would be about to appear again, he dove down into the dark hollow between roots and waited, counting again.

He risked a glance at Brite. Light cast on the path from the harbor brightened it enough that Walde could make out her shadowy form. She was bent double, pretending to vomit, waiting for him to reach the fence. His count finished. Glancing at the platform, he left the crack between roots and raced forward again. He stopped and started this way three times more before the fence's deep shadow enclosed him.

And now he had a conundrum. While he was safe in the darkness, that very same darkness concealed his path. Fortunately, he knew how roots grew very well, and by marking their pattern just beyond the fence's shadow, he could visualize their course through the darkness and walk accordingly. He stole a moment to reach down under the fence into the gap between roots where the fence posts had been driven. A stiff layer of wattle met his fingers. So they had sealed the area between the roots.

He straightened and fingered his bow. If Brite didn't succeed, he should have it ready. He could shoot the sentinel from the gate. Not with much accuracy in spare torchlight, but if he had to, he would do it. He slid the bow out of the quiver. The string was still attached to one end, making it easier for him to string the bow in the darkness. Still, his hands shook as he struggled to get it right. He was running out of time.

The moment he finished, he slid the bow over his shoulder and stumbled on, his gaze constantly flicking to Brite, who was unable to see him. She had mastered her moves. Weave, trip, and pretend to fall, hang over the ground for a few moments before righting herself. A few more steps, a few dry heaves. Down again. If the sentinel saw her, he must have been smiling.

The closer she came to the gate, the lighter her path became, until Walde could almost make out her features. The fence's shadow was also brightening, and the sounds of his footfalls, though faint, sounded too loud in the quiet night. He hesitated, then stooped down and took off his boots, securing the laces to his belt.

If the fence hadn't been curved, he could not have crept so close to the gate. Torchlight fanned over the fence, and still he couldn't see the guard—which meant that the guard probably couldn't see him. He slowed his pace, creeping along by inches.

A loud shout from close by made his heart lurch into his throat. Without thinking, he buried his palms under his quiver and held them there. Brite's drunken chortle answered the shout, and he heard the uneven patter of her footsteps coming closer, closer, moving off the main path and up a walkway that led to the gate.

"You look lo-lonely, honey," she cooed.

Desperately, Walde drew on the time he'd spent practicing in the corpse darkness to contain himself. The effort dizzied him, but the calm he sought settled over him, and he began moving again.

"You shouldn't be here," the guard warned.

"I know. But I–I got angry at someone back there."

"Are you alone?"

"Nooo…I'm with you. With you and…your big sword. How big *is* it, honey?" The nearness of her voice told Walde she'd stepped fully into the torchlight.

The guard gave a quiet chuckle. "Look at *you*."

"Look at *me,* honey."

Suddenly, she squealed, and there was a scrape and a thud. Another low chuckle. Walde couldn't wait any longer. Hand on the hilt of his dagger, he followed the torchlight to the corner of the gate, where he would be in full view of the guard but still hidden from the sentinel.

He froze there, hand clenching the dagger. The guard was kneeling on the ground beside her, hands sliding as he tried to roll her around. Brite squirmed away, laughing drunkenly.

Walde wanted to kill him. The urge wasn't fueled by rage—he was so tightly contained now that he couldn't have felt such emotion if he'd wanted to—but by a bone-deep compulsion he scarcely understood.

It would all have been over if not for a chance glance from Brite. A single, meaningful look. Walde's breath snapped back into his lungs, and he forced his hand off his dagger. It would've been easier to fight the rapids again than look away, but he did. He had to.

He passed under the torch and edged around the corner. If the sentinel had appeared then, Walde would have shot at him and then killed the guard, but when he looked up, it was just in time to watch him vanish around the trunk. Walde couldn't wait there for him to come around again, not without risking being seen by the guard. He would have to stick to his original plan.

Now. He padded through the gate and veered off the path as soon as he could. Planks were notoriously loud when trodden upon. Walde could not run on them in silence. Though the roots were shadowy, enough light spilled from the platform and fence to illuminate their backs. He located a hollow he'd spied from the neighboring Mothertree's branches and hopped toward it, all the while counting under his breath.

Before he'd even finished his count, he was lying down in the space.

He refused to think about what was happening to Brite. Refused to think at all. The sentinel came around again and paused to stare at the gate. What was he seeing? Walde ground his head into his hands and heard another squeal of laughter, this one edged with a note of desperation. A shaky breath tore out of him. A storm battered his calm. It would not hold up much longer.

The sentinel had moved on. Walde rose up out of the hollow and hopped over to the back of a thick root. Though he was close enough to the Reachers now to smell their stench and hear their exhausted snoring, he didn't dare look their way. His heart had betrayed him once already; he wouldn't let it do so again. He took an arrow from the quiver and set it to the bow but didn't draw. For a few moments, he simply stared at the spot on the platform where he meant to ambush the sentinel. There was a knack to shooting at elevated targets. He'd shot too high on his first attempts at it, even after his father had warned him not to overestimate the distance. Years of practice had made him better at it, but not perfect. And the dim light would make this a challenge, not to mention that the target would be in motion.

The sentinel's booted footfalls grew louder, and then the man appeared, his steps light as he made his way back to the place where he no doubt intended to pause and watch the scene at the gate. Walde stood barefoot on the root, his hair drawn away from his face, his wiry body almost graceful as it slid into an archer's stance. With steadied hands, he drew back the arrow and loosed it.

At once, he reloaded. The arrow had punched the sentinel in the shoulder, causing him to stumble back against the wooden railing. Another arrow flew. But it sped by the man's neck and vanished into the darkness. Wild-eyed, the sentinel retreated while reaching for his sentinel horn.

A groan of pain sounded from the gate.

Gritting his teeth, Walde loosed one last arrow.

And this time, it found its target. The sentinel slid to the platform floor, the arrow protruding from his neck.

It had all happened so quietly that the Reachers slept on. Clutching the bow, Walde wheeled around and was about to race back to the gate when he caught sight of a lone figure standing in the gate, her uplifted hand clutching a ring of keys.

They had done it. Walde stumbled back, dizzied. Then Brite was in his arms, and they were clinging to each other. She was stiff as stone and smelled of blood, but she was warm and alive. "Are you hurt?" he breathed into her hair.

"No. I'm fine."

He drew back a little and touched the hand that held the keys. Her knuckles were clenched and sticky. "Not my blood," she said, tugging her hand away.

He nodded tightly. "We have to free the Reachers—"

"I know. I'll unlock them. You go find your father." Walde paused a moment longer, searching her hooded eyes for pain. But she would not betray it, not now, and perhaps not ever.

He turned away, hopped up onto the wooden patio that surrounded the base of the First, and eyed the slack, chained bodies.

So many were hauntingly familiar, men and women from the Lakelands who must've been shipped down river after his father was. A terrible stench of bodily fluids bit into his nostrils. He tried not to think about how they had been living, exposed to the elements, soiling themselves either out of necessity or fear. As he came around to the opposite side of the trunk, a gleam of silvery light caught his eye. He quickened his step. If one of the Reachers had wakened, they might know if his father still lived.

The light brightened abruptly, and he halted, swallowing.

His father lay at his feet.

Walde hardly knew him. His skin looked sunken, and his lips were swollen over the gag. One of the bandages wrapping his hands had unraveled up to his fingers, revealing dark stains on the cloth. But for all that, Carrac was still very much alive. His eyes glittered like two burning coals. Walde choked and then stumbled to the ground. Light blazed from his palms, and he didn't care. He drew his dagger and slit the gag, peeling it away from his father's raw lips.

Tears tracked down Carrac's face, but he said nothing. Nothing needed to be said. Walde had come for him. He wiped tears from his own eyes and grinned. So much had happened since they had parted. How could Walde tell him that they had to go to the Woodlands to try to restore the First and help the cursed children grow? He shook his head. It was fanciful and foolish and wonderful.

His father lived, and he had found him.

Walde drooped on the trunk beside him, mouth working to form words. Ask how he was. If he could stand. But nothing came out. The roar of feeling inside him was overpowering. It played like a single note, gathering strength, storm-strong.

It was a reaching of sorts. He didn't see it that way then. He only felt, because feeling was life.

Without knowing it, Walde called out and something powerful answered him. Its presence rolled over him, as vast and wild as the sea. The world blurred, and he stepped sideways into another.

CHAPTER 18

...cannot go back to the way things were, and why should we when the land and all its riches stands empty, waiting to be used? The first steps are always the hardest, but we are not without aid. The future must be built on the past...
—A scorched fragment of a letter from Harborlands Elder Sel, found under a broken chair in a Woodlands meeting hut

Walde charged down the tunnel. There was no hesitation, no questioning. Dimly, he was aware of all he had left undone, even of the vulnerable state of his body, but he couldn't find the will to care. In the tunnel, all that mattered was the reaching.

Why was she so far away? She had seemed so close just before he'd plunged into the tunnel. But this was a different world, and when he found her, she wouldn't be a ghostly presence but the true being. The one called Thara.

Time passed. Not as it passed in the real world, in increments of light and darkness, but in a slow dripping away of strength. His concentration diminished, and he began to feel drained, thin. But he could not slow. Her presence was a growing flame ahead of him, and the closer he came to it, the harder he pressed, until it seemed he was fraying away to nothing, his thoughts, his memory, his very being, shedding like onion skin. Yet still he pressed on until he was no more than a stone hurtling in the darkness.

He knew nothing more until his mind screamed awake, as at a touch of fire. He had only grazed her before, and she had passed him knowledge. This…this was more than grazing. Nothing could have prepared him for the pressure on his mind, the heat of her, which, while not physical, was a burning all the same. Desperately, he fought the urgent need to pull away, to escape while he was still whole. But *he* didn't matter. So he clung on, writhing, until at last the pressure lifted and he felt an odd floating sensation.

For a time he rested, drenched in a peace so vast that the sky could not have contained it. And then she spoke, her voice entering his mind as if it were his own thought-voice.

"So it is you. I should have known you would be the one."

"The one…?"

"To cling on to the bitter end. No one has done it before. Many have reached but never clung."

Love for her moved through him, and for a long moment, neither spoke. "I need you," he said at last, and wondered why it had taken him so long to realize it.

"Of course you do."

"I don't want you to fade away."

A trickle of amusement emanated from her. Did she feel his emotions too? "I will not fade, Walde, at least not yet. That is not what you felt when you reached for me."

"You're right. It wasn't a fading, but a withdrawing."

"My links to you are weakening," she corrected. "When they weaken, they extend, and you must work harder to reach me through them."

"Links?"

"Every Mothertree has one. As a sapling, it develops in secret from its own heartroot. When the link dies, the tree dies, and my presence diminishes."

The tunnels. Of course. How could he have imagined there was only one? "What will happen if they all die?"

"Darkness and death. People must continue to learn from me, or they will eventually cease to exist. Like sparks flung from a fire, they will cool and fade out."

Walde recoiled from the thought. How could people allow such a thing to happen? Even animals knew what was needed to survive. If they were thirsty, they didn't turn their backs on water and walk away. And yet…wasn't that what his people were doing by turning their backs on the Mothertrees? Frustration and helplessness warred in him. "They think you're from the stars," he blurted. "That you fell like an unwanted seed and burrowed in. They think they need to get rid of you."

He sensed no surprise from her, only resignation. "Separation is the outcome of withdrawing, Walde. People have begun see themselves as separate from everything else, the trees, the sky, even the stars."

We aren't separate from the stars? "I don't understand what you mean."

"Ah, but you did. You glimpsed it the first time you touched me."

He tried to recall the knowledge she'd fed him, but like the stars, it was too massive for him to grasp. Still, a scent of it lingered, and he clung to it, as he had clung to her. He struggled to put it into words. "We are within the sky, not apart from it. We are children in a great womb."

Warm approval. "Yes. And children must grow."

"Yes." The knowledge filled him with rightness. "Yes. I understand. It's something I should have remembered."

"Do not be hard on yourself. No one grasps such things after a single reaching, but they must reach again and again."

Time was when Reachers could do that. Then the purges happened, and the elders seized power, and the Mothertrees gradually died. A question entered his mind, one that had troubled him since he'd learned he was a Reacher.

"Why do you—why do the links to you withdraw from negative emotions?"

"The links respond not to emotion, Walde, but to the ebb and flow of a Reacher's power." Once more, he didn't understand. Perhaps she sensed his confusion, for she went on, "Most of the time, Reachers are always reaching a little, whether they feel it or not. But strong, positive emotions like joy make them expansive, and that expansiveness compels them to reach deeper, to flow. Negative emotions, on the other hand, cause them to withdraw into themselves, and that ebbing is what causes a link to weaken and the power that livens a Mothertree to dwindle. Of course, it is natural for Reachers to experience strong negative emotions from time to time, but rarely do they all suffer at once, or for as long. There are so few Reachers left now, and most are suffering. If this ebbing continues, the links will fail."

"We can't let that happen."

His words felt almost menacing. There was a black desperation behind them, a readiness to do whatever was needed to prevent darkness and death.

Her voice slid quietly back into his mind. "Do not despair, Walde. All is not lost. You helped repair the link to this Mothertree. Given the opportunity, Reachers could restore the Firsts and grow other trees."

"I want to do that, but it feels like a dream. The elders have too much power now, and the people don't question it. The Lowlands culture is spreading. Soon, there'll be no going back."

"That time may come," she said, "but it does not have to be now. I would like to try something. A small thing that might set your people back on the right path."

Had Walde been in his body, his breath would've halted in anticipation. "What small thing?" he demanded when he could no longer contain himself.

A thread of amusement swept into him from her. "Curiosity is a powerful weapon when wielded with a light hand. I could draw on that emotion to work a change, but to do so, I would need a conduit."

"The link—?"

"No, a link is too fragile to bear such power. Only Reachers can traverse it. *You* would have to be my conduit."

Wonder and desire thrilled through him. "I'll do it," he said instantly.

"I knew you would. You would do it, even if it could cost you your life."

A silence fell as the meaning of her words hit him. "I might die."

"Yes."

He'd faced the prospect of death before. In the river, in the prison cell. Even reaching for her had brought him nearly to the brink. But somehow this simple statement of fact filled him with dread. "Will it truly help?" He didn't even know yet what "it" was.

"I hope so."

So there was a chance it would help, and there was a chance he would die. The scales tipped back and forth. "I'll still do it," he said before he lost courage.

"I knew you would." She had begun to withdraw from him. Even her thought-voice sounded distant as she added, "Cling on to life, Walde, as you have clung to me. Never let it go."

Walde scrambled after her presence. "Is this happening now?"

"It is. Prepare yourself."

"How?"

The heat of her brushed him then, like a warning. Walde had no arms to shield himself. No guard for his mind—or essence, or whatever it was that had entered this place. And even if he'd had a shield, what would be the point in thwarting her? He had agreed to be her instrument.

The thought changed his stance. He had been cowering. Now he stood firm and strong. He thought he heard his name, soft as a the faintest whisper, then something akin to heat seared through him and his whole being buckled as under intense pressure. This was well beyond what he had experienced before. He knew an instant of sheer terror, then his awareness diminished to a thread. For a moment longer she was with him still, holding him together as he became light.

Then he was flung away from her down the tunnel. A terrible crack sounded, and his whole being shuddered as if it would break apart. Light faded to darkness and then to something that was neither darkness nor light.

He floated, adrift and bodiless in a silent sea. The memory of a song danced around his periphery, too ethereal to grasp, too compelling to ignore. Where had he heard it before?

A Mothertree filled his mind, purple buds poised to blossom. Treelights blinked above him, and a crowd gathered on the paths encircling the trunk. Jak's long-fingered hands flowed like water over his harp, following Walde's lead. The dream song.

As soon as he'd named it, it strengthened. The notes shuddered through him, first with beauty and then with warning. Where was he? As he asked the question, his awareness intensified. Memories tumbled back. The sea vanished, and with a sudden, nauseating jolt, he felt his body again.

He was flat on his back, digging his hands into weedy earth. The dark pillar of the First loomed above him. Except now it wasn't completely black. Green shoots sprouted from the blunt knobs where branches used to be. And those were only the ones he could see in the torchlight from the sentinel platform. The First was very much alive.

"Walde!"

Brite's voice snapped across the compound. Other sounds reached his ears then. A pattering of footsteps. Distant voices. He tried to raise his head and was struck by vertigo. Someone grasped his wrists and hauled him to a sitting position.

For an endless moment, he simply stared at the familiar figure that crouched on the back of a root above him, at her rich, red hair tangled over her torch-brightened skin, her large, fevered eyes and compressed lips. His head shook, and he swallowed back a burning in his throat. He was in love with her. How had he managed to ignore that fact? He'd been squashing his emotions too well.

He lifted a blazing arm—arm? He tugged back his sleeve and followed the light up his forearm. Why was the inside of his arm alight now? He turned it, wondering at the brightness that radiated from him.

"Are you in pain?" Brite asked.

He struggled to stand. Brite hopped down into the space between roots. Before she could speak again, Walde caught her and dragged her into his arms. "Where's my father?" he breathed into her ear.

"Walde—" She broke away and grasped his face with both hands. "Listen to me. You passed out while I was unlocking the Reachers. Carrac said you were just reaching, and that he would try to waken you, so I kept on. But then the crack opened in the trunk, and the Reachers walked right in, all of them but your father. Once he saw the crack, he tried to drag you in, but I wouldn't let him. So we hid you here. And Carrac..." She shook her head. "He's wandered back to it, like someone spellbound."

A crack. In the trunk. Walde broke away from her and clambered up onto the root. The platform was shattered. Splintered boards stood up around it like loose teeth. The chain that had surrounded it lay limply on the wreckage. He followed the trail of damage around to the section of the trunk that was directly across from the gate. Then he halted, stunned. A gap the size of a door had opened in the trunk. The space inside it was lit by a silvery light that breathed up from the deeps of the tree. It was beyond enticing. He could scarcely keep himself from walking right in. *A small thing,* Thara had called it. He snorted. If the door had even half the effect on non-Reachers as it did on Reachers, the entire town would soon be clamoring to go into it. Where would they go? Had she created a separate realm for them, one that could be visited physically? He yearned to find out.

Carrac gripped the door's edge, as though blown by a strong wind. He started to say something but stopped as a series of horn blasts sounded, distant but forceful. The guards would expect answering blasts from the sentinel, Walde thought. When none came, they would rush in.

"The sound of that crack opening was deafening," Carrac said when the blasts had trailed to silence. He held out a bandaged hand. "Boy. Come."

Unable to help himself, Walde took an involuntary step forward.

"No!" Brite caught his arm and tugged him back.

I wouldn't have gone in, he told himself. He'd only meant to fetch his father. Gently, he unstuck Brite's hand from his arm and clasped it in both of his. "I'm not leaving you."

Brite nodded stiffly, and her face vanished behind a fall of hair. It was enough and more than enough to distract Walde from the pull of the crack. He stretched out an arm to his father. "Come with us!"

Carrac shook his head. Tears glistened in his eyes. "You'd better run, boy. You and your sweetheart."

This wasn't how it was supposed to end. Carrac was supposed to return with him to the Woodlands, grateful and proud of what his son had done. Perhaps he still would have, had Walde the time to explain things. But he'd run out of time. The distant, drunken sounds from the harbor had been replaced by an approaching rumble of running feet and excited voices. They would probably converge with the guards at the compound's gate.

Walde's jaw tightened as the terrible words choked out of him. "Farewell, then. Don't stay away long."

Carrac mouthed a word, maybe "go" or "no," then he took a step back and dropped. Walde half expected to hear a thud, but there was nothing. He had fallen right out of the world.

Walde dragged in a shaky breath. The insides of his arms were blazing, and he felt like he was going to be sick. Dousing his emotions took all his concentration, and he hated doing it. The darkness it brought was cold and deadening. But it was safe, and at that moment, that was all that mattered. He wheeled around and tugged Brite's arm toward the gate. "Run!"

As one, they raced across the space between trees and disappeared behind a Mothertree's trunk.

Read on for an excerpt from

Battle for the Woodlands
Book 2 of Mothertree

By W.K. Greyling

CHAPTER 1

"I have to piss."

Brite's reluctant whisper made Walde sit up in the darkness. He hadn't been asleep. Too much had happened this night to allow his mind to settle. His emotions clawed like chained animals at his carefully constructed calm. Fortunately, he had a measure of control over them. Singling one out and letting it rise to the surface was as easy as plucking a harp string.

Of course, he chose love. Who wouldn't? And the object of his affection was right beside him, unaware of his newfound feelings for her.

A shine of silvery Reacher light blossomed from his palms, and if he pushed his sleeves back, the entire underside of his arms. It illuminated the small space he and Brite were sheltering in.

His people called it the corpse darkness.

Many hundreds of years ago, a deep, rectangular hole had been excavated from a space between two massive Mothertree roots. Its four walls had been shored up with stone, and a door made from storm-felled Mothertree wood had been closed over its top. Holes carved out of the roots served as sockets for the door's wooden dowel joints. The pit's purpose was simple: to hold the bones of the dead. But after the Mothertrees were abandoned, the corpse darkness had been forgotten, its door concealed by vines and brush. Desperation had moved Walde to seek it out and use it as a hiding place.

He tried not to dwell on how many bodies lay under him. The bones were old and brittle and smelled faintly of ash.

Brite shifted to a kneeling position. She was tall, with dark auburn hair and a fey cast to her large eyes and wide lips. Walde's spare tunic hung on her slender frame like a night robe. She said, "I can't wait. I have to go now. And I'm not going in here. Do you think it'd be safe to go outside?"

They had been in hiding for at least an hour. Walde's face lifted to the shadowy door above. Curiosity nudged him. The muffled sounds that filtered into the pit offered little information about what was happening outside. "It should be, if you can manage it in the dark." He rose to his feet and grasped a handful of root hair. "I could go too."

"You mean…"

He grinned. "I mean to take a piss, not to stand around and watch you."

Brite returned his grin but then looked swiftly aside as if she'd been caught doing something embarrassing. She had been that way all night. Walde pinpointed it to the moment he'd agreed to stay with her rather than follow his father, Carrac, into the crack in the First Mothertree's trunk. Perhaps she was worried that she'd been too pushy.

The brightness in his hands and wrists had faded to a bare wisp. Only the strongest emotions produced Reacher light; maintaining such emotion required constant concentration. Gathering root hair around his wrists, he followed her up, and they shoved the door open together.

A cool wind, smelling of salt and oakum, brushed stray hairs from his forehead. A distant roar of agitated voices rose and fell with it. The sound was eerie in the darkness.

Brite whispered, "The crowd hasn't dispersed."

"No," he agreed. "In fact, it sounds like it's grown."

They stood under the boughs of an enormous dead Mothertree. Its bare, shadowy roots had once been covered by walkways. Now, only a few boards remained, many of them rotten. It was but one of twenty dead Mothertrees that ran alongside the harbor. Only one living Mothertree remained—the First—and it had become a doorway to some other place. Walde had unintentionally helped open the crack that now gaped enticingly at the base of its trunk. The sound of that crack opening had drawn both peacekeepers from the guardhouse and innocent partygoers from nearby harbor ships. Walde and Brite fled before they could witness what had happened, but from the angry clamor, it seemed the partygoers had spotted the glowing crack through the compound door and were subsequently prevented from entering it. Two huge trees now stood between Walde and the compound, preventing him from seeing what was happening.

He yearned to be closer to it, and not merely to satisfy his curiosity. His father had disappeared into that crack. Walde couldn't leave him. It would've been so easy to flee the Harborlands now, in the midst of such an uproar. Easy, and probably wise. He and Brite had killed several guards in order to free the wounded Reachers chained to the First's trunk. Indeed, they'd left a trail of death from the cell they'd escaped to the sentinel tower overlooking the compound. And while the city elders probably assumed he and Brite had entered the crack along with the other Reachers, there would doubtlessly be an investigation. Still, he'd come to the Harborlands to save his father, and he wouldn't abandon him now. Tomorrow he would have to leave Brite in the corpse darkness to investigate what had happened at the compound.

Thundering footsteps on boards made him shift his focus to the lamplit boardwalk at the harbor.

A group of men wearing unbelted jackets raced by, moving in the direction of the compound. Walde sensed purpose in their stance, and their unbelted jackets likely hid concealed weapons. He turned toward Brite, but she had drifted off into the darkness to relieve herself.

He refocused on the boardwalk. Would people be hurt or even killed because he had helped open that crack? He had hoped, perhaps naively, that the glowing hole in the Mothertree would have filled the elders with such awe that they would've allowed others into the compound to view it. The enticing glow had almost overcome Walde. Without Brite's restraining hand, he would have followed his father right in. The light must have stirred other people's curiosity, or onlookers would not have lingered at the compound. Perhaps if enough people joined the crowd, they could overcome the guards.

He refused to contemplate his worst fear—that the Reachers' physical needs weren't being met where they were, and when they finally had to leave, they'd walk straight into the drawn bows of their captors.

If their needs *were* being met, then they'd probably stay put for a while. Unfortunately, that meant Walde would have to remain in the Harborlands until the uproar subsided and he could return to the crack to retrieve them.

The uncertainty was frustrating.

Having relieved himself, he plodded back to the corpse darkness.

"Did you see anything?" Brite asked when they were safely inside, enfolded by blackness.

Walde used his Reacher light sparingly in the corpse darkness at night. A gap under the door's handle might leak a wisp of it onto the ground outside, alerting any nearby guards.

"No." He lay back into the hollow his body had made in the bone fragments. "I'm almost afraid to. People are going to be hurt tonight." And perhaps worse, he thought.

Brite said no more.

Walde tried to find sleep, but his eyes wouldn't close, even in the absolute darkness of the hole. A slow grimace pulled back the corners of his mouth. When one focuses on something they cannot do, the thing itself becomes so tempting as to be intolerable. That night, he simply wanted to feel.

He had been trained from the time he was a boy to stifle strong feelings, and until he'd become a Reacher, he'd believed he was good at it. Now that it was a matter of life or death, he'd come to realize how often he slipped up. When he had found his father alive and well at the compound, he had lost control. The blaze of his joy had been so powerful that he had unintentionally "reached," leaving Brite alone while he lay unconscious on the ground. When he finally woke up, dizzied and sensitized by all that had happened while reaching, it was to find a radiant Brite crouched like a sprite on the root. Once more, his emotions had run unchecked, and he'd been drowned by the realization that he loved her.

So much, so fast. For a short space of time, color and brightness had spilled into the grayness of his life.

And then he'd been forced to smother it.

He rubbed the unshaven scruff on his chin. This was foolish and indulgent. He ought to be getting sleep instead of yearning like a drunk for a few moments of gratification. It would do him no good to muddle over his relationship with Brite, to wonder if her affection for him could ever grow into something stronger. To consider all the reasons why he loved her and how wonderful her skin would feel under his hands—

He suppressed a groan and turned onto his side. When had he become so shallow and selfish?

"Walde…"

"Yes?" he replied, a little too quickly.

"Last night you asked me how I killed the guard after I escaped my cell. Do you still want the answer to that…or maybe the answer to another question?"

He grinned. "What do you want so badly to know?"

Brite's people were the descendants of tinkers and as such believed that everything came at a price, be it goats, favors, or information. Nothing, or almost nothing, was freely given. Brite still felt she owed him for helping her dispose of the body of a man she'd killed in self-defense, and nothing would convince her otherwise. To her, life was a pair of scales constantly tipping this way and that. Walde found it both frustrating and endearing.

He heard her sigh. "I want to know what happened while you were reaching. You told me you spoke to the tree god, to the one you call Thara, and that she used you as a–a—"

"A conduit."

"A conduit to help her open the crack. But I don't know why. I'd like to know what happened after you passed out."

He found himself nodding. He owed Brite this story, but he'd been holding it back for the simple reason that relating it would stir feelings in him he'd be forced to suppress. It was a poor excuse. "You remember me telling you about the tunnel?"

"Yes. It's your path to her. Your link."

"Link is the right word. The First's link was incredibly strained. In a healthy link, a Reacher only brushes Thara and is given knowledge. But this link was so damaged that I lost consciousness before I even got to her. When I did meet her, it was more than a brush—it was a collision. But I endured the pain and didn't let her go."

Brite must have sat up. The direction of her voice had changed. "Why?"

Why. He hadn't asked himself that question. "I don't know. Priorities change when you're reaching. It's like nothing else exists. Nothing else matters but communing with Thara." He swallowed tightly. "When the worst of it was over, a deep calm settled over me, and I sensed her there, all around me. I sensed her every emotion."

"Did she sense yours?"

"I thought she did, but I don't know. She told me I was the first to cling to her the way I did. She said that many have reached but never clung."

"I wonder what moved you to do it."

He snorted. "I don't know." He searched his mind for an answer. "When I left the Lakelands, it was to find and rescue my father. But then I learned about the dead Mothertrees and the children in the Woodlands who can't grow; I learned that elders here have been torturing Reachers in order to destroy the links, and that they did it openly. Because they could. Because they made people believe that Thara is really a parasite that fell from the stars..." His voice caught. He dragged in a painful breath. "I was so happy when I found my father. But I was also desperate. The two emotions twined and made me fire when I reached."

He sat up, felt the enticing warmth of her arm, and shifted subtly away.

Brite said, "Not everyone believes that lie about Thara. If they did, no one would be struggling with guards right now to be closer to the crack."

Walde wanted so much to agree with her, but there were too many other ways to view the situation. Perhaps the Harborlanders merely wished to satisfy their curiosity, and being deprived of the opportunity had sparked pent-up anger at the guards.

Brite asked, "Did you tell her about the lie being spread about her?"

"Yes."

"And…?"

"She didn't seem surprised. In fact, she told me it's the natural outcome of withdrawing from the Mothertrees, and, ultimately, from her. Her words were 'separation is the outcome of withdrawing.'"

Brite's hair flicked against her hand. Walde imagined her toying with it as her mind worked out the meaning of the words. "I see." She cleared her throat. "So what's the cost of separation?"

"Darkness and death. She said that Reachers must continue to learn from her and to pass on that knowledge, or people will cease to exist. Like sparks flung from a fire, we will cool and fade out."

Brite's voice sank to the barest whisper. "What else did she say?"

He pulled his knees up to his chin. She had told him not to despair. Given the opportunity, the Reachers could restore the First Mothertrees and plant others. Life could go on.

But that was before the Reachers had piled into the crack and disappeared. Walde had wanted so badly to go to the Woodlands with his father and Brite, restore the First there, and help the cursed children grow. Instead, he was trapped here, waiting. Was this what Thara meant to have happened? Or was Walde supposed to have followed Carrac and the other Reachers into the tree?

The thought startled a drift of light from him.

"What is it?" Brite's sleepy voice drifted up from the floor, where she had lain back down. He'd been so lost in thought that he'd forgotten to answer her question.

"I don't know. It's hard, not knowing where the Reachers are and how long they're going to be there."

"The tree god didn't tell you anything about the crack?"

"No." He shook his head roughly. "She just…said she would draw on people's sense of curiosity to work a change. When

I asked her if it would work, she said she hoped so. Nothing more." Sighing, he lay back down. "It's not that I don't trust her. I don't trust myself. And I don't trust that those in power here are going to respond the way she hopes they will. If the elders believe that the crack leads to Thara, they won't want anyone to go into it. If there's even a chance people will come back out knowing the truth, then the elders' power will be threatened."

"This might take a long time to settle." Brite tapped her fingers against something hard, probably a bone, he thought dryly. "I wonder if the First's new growth will make a difference to anyone. Before you reached, the tree looked dead. It still looks dead from a distance, but up close you can clearly see it has new shoots. When dawn comes, everyone else will see them too."

"But will they care? These same people abandoned their Mothertrees and seem to enjoy living like Lowlanders."

The Lowlands was a new settlement and until recently the only land where folk lived on the ground rather than in the treetops. The settlers had once been poor tinkers, but over time they had become wealthy and forgot what it was like to be of humble means. They paid the poor almost nothing to work their peat bogs and mines. Their corrupt legal system favored the wealthy, leaving the poor without rights. As a result, the place had become a hive of crime and injustice. Despite this fact, two of the three Mothertree lands had abandoned their dying trees and built new settlements patterned after the Lowlands.

He ran a weary hand across his eyes. The longer he considered the situation, the more complex it grew. And yet Thara had whittled it down to one word: curiosity. "What did you feel when *you* saw the crack?"

After a silence, she said, "Wonder. Simply wonder."

"Then others will feel the same. The glowing crack in the tree is compelling, and no matter what people have been led to believe, they'll be drawn to it. At the very least, they'll want someone to go in to get answers. Maybe the elders themselves will have to go in. Maybe that's what Thara foresaw."

Fabric rustled, and he felt the warm pressure of Brite's hand on his shoulder. "Do you wish you had gone in?"

"No." He touched her hand. Warmth filled his chest, and silver light sprouted around him. "I'm glad you pulled me back."

For several breaths, neither moved. The air seemed warmer, thicker, the darkness intimate. Walde didn't dare turn his head and look at her. He longed to discover if she returned his feelings, but this was the wrong place and time for it. If she did love him, then their relationship would change, and he didn't know if he could suppress the powerful emotions that would ensue. If he could, it would be painful.

More than that, it would be wrong.

He slid his hand away and turned onto his side. "I'm going to try to sleep. Sweet dreams, Brite."

***

When Walde finally succeeded in settling his thoughts, he slept like the dead. He woke gradually, blinking up at the smudge of light emanating from the gap under the door handle.

It was their second night in the corpse darkness, and they had grown comfortable there. The door was swathed in vine and moss. Walde had found it only because he'd been actively searching for it. The sea of bone fragments inside had been undisturbed, indicating that no one else had sheltered there. And who would? No sane person would want to open that door, never mind lie down on several centuries of human remains.

But Walde had discovered he could do many unthinkable things when he was pressed to do so. As could Brite.

He was amazed at how driven she was to help him. These were not her people. Until she'd met him in the Lowlands, she had never climbed an oak, never mind a Mothertree. "Reacher" and "Mothertree" were gossip words heard at Lowlander market stalls. They had little to do with the Lowlanders' lives.

But Brite had grown to believe in Walde's goal of restoring the Mothertrees. Comments she'd made hinted at a belief that folk needed Thara's guidance. She had cited her own land as an example of what would befall the world without it. Walde guessed that he had unintentionally blackened her land by his wistful descriptions of his Lakelands home. Well, so be it.

He shut his eyes and turned onto his side. For days he'd avoided thinking about his homeland. Before he had departed, only fourteen Reachers had been left to do their secret "maintenance" on the failing Mothertrees there. After the Lakelands elders had conspired with those in the Harborlands to drug and ship Reachers downriver, that number had likely dwindled to nothing. Without Reachers, the Lakelands Mothertrees would die.

Walde flinched from the thought.

He pushed his hands through his untidy brown hair. Brite might understand the severity of the situation, but she couldn't feel it in her bones like he did. She couldn't pine for a life she'd never had. For treelights and song rites. For living Mothertrees. The thought of it disappearing was beyond bearing.

His belly rumbled, and he swallowed back a stickiness in his throat. Soon, they would need to find a reliable source of food and water. They had already eaten half the mushrooms that carpeted the floor. If not for the food and drink they had nabbed from a guard's hut last night, they would've been in a bad way.

"Walde."

He jolted upright and found Brite's shadowy form standing over him. "I thought you were asleep."

"Listen. What do you hear?"

The tinge of fear in her voice unnerved him. He went still for several moments, hardly breathing. "I don't know. Birds."

"Those aren't birds."

The odd sound had grown louder. It was rough, toneless, and repetitive. It tickled his memory. Where had he heard it before?

When he remembered, his heart crashed painfully in his chest. "Dogs."

Reacher light flared, illuminating her wild eyes and pale face. "Guards will be close behind. What do we do?"

BOOKS BY W.K. GREYLING

THE AURE DUOLOGY

**Beneath the Roots*

**White Bird*

ABOUT THE AUTHOR

Canadian novelist W.K. Greyling lives in the maritime province of Nova Scotia. When she's not writing, she spends her time curating the music library for Ancient FM, an online medieval and Renaissance radio station.

Made in United States
North Haven, CT
25 June 2024

54062742R00157